PROLOGUE

'YOU DIDN'T NEED the police to tell you this was serious,' my soon-to-be fellow passenger mutters.

'That's enough talking,' the officer says. 'As we've already told you, anything you say can be used in evidence.'

If we'd been allowed to leave here before the police arrived, we'd have trampled each other in the rush. But it's too late for that now.

They're taking us two by two, flanked by officers, marching us out into the snow to be driven to the station. No one's been arrested. Yet.

At first, they let us all sit together in the same room. You'd think separating suspects would be rule number one. Still, they've been watching us like hawks, waiting for someone to slip. But they won't get anything from me.

A blast of icy air hits us as the lead officer steps back inside after conferring with someone in a white suit. I don't need to look again at what's behind that utility room door to remind myself of what they're walking into. Besides, the smell is already seeping out.

'Leave your belongings here,' the officer orders as he strides back through the door. His voice fills the hallway, low and sharp.

'Why can't we take our stuff?' Someone asks. 'What if—'

'Because this building is now a crime scene,' he snaps. 'Nobody's moving anything.'

A voice behind me mutters, 'It's a bit late for that.'

They're right. No one wanted to keep stepping over... it. So we moved it. And then we had to do it again. The utility room was the only option. Now the door looks too clean, too white and innocent. Like it's pretending there's nothing all that sinister lurking behind it.

'Will we be allowed to go home afterwards?' A small voice asks.

'It depends on what we find,' the officer replies. 'And what you tell us in your interviews.'

'What if there's nothing *to* tell?' I ask.

'Then you've got nothing to worry about.' The officer's voice is even, but his eyes tell a different story.

A sharp silence follows as we put on our shoes and coats. Outside, sleet pelts the windows like handfuls of gravel.

'Think also about whether you'll want a solicitor. You'll be asked again when we arrive.'

'Do we need one?'

I avoid looking at anyone, my thoughts locked tight inside my mind. *Do I need a solicitor?* Maybe. Maybe not.

Solicitor or not, the officer can ask as many questions as he likes when we reach the station.

I know what I did.

And I know what I didn't do.

1

FIVE DAYS EARLIER

'YOUR CARD HAS BEEN DECLINED, I'm afraid.' The assistant looks at me in that smug way people do when they believe they've got the upper hand. Just five minutes ago she looked like she'd been sitting at the checkout for the past eighteen hours straight. I've never seen someone look so bored, but now she looks positively animated. 'Do you have an alternative method of payment, madam?'

One thing which always winds me up is being referred to as *madam*. I'm thirty-two, not a hundred. But this is the least of my worries. That my card has been declined has become my most pressing concern.

Can today really get any worse?

'Just a moment.' I loosen my scarf, hoping to find some relief from the stifling heat in here as I fish around in my bag. 'Try this one.' I pass her my already maxed-out credit card, praying the powers that be might allow me to exceed my limit. I can worry how I'm going to pay it back at a later date.

'That one's also been declined.' She looks beyond me down the lengthening queue where people are beginning to shuffle and mutter as they wait with their tins of chocolates, crackers and rolls of wrapping paper. Everyone's gearing up for the big day in just over a week. I thought I was gearing up for it as well.

'Can you give me a few minutes? While I get something sorted?'

She raises her eyes to the heavens and presses a button on her tannoy. 'Supervisor to till seven.' The cheery Christmas music pauses as she makes her request, before it returns to its former volume. I wouldn't care if I never heard a festive song again for as long as I live.

By the time the supervisor arrives, the queue must be fifteen deep with furious-looking shoppers. The other checkout lines are just as bad, but at least they're slowly moving.

'This lady can't pay,' the checkout girl explains in an unnecessarily loud, sing-song voice. 'We need to put all this on hold while she sorts a new method of payment.' She gestures at my trolley.

'You could always take out a supermarket charge card.' The supervisor suggests, her lips pursed as she waits for me to answer.

'No thanks.' In the circumstances, I would normally have bitten her hand off, but I can't exactly admit that there isn't a cat in hell's chance I would pass a credit check. 'Just let me make a couple of phone calls. I'm expecting some funds into my account, but it looks like they haven't arrived yet, that's the problem.' I try to keep my voice airy and bright, though it's shaking with suppressed tears.

The woman plugs her key into the computer, presumably to save my transaction while allowing the assistant to move on to the next customer.

'You'll need to join the end of the queue,' she shouts after me as I scuttle to the packing area to find out what's gone wrong for me this time.

'Hi, this is George. Leave a message.'

There'll be no prizes for guessing what he's up to and with who.

'You said my maintenance money would be in today,' I hiss into the phone. 'Two months' worth. You promised. Call me back straightaway.'

I've never been as embarrassed in my life. Well, this isn't strictly true. I think of the time when I was caught with nappies under my coat when Hallie was a baby. It had been a choice between nappies or an extra six quid's worth of food. It wasn't my finest moment when the store detective put his hand on my shoulder as I was leaving the store.

I stare at my screen, willing my ex-husband to return my call. I have so much to do today. After getting the shopping home, I've still got Mrs Birch's house to clean, and then I was supposed to be picking up some presents. The kids know things are tricky and weren't exactly expecting much. Not like last year when I managed to afford a smart watch for Hallie and an Xbox for Barnaby. This year, they've lowered their expectations – Hallie has her heart set on a particular pair of trainers, and Barnaby just wants a new controller and game for his Xbox. But unless I get hold of the money George owes me, neither of them will get a single present.

Tears fill my eyes. Extracting maintenance from my ex has been like getting blood from a stone since he left us, but it's got even worse since he's moved in with the woman he left us for. I've heard every excuse under the sun for his non-payments, and it's getting to the point where I might have to report him to the Child Maintenance Service to force an attachment of earnings order. Now that he's finally holding down a job.

Where's the kid's maintenance money? My card has just been declined at Aldi.

I fire off a text message while continuing to stare at my phone screen as if something magic might suddenly happen.

Shit. What am I going to do? It's not as if I have many people I can ask for help. I don't have the time or energy for friends. Between working, caring for the kids and the house, and grieving for the end of my marriage, it's a miracle some days that I manage to get dressed and brush my hair.

But there's still Ruby. I don't know whether she keeps in touch with me because she genuinely cares, or simply because I owe her so much money.

'Hey, Aneka. I'm glad you've called. You've saved me a job.'

'How do you mean?' I sink onto a chair by the packing tables as shoppers buzz all around me.

'We haven't spoken for over a month.' She hesitates, and in the pause, I know what's coming. 'Really, if you can manage it, I could do with some of that money being repaid before Christmas.'

'Look, Ruby,' I blink back my tears as the bright store lights and the twinkling Christmas tree blur at the edges of my vision. 'I'm really sorry, but George hasn't paid the kids' maintenance, and he won't even pick up his phone.'

'I see.' Her voice is monotone. Great. I can't imagine her being on board with what I'm about to ask.

'He's left me in a right pickle to be honest. I'm not due to be paid from my shop job until the first week in January and only have a few bits of cleaning money to come in before then.'

'So you'll be able to repay some of that money *then*, is that why you've called?'

'Actually, I'm at the checkout in Aldi and my card has been declined.' I take a deep breath. 'I'm calling to ask if you could help me – just this one last time.'

My cheeks burn with shame. This new year, I've got to get my act together, no matter what it takes. I've got to dig us out of this hole.

'You want me to lend you *more* money?' She sounds incredulous.

'I'm sorry, Ruby. I hate to ask, but I don't know who else—'

'This is the other thing. You only ever call me when you need a favour. Never for us to get together or simply for a chat, or even just to see how I am for a change.' Her voice is rising.

'I would have done, of course I would, I mean, I was planning to, but—'

'Yeah, whatever.'

'Look, you're totally right.' The tears have finally spilt. I brush one from my cheek as a passer-by stares. 'I've been a useless friend, but I really am going to sort it all out.'

'You've got to. You can't go on like this.'

'Are you going to help me out this one last time? The checkout bill has come to a hundred and fifty pounds.'

'Bloody hell, what have you bought?'

'It's for next week, isn't it? I was just stocking up, buying some treats for the kids and some stocking fillers for them – as well as some food.'

'I wish I could help you. But I can't this time.'

My stomach twists. There is literally no one else I can ask. I've tried before to get an advance on the wage from my shop job, but the man in HR said that was something they never do.

'You already owe me over a grand, Aneka. Chris will have a fit if I lend you any more money.'

'Would he have to know?' Even as the words leave me, I know I'm overstepping.

'Like I've told you before, all our money's paid into our joint account. Plus, we don't keep secrets from one another.'

Unlike George did from me. At least Ruby refrains from saying this out loud. I didn't have a clue until it was too late, not only about his affair with the infamous Katina, but also about the savings he had blown and the debt he'd amassed.

'Please, Ruby. I wouldn't ask you if I wasn't desperate.'

'All this lending you money, I don't think it's doing our

friendship any good. Especially since you *never* pay me back. I try not to feel resentful, but you're not making it easy.'

'Look, I'm really sorry. Honestly, I'll pay you back, I promise - every penny.' I can't believe I'm being reduced to literally begging my friend. One of the women who was standing behind me at the checkout offers a sympathetic look as she passes, leaving a cloud of her perfume in her wake. Like a sympathetic look will help me at this moment.

'Sometimes you've got to hit rock bottom before you can find your way back,' my friend adds.

This is the last thing I want to hear.

'I don't want to be at rock bottom.' I wipe the tears that are now cascading down my cheeks.

'Then do something to change.'

2

TODAY JUST KEEPS ON GIVING. Someone's stolen the parking space right outside my house. We don't have allocated spaces on our terraced street, but the unspoken rule is that you don't park outside someone else's front door. With grey brick stretching as far as the eye can see, made even bleaker by the winter gloom, the only splash of colour on this street comes from our front doors and cars.

Now I'm forced to park a little way down the hill, which means I'll have further to lug my two heavy shopping bags.

There should have been many more bags if I hadn't been forced to put back nearly half of what was in my trolley. Since I'd already made the minimum payment on my credit card, I was able to spend the fifty pounds of space I'd created. So at least the kids and I can keep body and soul together.

What's she staring at? The woman parked in *my* space in her posh car, outside *my* house, is gawping at me as if I've done something wrong. I narrow my eyes, itching to ask what her problem is. If it were summer and her window was wound down, I probably would, but nobody's going to have their window open in these temperatures. I tear my gaze away from her and stare up into the sky, laden with snow. It's been forecast for the last couple of days, but so far, it's held off, thank goodness. My life feels tough enough right now without adding snow into the mix to slow me down.

'When are you picking me up again, Dad?'

I turn to the familiar voice of my son who's chasing his father from our door in bare feet.

'You haven't taken me anywhere since October.'

'We'll sort something out soon, I promise.'

Trying to avoid my eye and scuttle past me with a toolbox in his hand, George is heading towards the car parked outside my house. The woman at the wheel looks like one of the yummy mummy types who never bothers with me when I'm picking Barnaby up from school. Thankfully, there are also some down-to-earth mums at the school gates. Mums who don't think I'm beneath them just because I drive a battered Polo and don't wear designer labels.

'What are *you* doing here?'

'I needed this from the shed.' He rests the toolbox at his feet on the road beside the Merc he's evidently about to slide into. 'Katina's asked me to do a few jobs.'

'Katina, eh?' I peer through the car window to get a closer look at my adversary, rage pooling in my belly. At least now I've discovered the reason for her interest in me when I was walking past her car.

'I don't know how she's got the nerve to drive right up to our door after what she's done. The ink's barely dry on our divorce papers.' I should be saying what you've *both* done. But at times it's easier to blame her rather than him.

'Leave it out, Aneka. I've come here for some tools, not an argument.'

'So this is how you're spending the kids' maintenance money? I suppose you'll have bought her an expensive

Christmas present?' Curtains from neighbouring houses will no doubt be starting to twitch at my raised voice in the quiet of the street.

The boot of the Merc pops open, and George bends for his box. It's one of the final possessions he has to collect. Soon, he'll have no reason to return. He certainly doesn't seem bothered about seeing his children and has let them down more times than he's picked them up since he moved in with *her*.

'Not, now, eh, Aneka. Look, I'm getting off. There's no need for a scene in front of all the neighbours.'

'There's every need for a scene.' I step closer to him. 'You owe me two months' money.'

'No can do.' He shakes his head. He looks to have just had his hair cut. I can't remember the last time I could afford a trip to the hair salon. 'I can't sort anything until January.'

I drop the shopping bags at my feet. 'But I need it for the kids. For their food over Christmas – for their presents. What I've got here will just about see them over the weekend.'

His eyes widen. Blue eyes, which Barnaby has inherited, that once looked into mine at our wedding ceremony, making promises he never managed to keep. 'You must have allowed other money for all that, surely?'

'I spent what I had on the rent and the gas meter. You'd promised that money, George. I was counting on it being in my bank.'

'Like I've told you so many times, I can't pour from an empty cup. Since we split up, I've had to get back on my feet.'

'But you're working now, and look at you, all togged up in new clothes.' I pull a face at the sight of his jeans, designer sweater and pristine trainers.

'I have to look after myself before I can look after anyone else.'

'That's not how it works when you're a parent.' I'm shouting even louder. The kids will be able to hear every word, and I hate myself for carrying on like this, but the red mist has descended. 'Not that I'd expect you to grasp that after how you've behaved.'

'Don't start pulling me down.' He slams the boot lid.

'Me pull *you* down. How can you say that? After all—'

'Is everything OK?' The driver's door swings open, and the woman's mahogany hair, striped with caramel highlights, appears over the top of the car's roof.

'I'm just talking to my—' the word *husband* is on the tip of my tongue, until I remember the decree absolute so recently granted by the court. 'My children's father.'

'Are we leaving?' Her voice is syrupy sweet as she switches her condescending gaze from me and smiles at George. 'You said you'd be in and out. We've got things to do.'

'You said you'd be in and out, did you? You haven't seen your kids for over a month. And you call yourself a father?'

'Like I just told them – I'll make it up to them. I've just had a lot on.'

'You're a selfish—'

'George.' Clearly unaccustomed to not getting her own way immediately, Miss Caramel Highlights pouts, and looks like she might well be stamping her foot behind her car. 'If you don't get in here now, I'm setting off on my own.' She ducks back down, and her door slams.

'Run along, George,' I hiss as he hurries to the passenger side. 'Rest assured, you'll be hearing from the Child Maintenance Service. If you won't pay me, they'll *force* you to cough up.'

'You wouldn't dare get them involved.'

'Oh, you'll soon find out that I would.'

'I'll just pack my job in.' He opens the passenger side door. 'If you think—'

'And the award for father of the year goes to...'

'Mum.' Hallie's yelling from the front door. 'Please. Just stop.'

The engine of the Merc gives a throaty roar. How can he do this to us? He owed me a thousand pounds today. It took our separation for him to finally sort himself out and start holding down a job. Since then, the kids say he's stopped drinking, taken up the gym, and obviously moved in with *Katina*. She's very aptly named. The way she narrowed her eyes at me was extremely cat-like. And if she'd had a set of claws, I'm certain she'd have happily scratched my eyes out of their sockets.

As the car leaves me in its dust, I reach for the carrier bags at my feet, one of which promptly gives way from the weight of the tins it's holding. 'Bollocks!' I shout into the mist that's beginning to swirl around the houses. 'Hallie, give me a hand.'

Barnaby also rushes from the house, and together, the three of us gather apples, potatoes and tins of tomatoes and beans as they roll into the gutter.

'Shall I get the other bags from the boot, Mum?' Barnaby looks from the remaining bag in the centre of the pavement, and over to the car.

'This is all I've bought.'

'But we've hardly anything in the cupboards.' Hallie frowns. 'You open them up and out fly a load of moths.'

'It isn't that bad.' I laugh as I take a couple of oranges from Barnaby. 'We'll be fine. Meals might be a little more basic until I get some more money in before Christmas, but no one's going to starve.'

Apart from me, I don't add. They're right. There certainly isn't enough food here for a family of three, especially with a sixteen and an eight-year-old, both with decent appetites. So I'll have to survive on the bare minimum to ensure they both have enough to eat.

'You *are* getting paid again before Christmas, aren't you, Mum?' Hallie follows me through our door, and the heat of the hallway envelops me like a warm embrace. At least we've got a roof over our heads and the bills are paid. I've really been trying my best, though clearly, I need to try much harder.

'All being well.'

Somehow, I'll have to sort *something* out before Christmas. And if all else fails, I'll just have to rob a bank.

3

'DID your dad have much to say for himself?' I keep my voice nonchalant as I reach up to stack the pasta and rice in the cupboard. I should ask Hallie to do it, really, now that she's a couple of inches taller than me.

'Not really.' Hallie sounds downcast. 'I feel like I don't know him anymore.'

I want to tell her that George doesn't deserve her and Barnaby. But generally speaking, I try to keep my opinions out of our conversations. They need to decide what they think of their father for themselves.

'I asked him if he's planning to see us over Christmas,' she goes on, 'and he said he needs to see what's happening with Katina before he makes any plans. Like she's way more important than us.' Tears fill my daughter's eyes beneath the huge fake eyelashes she's stuck on. I've told her she doesn't need this kind of enhancement until I'm blue in the face. She's changed out of her school uniform into leggings and a jumper, looking way older than her sixteen years as she passes items to me to put away.

I feel wretched. And I'm going to feel even more wretched if

I can't put any presents under that tree for them both next week. I glance through the kitchen door into the lounge at the monstrosity we've dragged out of the loft for the last thirteen years, where it stands bedraggled and unlit in the corner. Even Barnaby doesn't get excited about it any more when it makes its annual appearance.

'Have you ever been introduced to Katina?' I've never asked this question of my daughter before. I've wanted to, but have always held myself back. 'I'm just wondering why she was waiting in the car like she was, instead of saying hello to you and Barnaby.'

'She doesn't like kids. Not that *I'm* a kid.' She points at herself, showing off the lovely red nails she's painted. 'But to be honest, I'm not fussed about meeting her anyway. Dad cares more about *her* than he ever has about *us,* so I'd probably say something awful.'

'It won't last,' I reply, immediately regretting my words. I'd love to be able to tell Hallie that relationships born out of affairs are built on the shakiest foundations. She doesn't need to hear my adult psychobabble.

'You've really hardly bought anything, Mum.' She pushes one of the loaves into the freezer, her ponytail swinging out behind her. 'Where's the crisps? What about biscuits?'

'Maybe it's time we stopped having so many goodies in the cupboards,' I reply. 'You should both be eating more fruit. More vitamins.' I point at the oranges and apples I've stacked in the fruit bowl. 'Look, I'll get something sorted before next week, I promise.'

Never make promises you can't keep. Grandad's voice pops into my head. How I miss his guiding hand. When he was around, I always had somewhere I could run for support. He was my anchor in life and the only family, besides me, George, and George's parents, that my children knew. His parents barely bothered with the kids *before* George and I separated, but since then, their contact seems to have reduced to birthday and Christmas cards. As for their other grandparent, my mother, the less said about her, the better.

It's soul-destroying to see my daughter's face etched with something that falls between sympathy towards me and misery for herself and her brother. They're both great kids and have put up with more than enough angst as the arguments and the subsequent divorce have played out over the last couple of years. Not to mention their father walking out to start a new life. Just like mine did.

'Would it help if I got a weekend job, Mum?'

Something inside me feels like it's giving way. Hallie already has several babysitting jobs and dog walking responsibilities, so she can afford bits and pieces for herself instead of having to ask me.

And if I know her correctly, she'll have also managed to save up to buy me and her brother something for Christmas. 'Don't be daft – besides, your exams are just around the corner. Hang on, love,' I reach for my phone, which is lying beside the empty biscuit tin. It's a number I don't recognise. Probably someone wanting money. If it is, I'll just end the call. 'Hello?'

Hallie pulls a face - probably at my telephone voice. I put a finger to my lips just in case she decides to poke fun. Perhaps HR have had a rethink and decided to let me have that advance. The man was firm, but there was definitely sympathy in his voice.

'Is that Aneka?'

4

THE MALE VOICE IS FRIENDLY.

'Speaking.'

'I'm calling on behalf of Sienna Milner, who leads wellness retreats.'

'Look, if you're trying to sell me—'

'No, it's nothing like that.' He laughs. 'She's asked me to call you because you have a mutual friend, Ruby – and she's passed on your number. I'm Vince. I work with Sienna.'

Their names don't matter. I just wish he'd cut to the chase – I don't have time for pleasantries. 'Oh – right.' It's also a little odd that Ruby's passed on my number to someone without checking with me beforehand.

'What it is,' he begins. 'Sienna's hosting a winter solstice wellness retreat in the Yorkshire Dales, and one of the helpers has let our team down.'

'Winter solstice, you say?' I glance out at the dusk that's falling beyond our brightly lit kitchen window.

'Yes, it's an escape from Christmas kind of retreat which runs from tomorrow until Monday. To be honest, we'll be run ragged without another pair of hands. Which is why she's asked me to get in touch.'

I hope Ruby hasn't told these people about the extent of my desperation for money. I might be struggling, but I'm proud, and what people think of me matters. Perhaps it shouldn't, but sometimes it feels like my reputation is all I possess. I certainly don't have much else. But whatever Ruby's been saying, I'm all ears at what's coming next. It's not as if I'm in a position to turn work away.

'Do you know much about yoga and meditation?'

'A little,' I lie as I lean against the kitchen counter. 'Would I need to?'

'It would be an advantage, but primarily your duties would be in the kitchen and ensuring the comfort of the guests.'

'Well, I'm good in the kitchen.'

Hallie sniggers, and I glare at her. But she's not wrong. There's a perpetual whiff of burning in this kitchen, no matter how hard I scrub at the oven.

'And I'd do whatever was needed.' Hark at me. I don't even know what the pay is, but whatever it is, I'll make things work so I can earn whatever's going to be offered. Hallie's watching me curiously as she fiddles with her bracelet. I'm going to have some explaining to do in a moment.

'There'll be some early starts.'

'I'm more than used to getting up early. I'm a single mum to two kids.' I need to ask whether I'll be paid before Christmas. But I'll wait until *he* mentions the money side of the arrangement.

'Childcare won't be an issue, will it?' For the first time in the conversation, his voice wavers as though he's uncertain.

'Not at all. I have lots of support with my kids.' My nose has probably just grown to half a foot long. The only support I get is from my greying, worn-out bras. 'Besides, the eldest one isn't really a child anymore - she's sixteen.' I turn away from her and busy myself making a coffee, now that we have some milk in the house.

'You don't sound old enough to be mum to a sixteen-year-old.'

'Thanks.' I smile. It's the first time anyone's said something nice to me today. 'So, the job - you say it starts tomorrow. And it's for three nights?'

'What job?' Hallie mouths at me, her eyes widening in what could be horror. 'You can't go for the full *weekend*.'

I wave her away and pull a face.

'That's right. If you say yes to this, we'll need you as early as possible tomorrow. The guests will be arriving from four, and we need to be ready.'

'I've got a job to do in the morning, and then I can be on my way.' Excitement flutters in my belly. However, this job *has* to pay me before Christmas.

'Sienna's asked me to check that you have a food hygiene certificate?'

The way he says it makes it sound like the job could hinge on my having one. 'Yes,' I lie again. 'But I'm not sure where it is.'

'It's fine. You've been recommended by Ruby, which Sienna says is good enough for her. Normally, she'd follow up with references, but in this case, she doesn't feel she needs to. There probably isn't time anyway.'

'Does this mean I've got the job?' I'm trying not to get my hopes up, as every time I do, they get slammed back down. Hallie's watching me intently as the steam from my mug curls into my face. I can't imagine she's going to be too happy about this.

'That will depend on whether the six hundred pounds for the three nights is OK?'

I want to tell him it's more than OK – it will practically save my life right now. I wish I could ask for an advance so I can leave the kids some money, but that might be pushing things. I don't want to do or say anything that could change their minds about hiring me.

'It's a hundred and fifty pounds per day as you'll be there the best part of four days,' he adds before giving me a chance to reply, as if he's trying to persuade me. 'And just between me and you, if you impress Sienna, there will be further retreats.' He lowers his voice, as though someone could be listening. 'The current chef, Nova, she's actually my mum, who you'll mainly be working with, she's well past retirement age, so Sienna's looking to train someone new up to her way of doing things.'

'Do you know whether she'll be able to pay me before Christmas. I—' I let my voice trail off. I nearly started wittering things like *I don't like to ask,* or *I'll understand if she can't,* but really, it's best if I just let him answer the question.

'I can mention it. I saw her pay the deposit for the lodge in cash, so I imagine she'll be happy to pay you when that gets returned.'

I want to clap my hands together. Grandad, wherever he is, must be watching over me like my guardian angel. I can't believe this chance has landed in my lap.

The money won't cover what I was expecting from George, but even if he doesn't come up with it until the new year, it will still be a Godsend to get it then. I'm driving on two bald tyres and the washer's broken down. At least I'll be able to buy a second-hand one in January, which would put an end to my having to wash clothes in the bath.

'My mum's excellent at her job but can appear a little fero-cious. But honestly, her bark's far worse than her bite. Trust me, I grew up with her.'

Great, a ferocious chef. I imagine a chef-white-clad, middle-aged woman, brandishing a meat cleaver every time I enter the kitchen.

'I'll text you the address, Aneka, and we'll all look forward to meeting you tomorrow.'

'What do I need to bring?'

'Warm things – you've probably heard there's some snow forecast this weekend, and comfy flat shoes. You'll be on your feet a lot of the time.'

'OK, that's great.' I can't believe this has been put my way, but it's reignited my faith in God, the universe, my grandad, whatever. 'I'll see you tomorrow.'

'Well bloody hell.' I rest the phone on the worktop. 'What a turn up.'

'Who was that? Where are you going?' Hallie's voice sounds almost childlike again as she fires her questions.

'I've been offered work until Monday,' I reply. 'But it means I'll be away.' I give her what I hope is an apologetic look.

'I gathered that. But where? What about me and Barnaby?'

'I won't be a million miles away. Just in the Yorkshire Dales.' It suddenly dawns on me that I might not have enough petrol to get there. Well, maybe there, but definitely not back home as well. However, it sounds like I'll be paid on the final day. So I'll be OK.

'For three nights.' Her face drops. 'You've never left us on our own overnight. Will Dad come and stay?' Her voice fills with hope. 'Are you going to ask?'

Chance would be a fine thing. My face drops, too. 'I'll have to call him.' But I already know there's very little chance. He couldn't get away from his kids and into that car with the glamorous Katina fast enough earlier. She seems to be all that matters to him these days.

However, I *have* to take this job. The kids are at school for their last day of term tomorrow, so they'll get their school dinners. Barnaby can go to breakfast club and after-school club, and there's enough food in the house to keep them going over the weekend, even if their staples are going to be jacket potatoes and beans on toast. 'It'll be fine, love, I'll be back before you know it and then we can have a lovely Christmas together.'

We can *now*. I've never been so relieved in all my life.

'Where are you going?' Barnaby appears in the kitchen with concern etched all over his face, the face which is so much like his father's, it sometimes hurts.

'I've been offered some work over the weekend, which will help me give some more money to Father Christmas.' Now that he's eight years old, I'm certain Barnaby doesn't still believe in him, but we still play the game. Christmas Eve, as always, will result in a mince pie, a carrot and a glass of Baileys being left out. Especially now that we can afford these items.

'Will you be sleeping there?' He's wearing the same expression as he used to have when he was experiencing night terrors a couple of years ago.

'I'm afraid so, sweetheart', – I tousle his hair, – 'but like I just said to Hallie, I'll be back before you know it.'

'I don't want you to go.' His eyes bulge with tears.

'I've got to. We need the extra money.' I hate that I've got to tell him this, but it feels better to be honest. At least by telling him the truth, he's more likely to understand. This final weekend before Christmas, in an ideal world, would consist of a panto, some shopping, a German market and lovely evenings snuggled at home with a Christmas tree that isn't bare and lopsided.

'But you need to be safe, Mum.'

'What are you talking about?' I bend to his level. 'Of course I'll be safe. I'm just going to help do some cooking and cleaning at a holiday weekend.'

'If you go there, you won't come back. We'll never see you again.'

Hallie and I exchange looks as if to say, *What on earth is he talking about*?

'Of course you will. Look, you'll be here with your sister, and—'

'Please, Mum, please don't go. Something bad's going to happen if you do.'

'Hey, hey, come here.' I reach for him, but he ducks out of my way and races from the kitchen like he's got the devil after him, slamming the door as he goes.

I stare at the door as his footsteps, now punctuated by his sobs, disappear up the stairs, followed by the bang of his bedroom door.

What the hell has got into him?

5

THEN

'CAN I ride my scooter to the park, Mummy?'

'Of course you can. So long as you don't go too far ahead.' I ruffle her hair, exactly the same colour and texture as her father's.

'Daddy lets me ride out in front.'

It's always the same. Good cop, bad cop. She's only four years old and can already play one of us off against the other. She's definitely a daddy's girl, which, on the whole, makes me happy. But I'm secretly hoping that to even things up, our next child, the one we've just started trying for, is a little boy.

Most of our friends are off travelling or building their careers before children, but all my husband and I dreamt about was having our own family. Building snowmen, waiting for Father Christmas and sharing bedtime stories. People told us to live a little first, but becoming parents has so far given us the happiest years of our lives.

'Hi Brenda,' my daughter calls over the fence to our next-door neighbour. Her garden puts ours to shame, the amount of hours she spends keeping it beautiful. Today, she's wrapping Christmas lights around one of her conifers.

'Well, just the person.' Brenda reaches into the pocket of her apron. '*I've got something for you.*' *She pulls out a Santa-shaped lollipop.*

'*Ooh, thank you.*'

'*You'll have to save that,*' I say. '*You could have a nasty accident if you were to fall off your scooter with a lolly stick hanging out of your mouth.*'

'*Daddy let me have a lolly last time.*'

'*Your mum's right,*' Brenda smiles. '*Anyway, I bet you're counting the days down now until the big day.*'

'*Six more sleeps.*' Her voice quivers with excitement.

'*And how's big school going?*'

'*I love it.*'

'*What about Mummy? How are you coping?*'

'*I just miss her,*' I laugh. '*It was the end of an era, having my little girl at home full time.*'

We've agreed that if I fall pregnant before the spring, I won't go back to work just yet, but if not, I'll have to find a part-time job. I love being at home full-time and really don't want things to change, but maybe I could get something at her school, or any school, so I'm only working in term time.

'*Come on, Mummy, we need to get to the park before it gets dark.*'

I laugh. She sounds just like me.

'*Duty calls,*' Brenda laughs too. '*Don't worry, I'll see you both for a longer chat some other time, all being well.*'

'*It always makes me nervous when someone says 'all being well' about seeing me again.*' I pull a face. '*It makes me wonder if they know something I don't.*'

6

I'VE STILL GOT NEARLY fifteen miles to go, and my petrol light has just lit up on the dashboard. My little Polo is good at limping along on fumes, usually, and I just pray it doesn't let me down. I'm already later than I'd like to be, as the cleaning job I had to finish this morning took way longer. Luckily, the family paid me my thirty pounds in cash, so Hallie and Barnaby have got a little money.

George, as I suspected, wanted nothing to do with looking after them over the weekend.

'You arrange these things – so sorting the children out is your responsibility.' It was a miracle he'd even answered the phone.

'I wouldn't have to take this job if you'd paid me what you promised.' I'd literally shrieked this at him, forgetting to keep my voice down while the kids got ready for school this morning. Barnaby was already upset.

'I've got a life to live as well,' George replied.

'You're their bloody father. And if you won't pay their maintenance money on time, the least you could do is keep an eye on them while I ensure they have some presents to open next week.'

But my pleas amounted to nothing. I couldn't have asked Ruby to help after her comments yesterday about my only being in touch when I want a favour. So I just sent her a text thanking her for recommending me for the job at the retreat. She hasn't got back to me yet, but I expect she's busy getting ready for Christmas. At least I know she still cares about me, as she wouldn't have put me forward if I'd truly blown our friendship.

The best I could do was to persuade my neighbour to be on hand if Hallie and Barnaby have a crisis. I hated asking her, but I've looked after her dog when they're away often enough and kept an eye on their house. One good turn deserves another, as I reminded her when she initially looked hesitant.

Barnaby clung to me when I dropped him off at breakfast club this morning. 'Please don't leave me, Mum,' he begged. 'You're not going to come back, are you?' There was such fear in his face as the bewildered breakfast club staff had to peel him from my leg.

'What on earth's the matter, sweetheart?' One of them said. 'Let's go over to the book corner and have a chat. You get going.' She gave me a sympathetic smile, which once again invited the tears.

'Thank you.' I called after them in a wobbly voice. I'd wanted to remind him not to fight with his sister and to keep the house tidy, but such talk might have made matters worse. Besides, I didn't really want the breakfast club staff knowing I was disappearing for the weekend and leaving Barnaby with his sister.

There's enough gas and electricity on the meters to keep them going, so my conscience is as clear as it can be under the circumstances. I hate living so hand-to-mouth and would have probably made my excuses to the landlord and not paid the rent until the new year if I'd suspected George might not transfer the money.

The first snow flurries are starting as I swap the main A roads for the more bendy and narrower B roads. I hope the snow doesn't lay until after I arrive. And even then, I hope it doesn't hang around as I need to get home on Monday. There's also the risk of the weather impeding the arrival of the retreat's guests. Without their attendance, I doubt I'll get paid.

'Come on, little car. Please get me there safely.' My voice is loud in the quiet. Well, I say quiet – I mean other than the shriek of the engine, which should have been serviced twenty thousand miles ago. The radio, which I could have switched on to drown out the noise and distract me from worrying, gave up the ghost around a year ago, much to the children's disgust. Now, when we go anywhere, they're usually plugged into their earphones.

The warning on my dashboard says I'm down to the last five miles. Oh God. The sat nav on my phone says seven miles. I have to get there. I can't be late. Plus, it's too cold to break down out here in the sticks. The temperature's only just above freezing.

I want to weep with relief as I reach a sign directing me to the private lane leading to the retreat venue. Whispering Pines, my destination, is way off the beaten track, nestled deep into a forest.

From the outside, the sprawling lodge with its dormer windows couldn't look any more inviting with lamplight shining from the windows as the snow continues to fall. It's heavier now and beginning to lay. I imagine Barnaby, who'll be in his art lesson. He'll be beside himself with excitement when he sees the snow from his classroom window.

That's if he's settled down as the day has progressed. The

last day before Christmas is always a fun day at school, so hopefully his mind will be diverted.

I wish I was picking him up and could take him to the park to play in it before it gets dark. Then I remind myself why I'm doing this. For my children. Only for my children. I've been backed into a corner and don't have any choice other than to leave them on their own this weekend.

I pull into the space beside an Audi. I'll leave my stuff here, in the boot. At least until I'm shown my room. I don't want anyone seeing that I've had to lug my belongings in an Aldi bag. This is certain to be different for the others staying here, with the nine-hundred-pound price tag attached to each of the retreat places.

'How much?' I nearly choked on my tea when Hallie read out what she'd found on Sienna's website.

'Four days, three nights,' she continued reading. 'Sumptuous vegetarian food at a beautiful venue – all workshops, classes, meditations and treatments included.'

'Treatments?'

Her eyes travelled down the screen. 'Massage, Reiki, Reflexology. What's that?'

'Feet, I think.' I replied. 'And I'm not sure about Reiki. I really haven't lived, have I?' *I've been too busy trying to survive.* But I didn't say this aloud. Not to my daughter.

I look back at my footprints in the freshly-laid snow as I wait at the door. It's like a scene from a picture-perfect Christmas card, though it's eerily silent. If it wasn't for the cars, I'd think nobody was inside the building. There certainly doesn't seem to be any sign of movement.

No one comes. I press the doorbell again.

Still, no one comes.

I glance at my phone and click on the message notification

in case there's been a change of plan. But no, the top message is the one I sent to Ruby. In response to the thank you message I sent for putting me forward, she's acknowledged it with a puzzled emoji instead of her usual smiley face, heart or thumbs up. She must have been using her phone without her glasses on and has hit the wrong emoji.

'Hello?' I push the heavy door, and a wall of heat hits me, just like when I got home yesterday – only this time it's from a crackling fire.

The air is thick with the scent of burning wood and something sweet, maybe incense, as I creep down the dim hallway. A floorboard groans beneath my trainers. It's warm and inviting, but a prickle of unease runs down my spine. I should have waited to be invited inside.

'Hello?' I call again, more quietly. What if they're all meditating, or performing whatever mystical ritual people do on wellness retreats? I might have pretended on the phone with Vince that I knew what I was getting into, but the truth is, I haven't got a clue.

'Who are you?'

I swing around at the voice behind me. Wearing a *Wellness with Sienna* apron across her slender frame, there stands a woman with a severe bobbed hairstyle and an even more severe expression as she looks from my scraggy ponytail down to my scraggier trainers.

'I'm erm. I'm here to help. I'm Aneka.' I hold my hand out, but the woman doesn't accept my greeting. I've had warmer welcomes from my former in-laws, and that's saying something. 'Are you Sienna?' I gesture to her apron.

'Of course not.' Her tone is snappy. 'But since you're asking, I'll tell you categorically, just like I told Sienna, that we don't need your help.'

'Of course we do.' Like a beacon of light, a woman with hair in three different startling shades of red comes bounding down the stairs. 'Aneka, hi – you made it. Welcome to Whispering Pines.'

'Of course I made it.' I smile back at her. 'So *you* must be Sienna.' There's something familiar about this woman, but I can't imagine where I could have ever met her before. It's probably just that I recognise her from her picture on the website. If a wellness instructor could have a 'look,' Sienna embodies it with her bright, flowing tunic, baggy trousers and bare feet.

She smiles back. 'Ignore our grumpy chef. She's just worried that you might upstage her. Nova, this is Aneka. Aneka, Nova. Now I need you to play nicely, Nova, you must show our new member of staff the ropes in the kitchen.'

Nova grunts about kitchen assistants who never last for more than five minutes and storms through a door next to the fire. I hope Vince was right when he said his mother's bark is worse than her bite.

'Ah, Carley.' A surge of freezing air brings a woman who's around my age carrying some sort of big case-type thing, which looks like it could unfold into a table. 'Just the person. I need to get set up for the first gathering ahead of our guests arriving, so I was hoping you might show Aneka around and let her know what she'll be doing.'

'She's here instead of Nancy, right?' Carley gives me a quizzical look. She's not friendly, but she's not unfriendly either. But she's so well put together with her perfect plait and her tunic and trousers combo that she's making me feel even more of a mess.

'That's right. Nancy said she didn't want to risk being snowed in here and missing Christmas with her family.' Sienna points at the fat snowflakes now steadily falling outside the cosy lamplit window. 'I thought she was pulling a fast one when she said it, but I dare say that if it carries on like this, her fears could be justified.'

I laugh but can't disguise the nerves jangling within it. The thought of not making it home to Hallie and Barnaby before Christmas Eve doesn't bear contemplating.

Perhaps this is what has sent Barnaby into such a tailspin. Though I have a nasty feeling in my gut that it could be something much, much worse.

7

'So that concludes your grand tour.' We finish up in a large, candlelit, almost church-like room where Sienna's rolling out exercise mats in rows of three. I glance up at the stained glass window above the arched door and the high, ornate beams criss-crossing the ceiling.

'This, a hundred and odd years ago, was used as a chapel of rest for the workers killed building the nearby viaduct.' Carley's voice echoes around the space as she points in what must be the direction of the viaduct. 'Which I think gives the whole place a really cool feel.'

I shiver. If she means *cool*, as in good and exciting, I really can't agree. Cool as in chilly, I most certainly can. Though I wish she hadn't told me about the chapel's former purpose. Now that I know, I can almost picture the scene.

'It brings a whole new meaning to corpse pose,' Sienna chuckles. I laugh back even if I have no idea what she means.

'Hopefully we won't have any corpses on this retreat.' Carley also laughs.

'I'd better get my stuff from the car,' I turn back to Carley. 'Can you show me my room?' I'm puzzled that she never pointed it out while she was giving me a tour. I kept expecting her to open a door and say, 'So this is where you'll be sleeping.'

'It's right here.' The dour-faced Nova enters the chapel from a side door, wiping her hands on her apron. She points at what looks like a bag of shopping on the ground near the far wall. 'Your airbed and sleeping bag are in there.'

I resist the urge to retort with *you're joking,* and instead I swallow as I cast my gaze around the room. 'Is there any heating?'

'It's on a timer,' Nova replies. 'So it goes off overnight. But that shouldn't cause you any bother. After all, you'll be asleep.'

'If one of the guests doesn't make it...' I glance out at the snow, certain someone will get stuck. 'Would I be able to have a proper bed if one became free?'

I also want to ask whether Nova and Carley already have real beds, but with Sienna watching, I have to bite my tongue. I've only just arrived – complaining about things isn't going to endear me to anyone. Still, asking about a bed seems reasonable. Surely.

'The therapists and other staff attend my retreats on a different basis,' Sienna says, as if plucking the thought straight from my mind. 'While you're being paid, the therapists aren't.'

'I do the massages and get the retreat in return,' Carley explains. 'But it's more than worth it to stay in a place like this for a few days.' She stretches out her arms.

I look at Nova, interested to hear what her 'basis of work' is. But she doesn't say a word. She's going to be a hard one to win over. I wonder what her problem is. It's got to be more than just being unhappy because of her impending retirement. I get a sense it's somehow being forced.

'It's alright – I'll be fine.' I inject a cheer I'm not feeling into my voice. I need to sound grateful. I *am* grateful. Without this work, there would be no Christmas for my children.

'You're going to have to be.' Nova looks at me like I'm something nasty she might have stepped in. 'Anyway, Sienna, if this snow continues, if we're here beyond Monday, do we have a contingency plan for the food?'

Sienna swings around to face her. 'What do you mean?'

'I mean, what happens when it's all been eaten?'

Sienna's eyes widen, then she laughs. 'Perhaps we need to be rationing everyone from the moment they arrive. I don't know, Nova – we'll cross that bridge if and when we get to it.'

Nova spins on her heel and heads back towards the door she entered by, clearly upset at her concerns being so easily dismissed.

'What are those?' I turn back to Sienna, who's now placing little rectangular pillows on everyone's mats.

'Lavender eye pillows for the relaxation,' Carley explains.

I look at one with longing. How I'd love just to lie down for half an hour with one of those across my eyes. From worrying about Barnaby to my hellish journey driving on petrol fumes, I'm exhausted. It's *me* who needs to retreat and be looked after for a few days. If only.

Shaking such daft thoughts from my mind, I ask, 'What will I be doing?'

'In short,' Sienna begins, 'you'll be making sure our guests are happy and have everything they need.'

'Which can be harder than it sounds,' Carley adds, thrusting her hands into the pockets of her tunic, probably to keep them warm. 'We sometimes get some *very* discerning guests.'

She sounds like she could have worked with Sienna for a long time. This bodes well. Nova's only leaving due to her retirement, which she evidently doesn't even welcome. Therefore, perhaps I'll have a job with Sienna for many years to come if I do OK this weekend.

'You'll also be under Nova's instruction in the kitchen,'

Sienna goes on as she begins dishing out a blanket for each mat.

'Which is also harder than it sounds.' Carley tugs me to one side, away from Sienna's earshot. 'I'd like to say, don't let Nova get to you, but that's easier said than done. What I will say is, impress *Sienna* over these next few days, and you might be able to take over from where Nova will hopefully be leaving off.'

'I really hope you *can* impress me, Aneka. Especially in the kitchen.'

'You weren't supposed to hear me, Sienna.'

She laughs. 'You know I have hearing like a bat.'

Cripes. What Sienna doesn't know is that I have a sign in my own kitchen, saying *I only have a kitchen because it came with the house.* What she also doesn't know is that my teenage daughter does more of the cooking than I do because I can literally burn water.

I'm going to have to be on the ball. I'll have to watch Nova. Listen to Nova, and somehow get on the right side of her so I can learn. Failing that, there's always the cookery channels on YouTube. That's if there's such a thing as wifi signal in a place this remote. The lane I drove along to reach the lodge seemed to go on forever, and get further and further into the wilderness with every yard.

The door Nova disappeared behind swings open again, and I'm half expecting her to be demanding I hurry along and start working instead of gossiping.

Instead, a man steps into the chapel, and I'm struck by how much like George he looks, except he's a little taller. Especially now that George is making more effort with his appearance for his posh new girlfriend.

'Ah, there you are,' Sienna exclaims. This man must be working for her as well, which might make the next few days a whole lot more interesting. No, I shouldn't be thinking along these lines. Men need to remain off limits, even good-looking ones with the swagger of Robbie Williams. Still, our eyes meet, and something definitely passes between us. Though what it could be makes me more than slightly uneasy.

I wish I'd made more effort, other than to wrench the first thing I could find from the ironing pile. Namely, faded jeans and one of Hallie's hoodies. I'm not wearing a scrap of makeup, and my hair is dragged back into a ponytail.

Men haven't been on my radar since George moved out, and it's not as if I've even got time for a relationship. As I keep telling myself, I need to focus on my kids. Men bring me nothing but heartache.

'Aneka, Vince, Vince, Aneka.'

'The pleasure is all mine.' He takes my hand, and I wonder for a moment if he's going to kiss it, but instead, he just drops it like a stone. Really, he's too old for me – I'd place him in at least his late forties, if not his early fifties. 'It's interesting to put a face to the voice.'

Interesting?

'Shouldn't you be setting up, Vince?' Sienna's haughty tone makes me worry for a moment that Vince might be her husband. Perhaps she likes an older man.

'Vince is our reflexology practitioner,' Carley explains, no doubt noticing me trying to work things out as I glance from him to Sienna. 'He's worked on every single retreat with Sienna.'

I want to ask exactly what a reflexology treatment consists of, other than being about feet, but obviously, I can't. When Vince phoned me yesterday, I made out that I'm familiar with what goes on at these retreats. If I'd have let on that I'm as clueless as I am, I doubt I'd have been offered the job.

'Three of the guests are arriving early,' Sienna says, her tone brisk. 'Just to make sure they can get here safely.' Right on cue, the doorbell echoes around the building. 'We've got all the staff here now, so this must be the arrival of our first guest.'

'Exciting.' Carley says in a sing-song voice as she breaks into a jog towards the door.

8

As it happens, it's the first *three* guests. The women stagger through the door, stamping snow from their UGG boots. They're each dragging a pink wheeled case and are laden with bags on their shoulders and yoga mats under their arms. They're huffing and puffing as if they've endured a mountainous trek instead of having just crossed the car park. The last one in shuts the heavy door with her foot. With that door constantly opening and closing, stoking the coal fire in the corner will be a never-ending job.

'Hello again, you guys.' Sienna flies across the hallway and greets them one by one with a hug. 'I'm so glad you made it.'

'So are we.' The eldest-looking woman of the three rests her bags at her feet. 'I don't suppose there's any chance of a hot drink?' With their shoulder-length, poker-straight dark hair, they must be sisters.

Sienna turns to where I'm loitering. 'Our new assistant, Aneka, will help you settle in and get you a drink.'

'It's lovely to meet you.' I beam at them in turn. 'What can I get you all?'

'Coffee for me – I'm Ana, by the way. And these are my

sisters, Ashleigh and Alexis. We're otherwise known as the A-team.'

'Oh, cool.'

'We'll have tea, please.' Alexis points from herself to Ashleigh. Hopefully I'll remember who's who, but I'm not confident. They look so alike, not just their hair but their faces, that I'll quickly forget their names.

'Ashleigh's getting married on New Year's Eve,' Sienna explains. 'So this is one of her hen parties.'

'One of *five* parties.' She scrunches her face in excitement. 'What can I say – I'm a very lucky lady.'

'Do you take milk and sugar?' I should ask how her wedding arrangements are going or whether she feels nervous, but after the year I've had, the last thing I want to talk about is anything to do with getting married. So I'll keep it to myself that I'm newly divorced. Nobody excited about their wedding wants to hear how badly wrong it can all go in the end.

'Milk, no sugar. We're all sweet enough.'

'Of course you are.' I smile.

'I'll sort their drinks,' Carley offers as she comes up behind me. 'You show the ladies to their rooms so they can offload their bags.'

'Excellent idea,' Sienna smiles. 'All the doors are labelled. Carley's given you the grand tour of the lodge, hasn't she, Aneka?'

'Yes, thanks. I know the way.' I just wish I were staying in one of those lovely ensuite rooms up there alongside the guests. I grab bags from two of the sisters and hoik them over my shoulders before reaching for a third bag to carry in my hands. 'Are you all alright to carry your cases?'

'Sure.'

I lead the way up the stairs. 'So how was your journey?' I should make conversation.

'It looks like we got here in the nick of time.' They all laugh.

'I kind of hope it snows on my wedding day,' Ashleigh says as we reach the top. 'It would be so pretty.'

I want to tell her how it snowed on my Valentine's Day wedding all those years ago. How I stood in the register office with a noticeable bump under my dress and my new in-laws shooting me sidelong looks of barely concealed disapproval. I was never good enough for George in their eyes. They'll be thrilled when they meet Katina, with her flashy car and too-white teeth.

The women behind me are still chattering about fairy-tale white weddings as I push the door into their room.

'Here you go.' I step aside and resist the urge to cry with envy. It's not just a room, it's practically a suite, rustic and cosy, just like the rest of the lodge. A bathroom and sitting area occupy the downstairs space, with a wooden spiral staircase leading to a sleeping loft. It's the only room in the lodge with its own upper level, which explains the dormer window I noticed from the car park. I'd be grateful just to sleep on their sofa.

'I'll leave you to get settled. Your drinks will be waiting downstairs when you've unpacked.' I bow my head as if I'm dealing with royalty. They're too busy chattering and taking in their accommodation with ooohs and aaahs to reply.

Carley's opening the door to our next guest as I arrive back at the foot of the stairs. 'Tracy,' she exclaims to the woman in a huge woollen coat. 'Vince never said *you* were taking part.'

'Only Alexander knew.' Tracy shakes her mane of chestnut hair behind her shoulders as she crosses the threshold with her matching pieces of luggage, the top of her head skimming the frame of the doorway. 'I wanted to surprise Vince.'

Damn. Vince has a girlfriend, wife or whatever role she plays. I should have known.

'I can't believe this weather.' She jerks her head in the direction of the door. 'Or how long I had to drive along that track. It's a ridiculous place to have a winter retreat.'

I'd like to point out that she's the ridiculous person for booking it if she wasn't prepared to take a chance with the weather, being that it's December. Instead, I say, 'Oh well, at least you got here in one piece.'

She glares at me as if wondering how I dare to give her my unsolicited opinion.

'Can I get you a hot drink?' There, the ultimate pacifier. 'While you get comfy by the fire.'

'Tea, strong, no sugar.' There's no please. There's no thank you. Then she turns towards the voices coming from the kitchen. 'Has Vince arrived?'

'I'll let him know you're here.' Carley points her in the direction of the lounge, and I watch her retreat along the corridor. 'She'll be a tricky one,' Carley hisses into my ear as Tracy disappears behind the lounge door. 'She came along last year when she and Vince first met, and just because she's his girlfriend, she behaved like the Queen of Sheba.'

My face must fall for Carley laughs. 'The best ones are always taken, aren't they? Though to be honest, I don't think he's quite as enamoured with her as he was when they first met.'

A man ducks under a doorway from the dining room. This one's younger than Vince, closer to my sort of age. He's got a weasely kind of look about him with his pointed face and sharp eyes, and though I hate to make negative first impressions, I can't help it.

'This is Alexander, our Reiki master,' Carley explains. 'He's also Sienna's husband.'

'You must be Aneka. Welcome to the madhouse.' Alexander, the Reiki master, whatever that is, actually seems friendlier than he looks. 'Hopefully, my wife won't work you too hard and you'll get a chance to join in with some of what's going on.'

I smile back. I'd like to tell him that I don't expect to join in.

Besides, if I'm busy working, the time will go faster, and before I know it, I'll be back at home with Hallie and Barnaby.

'I can't believe they're making you sleep in the chapel.' He pulls a face. 'But you know where to come if you're scared.'

I glance along the hallway. The last thing I want is for Sienna to hear her husband making such comments. I laugh, though the sound jangles with nerves.

'Since I'm already sharing my room with Sienna, can't Aneka bunk in with you?' He turns to Carley.

Yes, he's a lech. Great, this is all I need.

'Have you seen the size of the sun room, where I'm sleeping?' Carley pulls a face. 'It's hardly bigger than a postage stamp.'

As the doorbell rings again, the sisters are descending the stairs, wittering away about *who hasn't RSVP'd* and what *she'll say when she sees her* and how *she can't believe it.* I'd have loved to have made such a big thing for my wedding day instead of accepting the shotgun event George's parents insisted on for the sake of appearances.

'Have you gone to China for that tea?' A hostile voice echoes along the hallway. It must be Vince's evidently entitled girlfriend. I can't imagine for the life of me what he sees in the woman. Yes, she's pretty in a trophy wife sort of way, but in her case, beauty really is only skin deep. I sense Carley's right. Tracy's going to be extremely hard work this weekend.

'Coming,' Carley calls back. 'Whoops.' She hisses in my ear. 'I almost forgot about Tracy. You get the door, I'll get the tea and let Vince know his weekend has just become ten times more tricky.'

'I'll help Sienna set up for the opening circle,' Alexander says with a wink. 'I'd better earn my keep.'

As I open the door, the whoosh of freezing air brings a shower of snow onto the doormat. Before me stands a woman beneath her umbrella. The first thing I notice is her silly high heels. I don't know how she's managed to drive in them, let alone walk across the car park in the accumulating snow.

My eyes travel past her skinny jeans to her beautiful padded coat. Our eyes eventually meet, hers narrowing to slits as I stifle a gasp. Her eyes then widen, her expression filled with shock as we stand, our gazes locked for several seconds. I don't know whether to laugh my head off or run for the hills.

'I'm here for the retreat,' she eventually says. Her voice is more nonchalant than I would ever have predicted if I'd been able to forecast us coming together in this way.

I'm too gobsmacked to reply as I stand to the side to let her in, checking across the car park to ensure she's alone. I let a long breath out. She seems to be. For if she'd brought her partner, I'd *really* be in trouble.

I can barely believe the latest person to step into the lodge is none other than the woman who was waiting in the car outside my house yesterday. Yes, for the next three nights and four days, I'm going to be bowing, scraping, fetching and carrying for Katina, my ex's new girlfriend.

And I couldn't have a more ghastly feeling in my gut.

9

Two of the final three guests have just arrived, a mother and daughter, both with curly, bobbed hair, who finish each other's sentences and seem content to stay in their own little bubble. Their closeness hits me like a punch. I would give anything to have a mother I'd want to spend a weekend with, or more painfully, a mother who'd want to spend it with me.

Meanwhile, Tracy continues to hold court in the cosy lamplit lounge. I hate being judgmental, but I don't think she's spoken about anything other than herself for the past half hour. As I've bobbed in and out with tea, freshly baked scones and blankets to tuck around knees while the log burner gets going, I've learned that she owns a chartered accountancy firm with high-profile clients, she has a horse her mother is tending in her absence, her sister's just started biochemistry at Cambridge, and she herself trains every morning with a personal trainer. The others seem to hang onto her every word as she goes on... and on... and on.

'How come you're all wearing matching jumpers?' She addresses the elder looking of the three sisters, all sitting in a row on the largest and most comfortable-looking sofa.

'It's her hen do.' Ana points at Ashleigh. 'We're her two chief—'

'Ooh, when Vince finally gets around to popping the question,' Tracy cuts in. 'I'll have five bridesmaids and it will be a summer wedding, probably on an exotic beach. It'll be absolutely—'

'I need these lilies moving out of here – outside preferably.' The final guest, a red-headed lady who looks to be in her mid-twenties, has barely been led into the lounge by Vince, and she's already complaining. 'They'll give me a migraine.'

'This is Madison,' Vince announces, and I notice how he seems to be avoiding Tracy's eye. Perhaps the surprise she hoped to give him has turned out to be more of a shock. Meanwhile, the appreciative look Katina gives him as he strides into the room indicates more than a fleeting interest.

'Will they be alright in the hallway?' I slide the vase from the table.

'I need them completely outside.' Madison sniffs as she squashes herself into the remaining space beside the hen sisters. She crosses one denim-clad leg over the other and reaches for the blanket I've left on the sofa arm. 'I've paid enough to be here – I don't want it spoiling with a migraine.'

'I think they're pretty,' Ashleigh tilts her head to the side as she points at the vase in my hands. 'I've got lilies in my bridal bouquet.'

'They remind me of a funeral more than a wedding.' Katina wrinkles her freckle-dusted nose. 'Lilies represent death.' She gives me a pointed look as I turn to head for the door. Great. Not only has she helped herself to my husband, but she now wants to make veiled threats in my direction. No wonder she hasn't mentioned to anyone who she is. It's probably way more fun for her if no one knows how the two of us are acquainted.

'While you're taking them outside, I wouldn't mind a cup of tea.' Madison points at the mug in Ana's hand. 'Not one like that, though – it's way too strong for my liking. And if you could also change this blanket.' She rests it back on the arm of the sofa.

I give her my sweetest smile. After all, the comfort of these guests is what I'm being paid to uphold. 'What kind of blanket would you like, Madison?'

'One that's less scratchy.'

Katina scowls as I step back into the lounge and lift her empty mug from the table. 'Can I get you a top-up?' I attempt to force warmth into my voice. I refuse to sink to her level, no matter how loudly my thoughts are screaming, *How dare you scowl at me?*

I can't shake the growing suspicion that George has spent the kids' two months of unpaid maintenance on this retreat, as her Christmas gift. And now I'm expected to wait on her hand and foot for the next three days. George couldn't have planned this situation, but I can barely believe my rotten luck. Of all the people and all the retreats, how the hell have she and I found ourselves at the same one?

Yesterday, she mostly waited in the car while I confronted George, watching me with that smug, triumphant expression on her face. It was bad enough when she broke up my marriage, but I can't forgive how she pretends my children don't exist. Who gets involved with a man with two kids and then refuses to even acknowledge them, let alone meet them?

I pause in the hallway, the weight of it all pressing down. I genuinely don't know how I'm going to survive the long weekend, serving Katina, especially with her looking at me as though I'm something contagious.

Maybe I should just walk away now, before the snow traps us all inside this lodge.

'You OK?' Carley breezes from her room on the opposite side of the hallway. 'You could cut the atmosphere in there with a knife.' She nods in the direction of the lounge.

I grimace. 'They'll probably be fine once they all get to know each other.' I'm not going to tell anyone who Katina is. It's not as if it's anyone else's business, really, and it's also unprofessional for me to bring anything personal into my work. It's better and easier if nobody knows.

'It looks like Tracy, as always, and also Katina and Madison are going to cause all the problems this weekend.' Carley rolls her eyes.

If I were to tell *anyone* of the predicament I've found myself in, it would be Carley. I'd warn her that I'm likely to erupt with Katina if she continues looking at me like I'm something she's stepped in for the rest of the weekend. In the scheme of things, there aren't that many people here, so it's going to be impossible for Katina and me to keep out of each other's way.

A defeated feeling envelops me. Maybe I should just confess. Let Carley know it's not going to work. Take off, back into the snow while Sienna's busy setting up in the chapel.

My children's faces enter my mind. They need this money. I'm doing this for their Christmas presents.

'Here, give those to me.' Carley takes the empty mugs from my hands. 'Have *you* had a warm drink since you arrived?'

I shake my head.

'Tea?' She offers. 'Milk and sugar?'

'Just milk.' Tears burn my eyes at her kindness. I hope Sienna, Nova or Alexander don't come out here now and find me busy doing nothing. But I just need a moment to gather my thoughts.

As I watch Carley walk towards the two-way swing door back into the kitchen, I brush my unexpected tears away with my sleeve.

Really, I can't blame Katina for George not sending his

maintenance money. *He's* my children's father and the person who's supposed to be responsible for their welfare. Not *her*.

Perhaps speaking to the kids will convince me what to do for the best. As I wait for Carley to re-emerge from the kitchen, I press the button against Hallie's name and sink into the window seat.

'It's only me.' It's such a relief to hear my daughter's voice. 'Just checking you both got home safely from school in the snow.'

'Yeah, but Barnaby's still acting really weird. He's scaring me.'

'Oh no.' My heart sinks. I was convinced the last day at school before the Christmas holidays would have taken his mind off things. The children won't have been expected to do a stroke of schoolwork and will probably have spent all day playing games.

'He's convinced you're not going to come back home, Mum. That it will just be me and him on Christmas Day. And then forever. That's what he keeps saying.'

'I'll have another word with him in a minute.'

'I'd leave it at the moment. I've managed to persuade him to go on his Xbox so he's distracted for the first time since I met him at the school gates.'

'I should never have left you with him like this. I'm so sorry, love. I think I'm going to come home.'

'It's alright, Mum. You're there now. But can I ring you later if he gets upset?'

'Of course you can, and if he keeps on like this, I'll definitely leave.' But even as I glance from the window at the blanket of snow that's now covering our cars as the dusk darkens, I know it's going to be impossible to go anywhere until the snow subsides. I hate the darkness at this time of year, but at least it's the shortest day on Sunday and, after that, the darkness will start going the other way.

At least, I hope it will.

Besides, as I have to keep reminding myself, I haven't even got enough petrol to get home. Once I've got some money, I may have to ask Carley to drive me to the nearest petrol station to buy and fill a petrol canister. I'm not sure if my little Polo will even get me to the end of the track.

'It's fine, Mum. As long as we can keep speaking on the phone.'

I swallow the lump in my throat. Hallie's always had an older head on her young shoulders, and she's looked after her younger brother for years when I've needed to work, but this doesn't make me feel any less guilty for leaving them for so long. 'Text me first rather than ringing, love, as I don't always know where I'll be or whether I'll be able to take a call. I'll always ring you back as quickly as I can.'

'OK.' As she falls silent, it's on the tip of my tongue to tell her who's turned up here, but really, she doesn't need to know that I've got Katina to contend with. Instead, I bite my lip, promising that we'll speak later and that I'll also talk to Barnaby.

'One cup of tea for our newest recruit.' Carley emerges from the kitchen and presses the mug into my hands.

'Thanks, you're a star.'

'What's the plan then?' Tracy curls her head around the corner of the lounge, tapping the face of her watch. 'The programme says the opening circle starts at half past four.'

'Tell them we haven't come all this way in this weather to be stuck in a poxy room drinking tea all day.' It sounds like Madison. I've only spoken to her once, but she's made quite an impression.

I smile my sweetest smile at Tracy as I pass my tea back to Carley and rise to my feet. 'I'll see what I can find out.'

'Yes, I'm ready for them,' Sienna replies as I enter the chapel. It looks even more like a final resting place than it did before, now that it's just about dark outside. 'I might have known it would be Tracy who'd be kicking up a stink.'

'How well do you know her?'

'Well enough to know that she's only here to spy on Vince.'

'*Spy* on him? But why?'

'She doesn't trust him, that's all. But Alexander booked her in. I knew nothing about it until she'd already paid for a place.'

'Is she OK about not sharing a room with Vince?'

'She'll have to be.' Sienna gives me a strange look – as if I'm asking too many questions.

'Anyway, if you'd like to head to the kitchen now and help Nova with the evening meal, we'll be having a short meditation practice after the opening circle, and then, no doubt, there will be a few hungry mouths to serve.'

My mind flicks back to the children, and the fact that I only managed to leave jacket potatoes, pasta and a couple of sorry excuses for meals. But I'll make it up to them. That's the whole reason I'm here. When Barnaby is tearing open the presents he's been coveting, he'll forget all about the terrible feeling that something bad is going to happen to his mum.

But as I trudge past Sienna towards the kitchen, a cold prickle creeps up my spine. And for the first time since he got upset, a thought I've been pushing away forces itself to the front of my mind.

What if Barnaby's intuition is right?

10

THEN

THE SUN HANGS *low in a peachy sky, sinking behind rooftops. It casts the street in a somewhat eerie glow where everything looks beautiful but at the same time, sinister. The days are closing in earlier and earlier each afternoon.*

It's nearly the shortest day.

'Come on, Mummy!' My daughter doesn't wait for an answer. Despite my warning only moments ago, she shoots ahead on her scooter, pigtails flying, laughter trailing behind her like a ribbon in the wind. 'I'll race you to the slide!'

'No – slow down!' My voice cracks. I lengthen my stride, my trainers slapping the ground, my heart ticking faster with every rotation of her scooter wheels against the cracks in the pavement. 'What did I say?'

She doesn't hear. Or she chooses not to listen. Her excitement is louder than my caution.

That's when I hear the car. A guttural engine roar, sounding far away at first. Then the shriek of tyres. A sound that doesn't belong in our neighbourhood.

A prickle of dread crawls beneath my skin. I break into a jog. 'Wait!' I shout, sharper now. 'Stay with me! We're by a road!'

It isn't normally busy near the park. The engine is closer now, too close. The hairs on the back of my neck rise.

Another screech.

I look behind. A car's hurtling up the road, swerving wildly, as though it's being flung rather than driven.

My daughter is still ahead. Still laughing. Still unaware.

Time slows.

My legs are moving, but it's like I'm wading through water. My arms pump, my lungs burn, and my vision tunnels. The only thing in my focus is her small body on that scooter, directly in the path of the oncoming car.

The vehicle jolts right. Then left. The driver overcorrects. The bonnet lifts slightly as if the car is about to take flight.

I scream her name just as the car mounts the pavement, and a bang explodes into the quiet afternoon.

11

'As I said when you arrived, I don't need an assistant. I told Sienna this when she insisted on replacing Nancy.' Nova raises her voice over the dreadful music she's playing. Some kind of repetitive, grating drone, possibly from the seventies.

'But since you *are* here, you can peel and chop those apples ready for the crumble.' She points towards a huge bowl of apples on a surface which shines in the overhead fluorescent lighting.

'But–but, they'll be done in there in less than an hour. There isn't enough time to make and bake a crumble.'

'Of course there's enough time.' She arches an eyebrow. 'Sienna said you've worked in a kitchen before?'

Her words sound like a question more than a statement. I want to say, *of course, I've worked in a kitchen.* She doesn't have to know that it's only the kitchen in my own house.

I ignore her and head towards the apples. It's a mindless enough task where I can let my thoughts wander and keep my hands busy while I process my environment and how I'm going to navigate my way through the next few days.

'Get an apron on and wash your hands. Good God – did you

bring proof of your food hygiene certificate?' Nova shakes her head, the hat covering her coarse grey hair wobbling with the movement.

My cheeks flame. 'I turned the house upside down looking for it this morning.' I grin, hoping to forge some kind, any kind of allegiance with her, but as I might have predicted, she doesn't smile back.

'I can't let you work in my kitchen – not without sight of that certificate.' Nova looks more pleased than anything as she returns to the oven to check on what smells like a quiche. I'm so riddled with anxiety that the smell turns my stomach. 'You'd better go and speak to Sienna.'

'No, hang on. I've got one – really, I have. But, in any case, I couldn't go anywhere now, not even if I was forced.' I gesture through the large kitchen window at the snow. 'So it looks like you're stuck with me.'

'I hope you're not going to drive our new assistant away, Mum.' Vince strides through the kitchen, and something inside me once again skips a beat. *Stop it. Stop it. Stop it.* He's with Tracy. Coveting someone else's partner makes me no better than Katina. 'I'm just here to see what I can eat – I don't think I can make it through the welcome circle and the meditation without some food.' He grins at his mother.

Her expression softens, and she points to a tin. 'There's some cake in there. But don't go telling everyone you're getting special treatment just because you're my son.'

'It wouldn't do to have a reflexologist with no energy.' He tugs the lid from the tin. 'Have you tried reflexology before?'

I think he's talking to me – he must be, but since he hasn't said my name, I'm not sure. Regardless, I still flush to the roots of my hair. It's been so long since a man showed a flicker of interest in me that I can't stop my imagination from wandering at the prospect of being alone in a room with him. Even if he only means for *reflexology.*

'Aneka's here to work. You need to save the treatments for the paying guests.'

'Don't let my mother boss you around,' Vince says with his mouth full of cake. 'Once you get to know her, you'll find she's a pushover.'

Nova looks to be fighting a smile, which lights her face up at last. She's probably just being stern around me because she's fearful about retiring. She doesn't have an air about her like she could have a husband at home, so perhaps she's just dreading being lonely when her days aren't filled with work.

As I continue to peel apples, Sienna pokes her head around the door. 'I'm just about to start,' she tells me. 'But if you could come into the room in around an hour, I could do with your help at the end of the meditation.'

Sienna seems a little off with me, and I can't help but wonder if one of the guests has complained about something. Namely, Madison, Tracy or Katina. Now that I've decided I'm going to stay here at the retreat, I just want to impress my new boss. It's really kind of her to have given me this work on my friend's say-so. Without it, I don't know what I'd have done.

'I thought she was here to help in the kitchen.' Nova looks quizzically at Sienna.

'She's here as a *general* support,' Sienna explains. 'If you could just take a moment away from the apples and come with me, I'll show you what I want you to do at the end of the meditation.'

'It's OK. I'll do *her* work as well as my own.' Nova doesn't look amused in the slightest. Gosh, one minute she doesn't want me around, and the next, she's moaning because Sienna's taking me away. She's as tricky to please as Madison.

'I only need her for about five minutes now and then ten to fifteen minutes at the end of meditation. If you could come through to the chapel...' she looks at the clock as I follow her to the kitchen door, 'at 6:10. Then we'll aim to serve the meal at 6:30.'

'Sure thing.' I tug my phone from my apron, but just as I'm setting an alarm for 6:05 to make sure I don't forget, I notice a text and a missed call from Hallie.

> Barnaby's got himself into a state again Mum. I've tried calling you, but you're not answering. He's absolutely convinced that we're never going to see you again and keeps saying things like someone bad is going to get you. xx

This is all because of his bloody father. George has let Hallie and Barnaby down so often that it's little wonder our son has become so insecure and frightened of something happening to me.

> I'll call as soon as I can. xx

I slip the phone back into the pocket of my apron as I follow Sienna across the hallway. I don't want her to see me texting when I'm supposed to be working. I do want more of this work, which is why I pretended to have adequate childcare arrangements on the phone with Vince. But I'm going to have to sort something more satisfactory out for Barnaby. I just wish George would take proper responsibility.

Sienna flicks her red streaks of hair over one shoulder as she holds a door open.

'Welcome to the snug,' she says. 'My favourite room in the lodge.'

'I can see why.' I take in the window seats and the two-seater sofa I'd love to sink into. It's not as warm as it was in the kitchen, but it's still warm enough to earn its name as a 'snug.'

'Alexander and I have bagged this room.'

If I stood in the centre and stretched my arms, I could

almost touch either wall width-ways. So I wonder how two people are going to fit in this tiny space.

'The sofa folds out into a bed.'

'Oh.' I'd love to ask her why she couldn't have booked somewhere slightly bigger. Where her guests, herself and *all* her staff might have a proper bed and a decent space to escape to when off duty.

'I know what you're thinking.' She pulls a face. 'Why didn't I book somewhere with more room?'

'It did cross my mind.' I smile. Blimey, that's rather scary. She knew exactly what I was thinking, and not for the first time since I arrived. There is something wacky about her – I guess to run a 'wellness' retreat, you have to be slightly off the wall.

'I just love this lodge,' she replies. 'It's got such a good energy about it, don't you think? The moment I walked in for the first time, it just wrapped its arms around me.'

'I guess so.' Really, I haven't a clue what she's talking about, but I'll play along.

'Plus, we've got two people here we weren't expecting.'

'Oh?'

'Tracy was a last-minute booking as I mentioned.' She pulls a face. 'Which is why I've shuffled things around so she could go in with Katina.'

'Why isn't Tracy sharing with Vince? They're together, aren't they?'

Sienna narrows her eyes. She seems as enamoured with Tracy as I am. 'Vince is sleeping in the lounge, but I can hardly expect a full-paying guest to sleep on a sofa. It's warmer for him in there than where he slept last time, on the mezzanine level.' She points upwards, evidently referring to the spot on the landing which overlooks the kitchen. He'll be warmer than I'll be in that blinking chapel, that's for certain.

'Katina was none-too-happy to start with about sharing her

room. But I've knocked a couple of hundred pounds off her fee, which seems to have pacified her.'

'Who else was last-minute?'

'Carley.'

'Oh, right. She seems so part of things that I assumed she always had been.'

'She was supposed to be working at a solstice retreat down in Wales, but it's all snowed in. I was delighted when she offered her services to me instead. Anyway, have a lie down on that rug.' She points to the fluffy pile in front of the sofa.

'Why?'

'So I can show you what I'll need from you at the end of the meditations.'

I lay on my back on the floor, feeling decidedly uncomfortable. Is this some sort of a trick or test?

'Close your eyes, Aneka.' Sienna's voice is soothing. Perhaps I'm just being paranoid.

I do as she asks and wait, listening to the rattle of a lid being removed from a glass bottle and then the sound of her hands as she rubs them against one another.

'That smells nice.'

'It's bergamot, geranium and ylang ylang.' She says. 'Uplifting. I'm glad you like it. Hopefully the others will too. You'll crouch behind the head of each guest,' she explains, 'and start by placing your hands on their shoulders, first on the edges and then you'll press onto their collar bones.'

It's been so long since I've felt anyone's hands on me, I freeze as Sienna presses down.

'Gosh, I've never felt anyone so tense. Try to relax, Aneka. We don't want that kind of energy in our meditation.' She laughs, though I sense she's being deadly serious.

I'm dying to tell her that one of our guests is the bitchy new partner of my ex-husband, and the thought of getting up so close and personal to her is unthinkable, but I don't want to do anything that could jeopardise my prospects.

I'm also unsure of how I'm going to feel being so close to Vince and Alexander. I might be lonely, but after George, I feel nothing but discomfort around men. I have discomfort around *anyone* if I'm honest. Other than my children, I don't let anyone get near me. It's safer that way.

'Then I want you to cup your hands firstly around the base of each person's skull.' She demonstrates, and strangely, I find myself relaxing slightly at the unexpected touch of another human. Her hands are so warm it's impossible for me not to sink into the rug. The mixture of the floral and citrusy scent is also more intoxicating than I would have expected. 'Then move your fingers to the temples, round to the crown and lightly massage for a few seconds.'

I didn't realise what a horrible headache I had before I felt the circling of her fingers against my scalp. Now I don't want her to stop. But all good things must come to an end.

'Is that OK?'

I nod, still wondering how the hell I'm going to deal with Katina when it's her turn. Perhaps I'll just sidestep her. I don't think I can bring myself to make any sort of contact. To be honest, I still can't believe she's at this retreat and keep wondering if it's some kind of set-up.

She and George have been cruel enough to me already. There isn't really anything else they could do to me.

Is there?

12

THE CHAPEL IS IN SILENCE. For a moment, I wonder if anyone's inside. The door creaks, but nobody stirs. The guests look like they're dead, laid out on mats with blankets covering them. For a moment, I wonder if Nova's poisoned the scones we served with the arrival drinks.

Sienna nods and smiles at me from where she's sitting at the front, serenely bathed in candlelight, which is reflected in the huge window behind her. The snow is falling in huge flakes, casting an eerie light into the chapel. I really hope Barnaby's going to be alright, as there's no way on this earth I can get the car out of here in the foreseeable future.

'We have an extra gift to end the meditation,' Sienna explains in a gentle yet authoritative voice. 'It will involve a little pressure on the shoulders and a brief head massage with some essential oil. If anyone would prefer not to receive this, please raise your hand.'

As I might have predicted, everyone remains still on their mats. Sienna nods at me, which I take as my signal to begin.

I've never done anything like this. With shaking hands, I unscrew the cap from the bottle of the oil and tiptoe to the person nearest me – luckily, it's Carley. If I mess up, she'll be the least likely to complain. My knees crack as I crouch behind her, and I can only hope I don't stink of the onions Nova forced me to chop up for the side salad. I told Nova what was being expected of me, but she seemed completely disinterested. Every time I try to talk to her, no matter how friendly I am, she seems to look straight through me – almost as if I don't exist.

I press on Carley's shoulders in the same way Sienna pressed on mine in the snug. After several seconds, Carley lets out a long breath. Meanwhile, Sienna's waxing lyrical about how we are all at one with nature, how we are the trees and the trees are us. A gentle snore emits from the woman several mats down, one of the hen sisters. The person on the other side of her tuts – the lovely Tracy. Carley seems to relax some more as I apply the same treatment to her head that Sienna gave to me, and I also relax. I really can do this.

Carley's eyes remain closed as I leave her to move to the first of the hen sisters, who also takes deep breaths, inhaling the scent of the oil as I apply the same pressure to her shoulders and then to her head. It's the same with the other two sisters.

Sienna smiles at me again as she continues to relay what must be her meditation story. I didn't really have a clue what to expect when I walked into the chapel. However, perhaps this is a world I could inhabit – a calm, tranquil bliss with the snow falling outside, no worries about bills and no children demanding to know what's for dinner, much as I miss them.

I continue working the room, my hands shaking when I arrive at Vince's mat. He squints his eyes open, which is unnerving as I administer his head massage. My hands are still shaking as I move forward to Alexander the lech, half expecting him to grab hold of me and jump on me. Sienna talks about energies, and one thing I do know is that he's not emitting a very nice one. He might be handsome, but he's a creep. Sienna could do much, much better.

Thankfully, he barely stirs.

As I reluctantly move backwards to Tracy, I expect her to snap at me, either that I'm digging my fingers into her or pressing down too hard, but she seems as relaxed as the others. It's the same with Madison, the other participant I'd expect to complain. Finally, I'm at Katina's head. She's the last person.

I hesitate. Sienna's still watching me. She sounds like she's wrapping up the meditation.

'We will shortly be leaving this sunny meadow behind and heading back to the gate,' she says in a soft voice.

I take a deep breath and try to calm myself. I've been fine so far. It's just another set of shoulders. Just another head. The fact that they belong to the woman whom my ex is doing everything he couldn't, or wouldn't do or be for me is besides the point. The fact that she seems to be partly responsible for his constantly letting the children down has to be put aside. I'm here to do a job, and our family's Christmas depends on me. I rub my hands with the oil and press down on her shoulders.

However, I can't help but imagine what it would be like to move my fingers around her scrawny neck and squeeze. I could really put her into this yoga corpse pose Sienna keeps mentioning.

No Aneka. Honestly, I've never had such a dark thought. Not even when things were at their very worst between me and George, when he announced the affair I'd long suspected.

'Owww.' The whole room jumps as Katina shakes my hands from her shoulders. 'What the hell are you doing? You were pressing me into the floor.'

'I wasn't,' I gasp as Sienna rocks herself onto her knees to gain a better view above where the others are lying. I rise to my feet and step away from Katina's mat. Sienna has stopped speaking, her mouth now hanging agape. Everyone else in the room is rolling onto their sides so they can see what's going on.

'Well, she did a good job on me,' Vince says as he props

himself up onto one elbow. I smile at him. Tracy is also sitting up, and her scowl could literally curdle milk as she looks sideways at her boyfriend.

'Don't let her near me again,' Katina snaps, and she wags an accusing finger in my direction. 'I don't trust her one iota.'

'What on earth happened?' Sienna's puzzled expression deepens.

'I–I really don't know.' I edge further away from my adversary. 'I'll go back and help Nova with the meal.' The best thing now is for me to slink from the room in much the same way I entered.

Is Katina going to spill the truth about our connection? Should I say something to Sienna before Katina gets the chance?

Perhaps I did press too hard on her shoulders.

Perhaps I should have pressed harder.

13

'THIS SOUP'S TOO SALTY.' Madison pulls a face as she drops the spoon back into her bowl. 'And can we have the heating turned up? It's freezing.' I'm quickly getting the measure of this woman. *Moaning Madison.* Honestly, I've never heard anything like it. Moan, moan, moan.

'I assume this is gluten-free bread you're serving?' Tracy pokes at the roll like it might bite.

'I believe so.'

'I think the food's lovely, and that you're looking after us brilliantly.' One of the hen sisters smiles at me as I offer the bread basket at their table.

I can't remember which is which sister. Their names have stuck with me, Ana, Alexis and Ashleigh, but they look and sound so alike with their button noses, and startling blue eyes which look too large in their faces, that their names have become almost interchangeable.

'Is this soup dairy-free?' Madison asks as she fills her spoon and empties it back into her bowl. 'It had better not contain cream.'

'Would you like me to double-check with Nova?' I look from Tracy to Madison.

'If you're not too busy.' Madison's words are polite, but her voice drips with sarcasm. 'And can you find out if wine is being served with our food?'

'It's a wellness retreat.' Sienna smiles as she takes a seat among them. 'But like I said in the welcome emails, you could have brought your own.'

'Can you also find out where Vince has disappeared to?' Tracy calls after me, her piercing voice shredding what's left of my frazzled nerves.

I'll perhaps linger in the kitchen now that Sienna's there to absorb their questions and criticism. But I'd still better check with Nova about the gluten and dairy-free status of what I've just served in the dining room. I wouldn't want to be held responsible for any nasty reactions to their food.

'Tracy's asking where you are,' I tell Vince. He pulls a face as he turns to the door.

I head towards the sink where Nova's washing her hands. 'Two of the women have asked—' I begin.

'We refer to our attendees as gentlemen or ladies,' Nova cuts in. '*Ladies*.' She gives me a withering look as she repeats the word as if to suggest I would have little idea about the word's definition.

'Can we start again, Nova?' It's just the two of us in the kitchen, so I'll take this chance to appeal to her good side. I know she has one, as I saw it on display with her son. 'I'm not sure what I've done to upset you, but I'd really like to make amends.'

'We're here to work,' she reminds me for what feels like the umpteenth time since I arrived. 'Not to be friends.'

'But surely, it would be much easier and nicer if we were.'

'Ah, Alexander.' Her voice and face soften in the same way I noticed earlier when she spoke to her son. 'Are you already back for seconds?' He's wearing the same pale grey tunic and loose trousers ensemble that Carley and Vince both wear, emblazoned with *Wellness by Sienna* on the pocket.

Alexander isn't smiling back at Nova. Instead, his full attention and his smile seem to be on me. 'What was all that about in the chapel?'

'I really don't know, but whatever it was, it seems to have blown over.'

He nods. 'Other than that, are you settling in, Aneka?' He brushes up a little too close to me as he passes. Meanwhile, Nova's watching intently. But I'm doing nothing wrong, and no one can suggest anything different.

'Erm, yes, thanks.' I reply. 'It's a lovely place.'

'Well, that's good.' He winks. 'Because looking at that snow, we could be all stuck here over Christmas.'

Nova's smile fades as quickly as it arrived. From his tone of voice and the curve of his smile, I'd hazard a guess that Alexander is flirting with me. But surely not. I mean, not right under his wife's nose.

I'm certainly no match for Sienna. She's got something about her that I'll possibly never have. Plus, I've lost so much weight since my split from George that people have started to comment. One well-meaning 'friend' even suggested I look like a coat hanger. Somehow, I've got to get myself sorted out. Perhaps spending time in such opulent surroundings amongst these seemingly affluent people will somehow translate to me. God only knows I could do with a turn in my fortunes. With the mother and husband I've had, I've had more than my fair share of rotten luck.

'In the nicest possible way, I hope we're not stranded over Christmas,' I reply. 'I have two kids waiting at home.'

'Oh?' He arches an eyebrow. 'I didn't realise you were a mum. So I take it there's a Mr Aneka?'

I shake my head. 'The divorce came through last month.' The words still land like a punch to the gut every time I say them aloud. This will be my second Christmas since George confessed to his new and exciting affair with Katina.

The woman, whose voice I can now hear cutting through the scraping of cutlery and the clinking of glasses, sharp and unmistakable. She's probably bitching about me. The more I consider it, the more convinced I become that she's been complicit with me in keeping our connection hidden because it gives her power. If she complains about me while everyone remains oblivious to our history, her words carry weight. But if it comes out that she stole my husband? Suddenly, she's the other woman. And perhaps, just perhaps, there's a small part of her that carries even a molecule of shame for what she's done to me and my kids.

'Fresh meat back on the market then.' Alexander offers an approving nod. 'That's what I like to hear.'

Ugh. What an ugly remark. I grab two jugs of water and resist the urge to tip them over his smarmy head. Even if his wife wasn't in the next room, what right does he have to refer to me as *fresh meat*?

I'll have to continue being civil, but from now on, I'll be staying well out of his way. If Sienna hears him talking to me like he does, she could think I'm somehow encouraging him. I pause in the centre of the kitchen. Thankfully, she sounds like she's busy in the dining room. Busy listening to Tracy, who's taken over from Katina and sounds to be holding her audience captive with whatever story she's regaling in her commanding voice.

'What are you waiting for?'

Nova looks like she might explode with rage. Reading between the lines, it seems she has a soft spot for our boss's husband and doesn't want him flirting with the likes of me. As I head through the swinging door, it dawns on me that I didn't

even find out what I came in to ask. The gluten and dairy information. Oh well, if those spoiled 'ladies' are affected by what
they're eating, I'll just have to play dumb.

As I swap the heat of the kitchen for the cooler dining
room, Tracy's still on her self-imposed stage. One of the sisters
is nodding and laughing as she speaks, and Brittany, the
youngest guest here, is watching her with what could be wide-
eyed wonder. She's clearly impressionable and probably in awe
of this confident and sophisticated woman. Then I realise she's
filming her on her phone. That's interesting. At some point, I'll
have to find out why.

'My daughter and I came here to have a break *together*.' Her
mother, Olive, hisses as I rest the jug onto their table. 'To chat
and catch up.'

'I understand.' I take her glass and fill it with water.

'Brittany's had a really tough time lately,' she goes on. 'Isn't
there somewhere quieter we can take our meals? Somewhere
where we won't be subjected to *her* life story every time there's a
lull in everyone else's conversation?' She tips her head in
Tracy's direction.

'I'll ask Sienna when I get a chance.' I get where she's
coming from. The retreat really does seem to be the Tracy
show. Even Vince looks bored with whatever story she's telling,
and he's supposed to be in a relationship with the woman.

'Brittany, turn off your phone.' Olive narrows her eyes at her
daughter.

I move away to rest the other jug on the table where Tracy,
Katina, Madison, Carley and Sienna are sitting, resisting the
urge to empty it over Katina's perfectly curled hair. She's
texting, but she covers her screen as I approach. I bet she's
texting George.

Don't stop on my account. Thankfully, I prevent myself from
saying the words aloud.

'Why won't this bloody message send?' I glance at her phone, noticing the heart next to George's name, and my gut twists. She *is* texting him.

I wouldn't be human if the shadow of jealousy didn't fall over me. Why did I marry someone who would eventually let me down so spectacularly? Maybe it's all my fault. Perhaps, like Mum used to tell me on the rare weekends I stayed with her when I was growing up, maybe there *is* something inside me which brings out the worst in people. I mean, look at things since I've arrived here. Nova can't stand me. Tracy, Madison and Katina are ordering me around like I'm some kind of slave, and Alexander seems to have taken an extremely unhealthy shine to me. I only hope he doesn't act up in front of Sienna. I have six hundred pounds riding on this, and I need the money I've been promised more than I've ever needed anything.

'I hope it's something more appetising for the main course.' Madison pushes her soup bowl to the centre of the table. 'Even if you *had* confirmed its dairy content like I asked you to, it was still too salty.'

'It's dairy-free,' Sienna smiles. 'As you requested. Quiche and salad are the main course,' she continues. 'Followed by apple crumble. All we want to do is to take good care of you all this weekend.'

Madison has the grace to look slightly ashamed of speaking to me like crap in the face of Sienna being so pleasant. It's probably the best way to deal with moaners and narcissists. Kill them with kindness.

'Yummy.' Carley pats her stomach. 'Aren't you sitting down to eat yet, Aneka?'

'I put a slice of quiche for you on the plate nearest the microwave,' Vince says. Tracy glares at him like she always does when he speaks to me. 'To make sure you get some.'

'And there's plenty of soup left,' Carley adds.

'Yeah, you look like you could do with a good meal inside you,' Katina adds.

'Thanks for your concern.' I glance at Sienna to see if there's any reaction, but her attention is still on Madison. I wish I could stick up for myself. I could tell Katina that if her boyfriend were paying what he's supposed to towards his children, I wouldn't be forced to skip meals to make sure they have everything they need.

'I'll get a chance after everyone else has eaten,' I mumble.

'Get your dinner *now*, Aneka.' Sienna jerks her head up. 'Goodness, please forgive me, I never thought. Here you are, running around after everyone, and you haven't eaten a thing since you arrived. Go on, *I'll* serve the main course.'

'And I'll do the pudding,' Carley offers.

'We've got ninety minutes after dinner before the sound bath,' Olive remarks to Brittany as I sit at their table. 'I say we have a dip in the hot tub once our food has settled.'

I glance from the window at the steam escaping around the edges of its lid. What I wouldn't give to sink into that for just five minutes. I've been on my feet since I arrived here nearly five hours ago.

'Is there something wrong with the phone lines?' Katina calls across the room. 'I can't get wifi to work either. It's really not good enough.'

'It's probably because of the weather,' Sienna replies as she sets a plate of quiche in the centre of their table. 'I'll take a look at the hub in a minute.'

'My phone's offline as well.' Tracy rests her phone on the table. 'It's just as well you're here and I don't need to text you, Vince?' She nudges him, and he grins back. It's the first time I've witnessed much communication between them since Tracy arrived.

Madison was right about this soup. It *is* too salty.

'We should have a no-phone rule at the dinner table.' Tracy glares at Brittany, who's holding hers in the air as if trying to find a signal. 'Aren't we all here to get away from the usual way of doing things?'

'I'm writing a blog about the effectiveness of wellness retreats,' Brittany explains in a surprisingly clear and loud voice. 'But I'll be sensitive and careful, and I'll try not to film faces.'

'No, that's not good enough,' Madison says. 'And I'd agree with a no phone rule.'

Tracy nudges Katina, and they both giggle. I imagine they'll be saying that Madison wouldn't have anyone to call or text.

'I, for one,' Madison goes on, 'don't particularly want to listen to someone's conversation or their tap, tap, tapping of a text when I'm trying to eat. Nor do I want a phone stuck in my face each evening under the guise of research for a pointless blog post.'

'You could always sit somewhere else,' Katina smiles at her. Yet it's a smile where her lips merely turn upwards; it doesn't reach any other part of her face.

'Maybe it wouldn't be such a bad thing if the phones and internet *had* gone down,' Sienna turns back from the door to gain everyone's attention. 'You did all say you wanted a break from your Christmas preparations on the questionnaire.'

'But I've still got so much to do,' one of the A sisters wails. I think it's the one who's due to get married in less than a fortnight.

'I can't believe we haven't even got so much as a Christmas tree here at the lodge,' Madison mutters. 'When you said, there'd be no sign of Christmas—'

'I meant there'll be no sign of Christmas.' Sienna's dimples deepen. 'I'll be back in a few minutes. I'll go and check this internet.'

'You'll never guess what happened to me when I went Christmas shopping last weekend?' Tracy begins, looking around to see whose attention she might have gained as she embarks on yet another tale. Two of the sisters and Brittany's heads jerk up from their quiche.

Here we go again.

14

TRACY IS STILL in the throes of her tedious Christmas shopping story, involving an assistant who didn't give her the service to which she felt entitled. However, it's Katina's conversation I'm interested in as she tells Madison about her new venture, as she describes it.

'There'll be so much more than at this retreat,' she explains. 'Life coaching, hot stone massage, a silent disco... Give me your number and I can keep—'

She stops short as Alexander returns to the dining room.

'We've had a look at the hub and it seems the weather might have brought the wifi down.' He gestures to the window. All that can be seen beyond it is the lights surrounding the sauna and jacuzzi and the ever-thickening snowflakes.

All conversation stops as everyone reaches for their phones, me included. Sure enough, there are three dots where there is normally a connectivity icon. Until the wifi comes back up, I can't even reach my children to check they're OK. Barnaby will never get to sleep tonight without speaking to me and having his mind put at rest. I can only hope and pray this outage is just a temporary blip.

'I asked for a fresh towel to be left on my bed for the hot tub,' Katina scowls as she leaves her room. 'Don't think I haven't noticed how you push me to the bottom of your list every time I ask for something. And don't think anything will stop me from complaining about you to Sienna.'

'I've been rushed off my feet.' It's on the tip of my tongue to add the word *sorry* like I would with any other guest, but she's so rude that it would be almost criminal to apologise. Plus, she's George's girlfriend – the last person I should be trying to appease.

'It's hardly strenuous to fetch another towel,' Katina says, twisting her hair into a ponytail as she fixes me with a cold stare. 'Or are you ignoring me because I'm with George now—and he's done with you?'

I cast a quick look along the landing to make sure we're alone. Most of the guests are either in the hot tub, sweating in the sauna, or sprawled in the lounge where the radio's been switched on to catch weather updates, much to Olive's annoyance. She's made it clear they came here for *peace and quiet*. Personally, I'd take static noise and news bulletins over another minute listening to Tracy's autobiography.

I step forward, closing the space between us, keeping my voice steady. 'I'm here to do my job, nothing more. I just want to get through the weekend and then go back home to my children.' I drop my voice even lower. 'As for George, you're welcome to him.'

'He's totally over his previous life.' Katina points at herself. 'He's moved on.'

'Well, isn't he the lucky one?' I regret the words as soon as they leave my mouth. I'm stooping to her level.

'He is actually.'

'Listen, I don't care who he's shacked up with. All I care

about is that he keeps letting our children down. They're all that matter to me.'

'What are you even doing at this retreat?' She steps closer, and for a moment, I worry she might give me a slap. 'It's like you're stalking me. George thought the same when we spoke before the wifi went down.'

'*Stalking* you?' I stifle a laugh. 'I'm only here to earn some money so my children can have some sort of Christmas.'

'Perhaps I should take my concerns to Sienna,' she goes on. 'How you've taken this job under false pretences just so you can wage your vendetta.'

'I only clapped eyes on you for the first time yesterday.'

'George thinks you've been hanging around us for weeks,' she goes on. 'He's told me how jealous you can be. Well, I'll tell you something that will really shut you up, shall I?'

'What's going on?' Carley appears at the top of the stairs, sporting a *Wellness with Sienna* hoodie over her tunic, and her wavy hair loose around her shoulders. 'Is everything OK, Aneka?'

'Absolutely fine.' Katina smiles sweetly. 'I was just complaining about the phone lines and the lack of towels.'

'The weather's hardly Aneka's fault.' Carley's frown deepens. 'Why don't you just forget about your phone and go and relax with the others?'

'I'd relax in the hot tub if she'd get me a towel like I asked.'

'Aneka might be on the staff here, but Aneka has a name. So I'd appreciate you using it.' Carley's eyes narrow. 'She's here to look after you, not to be spoken down to.'

'I'll wait at the hot tub for my fresh towel then, shall I?' Katina flounces along the corridor.

'I'll bring you one shortly,' I call after her.

Carley comes closer, her green eyes troubled with concern. 'Honestly, some of these guests.' She shakes her head. 'Look, I know some of them are worse than others.' She lowers her voice to a whisper as if remembering herself. 'But just let it all go over your head. It's them with the problem.' She squeezes my arm.

'I know.' It's on the tip of my tongue to divulge mine and Katina's connection, but once again, my pride and need for privacy are stopping me. I don't want anyone, not even Carley, who's been so friendly, knowing about my business.

'Have you eaten yet?'

I nod.

'Properly?' Carley asks, genuine concern in her eyes, and it's almost my undoing. 'I only saw you with the soup.' I blink hard as a rush of tears threatens. There's no way I'm telling her the truth, that I only forced down a few spoonfuls of soup and a roll of bread, just enough to keep body and soul together. I couldn't bring myself to eat a three-course meal, not when Hallie and Barnaby are at home with nothing but a few meagre supplies. With this weather, they won't even be able to get anything extra with the money I left. Nothing will be delivered. And they'll be stuck in the house all weekend. Fed up. Waiting for me.

'Yes, I'm fine.'

'Listen.' Carley glances at her watch. 'I've no massage bookings until tomorrow, so if you want to drop her ladyship a towel off and then make the most of me for half an hour before the gong bath, you'd be very welcome.'

'How do you mean?'

'For a quick back, neck and shoulders, that's what I mean,' she replies. 'You look like a coiled spring – you have ever since I clapped eyes on you.'

'Won't I get into trouble?'

'I'll cover,' she says. 'I'll tell Sienna I gave you a job.'

'Such as?'

'Don't worry, I'll think of something. Come to the sun room in five minutes.'

'Lie still and try to relax. Close your eyes.' Carley's voice is soothing, but trying to relax is an impossible request. Not when I feel like at any moment Sienna, Alexander or Nova could burst in here and demand to know what the hell I think I'm doing.

This is what the guests in the chapel will have experienced before. The rattle of a lid against a glass bottle, the aroma of whatever it is, the sound of hands rubbing together, then the firm sensation of being pressed down.

'This is the first massage I've ever had.' I keep trying to lower my shoulders from my chin and let my limbs unwind, but it's almost impossible.

'Blimey.' Carley's voice is filled with shock. 'It sounds like you need to carve out a little more you time.'

'Chance would be a fine thing.'

'Enough talking.' Carley cups my chin. 'Try to also relax your face. Look, you're even clenching your jaw.'

'I feel like I might be getting a migraine.' I stare at Carley's white pumps through the hole in the treatment bed, wishing there was a lock on this door so I could try harder to relax.

'It's no wonder with that jaw. Hopefully, this will ease things. I'll give you a five-minute Indian head massage after I've worked these shoulders.'

'Sounds wonderful.'

'Right, that's enough. Stop talking, moving and clenching, keep your eyes closed and relax.' She elongates the last word as she drips oil down the length of my spine.

'Yes, Mum.' I force a laugh.

As Carley's hands work over my shoulders, kneading into the knots that have become a permanent fixture in my body, I try, really try, to surrender to the calm she's attempting to coax from me. To let myself melt into the table instead of spiralling into the usual storm inside my head.

There's always so much mind chatter. A relentless monologue of *where I have to be, what time pick-up is, what Hallie needs for school tomorrow*, or *whether there's enough pasta in the cupboard for dinner*. It's constant and exhausting.

But today, the noise has taken on a different pitch, higher and sharper. For the first time in ages, my mother's voice has pushed its way back into my consciousness. Usually, I manage to keep her buried deep enough that I can almost pretend she doesn't exist. But being here and leaving my children behind has shaken something loose.

Maybe it's the mother-daughter duo on this retreat, all soft smiles and mutual affection. Maybe it's Katina, who looks at me like I'm totally insignificant. Or Tracy, whose need to be admired feels like a mirror held up to the woman who gave birth to me, but that's pretty much all she can claim any credit for. Either way, the comparisons are clawing at me, and my mother's presence, unwanted and unwelcome, swells in my mind like poison.

I squeeze my eyes shut, desperate not to hear her voice. Not to see her face. But memory is ruthless.

The last time she had any real power over me was after Grandad died, four years ago. He'd changed his will, leaving half of everything he owned to me and the other half to his sister. He'd done it not long after I'd gone to live with him, when I was two. But because the document wasn't properly witnessed, it meant nothing. She made sure of that. And she made sure I got nothing.

Nothing, except the reminder that in her eyes, I never had any worth to begin with.

'It obviously wasn't meant to be.' A smile had stretched across my mother's face when I called around to reason with her. 'You'd only fritter it away in any case.'

I considered taking her to court, but I couldn't afford the costs if I lost. Besides, in law, Mum was Grandad's next of kin, even though they were estranged.

'Just a thousand pounds would help me and the kids out no end,' I'd pleaded.

Her reply? 'It's not my problem if the only man you've managed to attract is an idle slob whose fancy ideas are bigger than his work ethic.'

And now, as I lie on this couch trying to melt into thirty precious minutes of relaxation, the harsh words she spouted whenever I tried to see her over the years won't leave me alone.

'Wherever you go, you give off bad vibes. Then you wonder why no one wants to be around you.'

'Having you ruined my life. It's no wonder I suffered so badly with postnatal depression.'

'It's your fault your father left. You came between us.'

'If I knew then what I know now, I'd have never had kids.'

'You'll never amount to anything. Cleaning is pretty much all you're good for.'

'When Hallie and Barnaby are old enough to make up their own minds, they'll see you for who you really are.'

So yes, when I watch the likes of Olive and Brittany deep in conversation and enjoying their time away from the usual routine together, it fills me with a sense of longing so deep, it's like it could split me in two.

Worse still, when I consider how I've abandoned my children this weekend, coupled with Barnaby's fears over losing me and the perpetual cycle of poverty I've exposed them both to, I keep fearing that history is somehow repeating itself.

Am I, without realising, just as bad as my mother?

15

THEN

FOR SEVERAL SECONDS, *I'm rooted to the spot, the horror of what I've just witnessed making it impossible to react, to move, or to even call for help.*

My baby, my beautiful girl, is motionless at the side of the road, her mangled scooter just inches away from where she's lying. And the driver responsible is trying to turn, risking hitting her once more.

'No,' I scream as energy finally floods my body and I rush towards my daughter, ready to hurl myself in front of the car if it means she won't be hit for a second time.

But with a screech, the driver is now hurtling away from what he or she has caused. They haven't stopped to assess their damage, they haven't stopped to help, to even call an ambulance. No, in their cowardice, they've turned their car in the road and gone back in the direction they arrived.

Except they've now ruined our lives.

I crouch by my daughter, feeling for a pulse. Please, please, please. 'Help, somebody, please,' I scream into the street. Thankfully, residents are leaving their fairylight-lit houses, coming to see what the bang was, wondering who the distraught woman might be. 'Someone, call an ambulance.' I sound like a wounded animal.

'Did anyone get a look at the car?' A voice asks.

'I got part of the number plate,' comes a reply.

'It all happened so fast,' says another.

'Please just help her,' I sob as I lay my coat over my daughter. I want to cradle her in my arms and rock her better, but I don't want to worsen any of her injuries.

'Is she breathing?' A man asks.

'The ambulance is on its way.'

'What's her name?'

'Please, please wake up,' I urge her. There's a pulse, but it's so slow, I fear it's going to stop. 'I can't lose her,' I cry. And then another realisation hits me.

'How the hell am I going to break this to my husband?'

16

'WHAT ON EARTH do you think you're doing?' Nova's voice is enough to splinter teeth. 'Wait until I tell Sienna!'

I leap up from the bed, forgetting I'm wearing nothing on my top half.

'Ugh, do you really think I want an eyeful of that. Get some bloody clothes on.'

I clasp my hands across my chest. 'Close the door,' Carley shouts. She's normally so chilled that it's a surprise to hear her raise her voice to such a level. But it's too late. A grinning Alexander has already had a good old perve at my boobs as he saunters up behind Nova.

My half hour on Carley's couch was just about starting to take effect, but all that's gone to shit.

'I was getting a migraine.' My head swoons with the sudden movement as I lower my feet to the ground, covering myself with a pillow. 'Carley offered a massage to help my head.'

'You're here to *work*.' Nova shouts the last word as she steps further into the room. 'I knew as soon as I saw you that Sienna had made a mistake.'

'Ah, come on, Nova.' Carley rushes to the door and closes it in Alexander's face. 'I know you're finding the prospect of retirement difficult, but there's no need to take it all out on Aneka.'

'She's after my job.' Nova's voice is needle-sharp.

'What are you talking about?' My raised voice in an attempt to defend myself also comes as a shock. But I'm pig-sick of people talking to me like I'm worthless. It all started with my mother, of course, but lately, negative judgment seems to be all I come across. I'm beginning to wonder if everyone's right. Maybe I should crawl back under my stone and rot there.

'I heard you this afternoon.' Nova swings around to face Carley, her hat nearly leaving her head with the motion. 'Telling her to make sure she impresses Sienna enough to be my replacement.'

'You owe Aneka an apology, Nova.' Carley passes me my *Wellness with Sienna* t-shirt from the chair as I fasten my bra.

'And don't think I haven't noticed you making goggle eyes at my son.'

'Stop changing the subject, Nova.'

'I'm only here to work and then get home for Christmas,' I protest. 'Just as we all are.'

'He's already got a girlfriend,' she continues, contempt written all over her face. 'But in any case, he's way too good for the likes of you.'

'Enough.' Carley shouts. 'Come on, Aneka. We're going to see Sienna. We'll tell her ourselves that I offered you a treatment. This shrivelled up old prune here is only jealous because I'd prefer to immerse my hands in a boiling vat of chip fat before I'd place them on her back.'

They glare at each other for several seconds.

'Seeing Sienna won't be necessary.' Nova's tone has softened. In fact, she appears to have suddenly done a full three hundred and sixty-degree turn. 'Let's not make things worse.'

'I fail to see how they could be.' I step closer to her now, fuelled by the fear which has emerged in her face. Good. For the first time since I arrived, I've got the upper hand. 'Whatever your problem is, it's not my fault, and I won't allow you to punish me.'

'What's all the noise about?' The door's pushed open again, bringing me face to face with the last person I want to see, Katina. 'Oh, I might have known you'd be involved.' She laughs. Thank goodness I got my top on before she burst into the room.

'Just leave me alone, alright?'

'Oooooh, that tone sounds almost like a threat.' Katina throws her head back and laughs. 'May I remind you that I'm a paying guest? One word to Sienna and I can have you sacked.'

'What is it with you towards Aneka? I've noticed all your looks and sniping.' Carley points at Katina. 'Come on, there's no need to involve Sienna. We'll have it out here and now. We've got three nights, and possibly longer, to spend under this roof together.'

I shiver, even though the room is warm. The prospect of spending three nights in Katina's vicinity is chilling enough, but the thought of any more is enough to bring me out in hives.

This is Katina's chance to tell Nova and Carley that she's with my ex. But she doesn't. And I don't want to give Nova anything she can lord over me. I get the impression she'll use anything she can to gain one-upmanship. Especially with Sienna.

'Go on, I'm waiting for an answer.'

But Katina stays quiet. As I've been hoping, she'll realise how bad she'll look, after all, she effectively lured a married man with two children away from his family. Not that I'm saying George is without blame for allowing himself to be lured.

But I'm also tired of coming across as the underdog, a complete victim. Nor do I want anyone here to know how financially broke I am. I'm not sure how I'll deal with this situation yet, but I will.

But for now, I just want to get away from both Nova and Katina.

Before I do or say something I come to regret.

17

THE NEXT HOUR is spent buzzing around like a bluebottle as I satisfy the guests' requests for warm towels, fluffy robes and hot drinks. The outdoor area looks like something from a Nordic holiday brochure as guests bask in the bubbling tub, the steam room and the sauna. I want their lives of ease, and as the hours I'm around these people tick by, I'm becoming more and more resolute.

No matter what it takes, I'm going to free myself from debt and be a success. Never again am I going to be reliant on my ex-husband's maintenance money for survival. Never again am I going to drive my clapped-out car on petrol fumes to a destination that risks me not getting back home to my kids before Christmas. It's time to stand up and be counted.

In a rare breather between requests, I slip my phone from my apron. There's still no service. It's nearly 8 pm, only an hour before Barnaby's bedtime, and I'm beginning to lose hope of speaking to him tonight.

The guests will shortly lie down for their final event of the evening, their eagerly anticipated gong bath. I'd like to Google what this entails so I don't look like a total klutz if I'm asked to assist with the proceedings, but obviously, nobody here can do any Googling.

'Are you ignoring me?' Another voice I've come to hate is far too close. I jump around like I've been scalded. Tracy. Clad in a white bikini, she looks like a catwalk model. As if I could have got excited when I first clapped eyes on Vince. As if he'd ever look twice at me when he's got a woman like her on his arm. However, they've seemed as distant as two bookends since she arrived.

'What?'

'I asked for some prosecco glasses for myself and Katina.' She gestures towards the hot tub.

'I doubt you'll be allowed glass in the hot tub,' I say. 'I'll have to check with Sienna.'

'Why?'

'If a glass gets smashed, the facility will be ruined.' Hark at me, Miss Jobsworth. I just don't want to take orders from this woman. She's the epitome of the word narcissist. One in ten people is said to be affected by the disorder, yet I seem to be a beacon for them. Wherever I go and whatever I do in life, I seem to magnetise them into my presence.

'*If* a glass gets smashed...,' she begins. 'Sorry, what's your name again?'

'Aneka.'

'An-e-ka.' She twists the syllables around in her mouth like she's getting ready to spit them onto the ground. 'If a glass gets smashed, you'll just have another mess to clean.'

'Bitch.' I mutter as I shuffle away.

'Pardon?'

'Nothing. I'll get your glasses.' I don't add that she'll be lucky if I don't smash them over her head.

'You're doing a great job.' Olive and Brittany step from the warmth of the lodge onto the freezing veranda, both wrapped in white robes. 'We've been watching you, haven't we, Brittany?

Well, *she's* been filming bits and pieces for her blog post.' Her daughter nods. 'You've got some tricky customers here and you probably don't realise how well you're handling it all.'

'Really?' Something inside me brightens. 'Well, thank you. I needed to hear that.' I give her the biggest smile I can muster as moaning Madison calls from behind them. 'I've been waiting for twenty minutes to get into that steam room. Can't you tell those sisters, whatever their names are, to come out and let someone else have a turn?'

'Don't forget what I said.' Olive reaches for my arm and gives it a squeeze.

'I need your help to unload the gongs for Sienna.' Alexander catches my arm as I head towards the kitchen. 'Now that you're wearing some clothes. To be honest, I almost didn't recognise you.'

'What's that supposed to mean?' Sienna steps out from behind the kitchen door and looks from her husband to me. 'I do hope you're not being inappropriate again, Alexander. First Nova, then Katina and now Aneka. Is no one safe?'

I'd love to hear what he's said to Nova and Katina, but I should keep well out of their argument. However, at this exact moment, there's nowhere to run.

'I erm, I was getting changed,' I mumble. 'Alexander walked in by mistake.' The last thing I want is to get on the wrong side of my boss. If I'm going to move forward and keep to my resolve, Sienna will be a big part of my kick from the starting block. Not that I'm even on the starting block. With my debt and overdraft, with the things that need buying and the items which need replacing, I'm way, way behind the starting block. If only Grandad had thought to have his new will witnessed. He'd be spinning in his grave to know that Mum got *all* his money.

'I see.' Sienna nods. 'What's he asking you to do now?' She's avoiding my eye but staring straight at her husband. She's probably used to his philandering. To be honest, the fact that he's so blatant probably means there's no need for her to worry. It's the quiet and sneaky men who are cause for concern. Men like George.

'Erm, I've been asked to help unload the gongs.'

'Vince can do that,' she replies without taking her eyes from Alexander. 'They're very heavy. Go on.'

We watch as Alexander obediently scuttles into the kitchen.

'You can start rounding everyone up if that's OK.' Sienna's voice echoes around the hallway. 'Usually I'd put a message in the WhatsApp group, but clearly we don't have any access to comms with this dratted internet being down.'

'Is it likely to come back on?'

She shrugs and looks apologetic. 'It could, but in my experience, out here in the sticks as we are, it's unlikely to be fixed until the worst of the snow has passed.'

'It's just that I need to check with my daughter that my son's OK. He's only eight and was really upset the last time we spoke.'

'Really?'

'It's probably nothing. Just angst because his routine's different this weekend.'

I wish I could confide properly in Sienna. I feel like I could trust her, but she's mostly running around, either setting things up, going through her notes or leading the group. I'd like to ask her if she's got kids, so I could get a sense of whether she'd understand.

I'm sure most people would sympathise with what I experienced with Barnaby's outburst this morning. But Sienna would maybe have a psychoanalytical explanation for why, when I kissed the top of his head at the school gate, he genuinely feared that it would be the last time he would ever see me.

18

I STAND in the corner of the room, unsure what to do with myself as I wait for the nod from Sienna to say it's time to begin. The guests are lying on their mats, once again covered in blankets as they wait for me to attend to them.

After this, it's the final offering of the day – cocoa. Nova's retired for the night already, muttering something about there being no point in having a dog and then barking yourself. Charming.

Once they've got their drinks, it will be bedtime. As for what this will mean for me, I haven't a clue. Perhaps Nova will have left me a list of further jobs to do while everyone sleeps. That's how my life feels. But this Cinderella isn't going to the ball this weekend.

I'm suddenly reminded of being fourteen when everyone in my class, and I mean *everyone*, was excited about the French exchange. I might have been living with Grandad, but because he'd never legally adopted me, Mum's signature was needed on the consent form so I could take part. But she wouldn't sign.

'Please, Mum.' I'd stopped by while I was doing my paper

round. 'I'll be just made to stay in school and work while everyone else is in France.'

'Why should *you* get to go to France when I've never even been abroad?'

I fought back tears as it always irritated Mum even further when I cried. When I stayed with her some weekends when Grandad needed a break, I'd learned to cry silently into my pillow where she couldn't see or hear. 'Please. I'll save up my own spends from my paper round and babysitting money.'

'I could have travelled the world if I hadn't had *you*.' The way she said *you* was as if she were addressing someone she hated. I think perhaps, she did. And still does. 'Besides, do you really think Grandad would want some foreign stranger staying in his house?'

When I became pregnant two years later, Grandad no longer made me stay with Mum at weekends. By the time the baby was born, George and I had left his parents' house, and the council had given us a flat. Though sixteen and terrified, I had every hope that I'd now have my own little happy family. Me, George and our baby girl. Little did I know that I was jumping out of the frying pan and into the fire.

As I make my way around the head and shoulders of each person, administering the oils, pressure and brief scalp rub in the same way I did before, the vibration of the gongs at the front thuds through my body. It's a peculiar feeling, shaking me from the inside.

And it feels good – almost cleansing. Rather than continuing to live as an underdog, I'm beginning to feel as if I, too, can rise. My past no longer has to determine my future.

Who are you trying to kid? Once again, it's my mother's voice. I haven't seen her for five years, but she's always there, needling and mocking. *You'll never amount to anything. You don't deserve to.*

I scrunch my eyes together as I move from one person to another.

'Owwww.' I nearly jump out of my skin as Katina sits bolt upright from the mat as though she's been catapulted from the floor. 'What the hell are you trying to do? I said earlier that I don't want you anywhere near me.'

Sienna silences the echo of her latest gong beat, and the rest of the attendees prop themselves onto their elbows to see what the commotion could be.

'What on earth's happened this time?' Sienna rises to her feet and threads her way through the bodies on the ground.

'She,' Katina points an accusing finger in my direction. 'She was digging her fingers so hard into my skull, it was like she was trying to scoop my brains out with her hands.'

Thinking of Mum has sent me into some kind of autopilot mode, and if I were forced to be honest, I have little recollection of what I might have been doing before Katina reacted. Shit. Turning Mum's words over in my thoughts whilst at the head of my ex-husband's spoiled and nasty new girlfriend means maybe.... No, surely I wouldn't. I've always been appeasing. Violence isn't in my nature.

But maybe I've reached the end of my rope.

'Aneka?' Sienna's usually smiley and zen face is teetering into concerned angst. I've interrupted her therapeutic gong bath and upset the day's end for the whole group. Damage limitation is now called for. Plus, it's the second time today this has happened.

'I'm so sorry,' I blurt. 'But everyone else seemed comfortable with the level of pressure, and I really didn't do anything different with Katina, but maybe—'

'Yes, she did do something different.' Katina's face hardens. 'This is all because I've complained about her a couple of times since I arrived. Why didn't you listen when I said I didn't want her to touch me?'

A titter of conversation echoes around the chapel. Hopefully, most of the other guests will disagree with Katina. Except Tracy and Madison, who are impossible to please anyway. But the others have seemed happy enough with my attention.

'You need to give her some lessons in customer care. And I mean it this time – I don't want her anywhere near me again.'

'We'll have a chat afterwards.' Sienna looks from Katina to me.

Oh God. I need this job. I desperately need the money. So if Katina's ruined it all, I don't know what I'll do.

19

'Can I trust you not to have put something in my drink?' Katina snaps as she reaches the front of the cocoa line.

'I'm sorry if I hurt you,' I begin, but she waves away my apology.

'I don't want to hear your platitudes,' she snaps. 'Just stay away from me, do you hear? Wait until I tell George.' She lowers her voice, seeming to be enjoying our little secret.

Sienna hasn't spoken to me since the incident in the chapel, but I feel that to tell her how I know Katina would only invite questions of why I never divulged anything when she first arrived.

'Is this all there is?' Madison glares at me as I ladle cocoa into her mug. 'What if I'm hungry? Isn't there any supper?'

'You can help yourself to fruit.' I give her a similar apologetic look to what Sienna gave me when she broke the news about the internet.

'I want more than fruit.'

One of the sisters, Alexis, Ashleigh or Ana, clears her throat behind her. I still can't remember who's who out of the three of them. Miraculously, their presence encourages

Madison to stop demanding what I can't give her and to step to the side.

'You OK?' Carley reaches me, and I press a warm mug into her hand. 'For the record, I believed you back in the chapel. That little head rub you gave me in the gong bath was exquisite. Katina's just being a drama queen. She really seems to have it in for you for some reason.'

'I'm just worried about what Sienna might say when she speaks to me after I've finished serving the cocoa.'

'Sienna likes you.' Carley's face breaks into a smile. 'She thinks you're a great addition to our little team.'

'How do you know?' Something within me lifts. Maybe I'll be offered future work after all.

'I heard it straight from the horse's mouth.' Carley narrows her eyes in Katina's direction. Katina is pretending to listen to Tracy, who is, inevitably, talking about herself. I swear, if Tracy could clone an audience just to admire her, she would do it in a heartbeat.

A sliver of envy curls inside me, not because I want to be like Tracy, but because I can't imagine ever having that level of unshakeable self-belief. With a mother who dismantled my confidence piece by piece and a husband who walked away without a backward glance, how could I ever have turned out any differently?

Across the room, Olive and Brittany sit together, older and younger versions of the same person. A mother and daughter at ease in each other's company. I've spent my life watching relationships like that from the outside, always wondering what it must feel like to be loved without condition. It's not that I want *my* mother. I just wanted *a* mother.

People love to say it: *You've only got one mum, you should make peace while you can.* As if the title of mother alone absolves her of all wrongdoing. They tell me I'll regret it when she dies, but they don't understand.

I still check in on her occasionally – Facebook stalking, more from morbid curiosity. She's in her mid-sixties now and looks disgustingly healthy, like she'll go on forever. It's the good people who get taken too soon, like my grandad.

'What was the problem earlier between you and Katina? I take it there was no truth in her accusations?' Sienna looks mildly worried but is still calm and friendly. I want to tell her how much I like the jumper-dress she's now wearing. But that wouldn't be appropriate given the question she's just asked.

'Of course not.' I shake my head. 'Look, I'll tiptoe even more carefully around her for the rest of the weekend.'

Sienna's face dimples as she smiles. 'Look, I'm aware we've got one or two tricky guests on this retreat, but we'll all support one another.'

My shoulders relax as her words wash over me. I should have known that someone like Sienna would stand by the staff she's chosen.

'But one thing we have to honour in this game,' she continues, 'is that the customer is always right. Even when they're not.'

Now that she's mentioned 'supporting each other,' I want to blurt about the way Nova's also treating me, but it feels like a step too far.

'Get yourself a decent night's sleep.' Sienna rests a hand on my arm. 'We've got an early start in the morning.'

It's on the tip of my tongue to ask if she has any calming magic tricks to stand a chance of getting much sleep in the spooky and draughty former chapel of rest, but again, I'd better keep quiet.

I'll be fine. I've no other choice.

20

THEN

*S*HE LOOKS IMPOSSIBLY *small beneath the tangle of wires and tubes, the rise and fall of her chest barely perceptible as the ambulance hurtles through traffic, blue lights flashing across her pale skin.*

In any other circumstance, she'd be excited to be in an ambulance– nee-naw, nee-naw – she shouts it every time one passes us on the road. The sound echoes in my mind, and I clutch her cold hand beneath the blanket, willing warmth back into her fingers. Willing life back into her.

'What's our ETA?' the paramedic at her side calls forward, her eyes never leaving the monitor.

'Six minutes, maybe less if the traffic keeps clearing out of the way,' the driver shouts. 'The paediatric trauma team is on standby.'

Six minutes. It might as well be six years.

'I can't believe this is happening,' I hear myself say, my voice ragged. 'Please, please tell me she's going to be alright.'

The paramedic reaches out and squeezes my shoulder. Her eyes are kind, but too calm. Too professional. 'Leeds has one of the best emergency departments in the country. They'll do everything they can.'

That's not an answer.

My daughter lies eerily still, only the steady bleep of the heart monitor assuring me she's still alive. The blanket hides her injuries, mercifully, maybe, but it also makes her look like she's simply sleeping.

'She hasn't woken up once since she was hit,' I whisper.

'Sometimes that's the body protecting itself,' the paramedic says gently. 'It shuts down what it can't cope with.'

The ambulance swerves past a queue of cars. Outside the window, the town hall clock flashes past. So do the endless rows of Christmas lights.

'Less than an hour ago, she was riding her scooter, laughing. She wanted to race me to the park.' A sob claws to the surface. I bow my head, hands over my face.

'I'm so sorry,' the paramedic says.

'Is she going to need surgery?'

'That'll be down to the consultant. Do you have someone meeting you when we arrive?'

'My husband's on his way from work.'

He doesn't know the details. I couldn't form the words. But he'll have heard the terror in my voice.

'Three minutes,' the driver calls.

I lean over her, brushing my thumb across her cheek. 'Hang on, sweet pea. Mummy's right here.' My voice breaks. 'Everything's going to be alright.'

But I don't know if that's true.

21

I'VE BEEN FANTASISING about this all day. If I'd known there was a hot tub, a sauna, and a steam room, I'd have packed my swimming costume, even if it is threadbare from years of chlorine at the local baths with Hallie and Barnaby. Instead, I'm sitting here in my greying bra and knickers. But everyone else has gone to bed. No one's going to see what I'm wearing.

No one ever really *sees* me anyway.

The heat enfolds me the second I lower myself into the water. Jets hammer at the knots in my lower back, the kind that feel carved into my spine from years of stress, cheap mattresses and financial anxiety. The water bubbles up around my shoulders, and the night air, sharp with the cold, almost melts away. For the first time in what feels like forever, I exhale without my breath trembling.

Only my head feels cold. I consider dunking it completely, but suddenly remember. I once watched a film where a woman's hair got caught in the filters, slicing into her scalp. She didn't make it out alive. My mind flickers to Katina's hair, those perfect highlights. I shake my head. *Stop it, Aneka.*

I tip my head back and stare up at the canopy. Beyond it,

snow-laden clouds move slowly across the sky. The world is quiet. No sirens, no children arguing, and no final demands popping through the letterbox.

All that's missing is a glass of wine. Then this would be perfect. Almost enough to make me forget reality still exists.

Through the veil of falling snow, I glimpse the dark slope of the lodge roof and the ghostly shapes of trees. This place should have been even more of a haven for the guests – woodland walks, icy lake dips for the brave, and hikes through the peaks. Instead, the weather has imprisoned us indoors.

I slide deeper into the water, stretching out my legs until I almost float. Maybe I could stay like this all night. Maybe I *should*. For once, I feel safe and warm.

The thought once again rises, *why can't this be my life all the time?*

If Sienna keeps offering me weekend work, and if Barnaby can manage without a meltdown when I'm gone, maybe I could build something. A cleaning business. My own hours. My own money. A future.

More than just survival.

One day, I could even give other women jobs. Women who have heard all their lives that they are not good enough.

Maybe, if I make it, I'll finally be able to silence my mother's voice. That relentless, wasp-like buzzing in the back of my skull, always reminding me of where I came from and who she believes I really am.

Maybe, just maybe... this weekend is the start of something.

Sometimes you have to hit rock bottom before you can claw your way back. Ruby's words creep back to me, the ones she said yesterday over the phone in her no-nonsense voice.

Rock bottom. I know what that means after standing at that checkout, heat rising in my cheeks as the till assistant, smirking like she'd been waiting all day for it, as she announced *your card has been declined.*

All I could see was Christmas Day – with the three of us around the table, not with a turkey and all the trimmings, but with beans on toast. No gifts under the tree. Just my children trying to be brave, pretending not to care.

That has to be it. My rock bottom. My turning point. There's only one direction left to go. Up.

'Penny for them.'

'What?' My eyes snap open.

Vince stands at the foot of the hot tub steps, snow melting on the hard plane of his shoulders. His expression is unreadable, studying me as though he's caught me doing something I shouldn't.

'Where's Tracy?' I turn sharply, scanning behind him. The last thing I need is her droning commentary added to the night.

'She's gone to bed.' But Vince doesn't sound bothered. 'She and Katina are sharing a room, so she's left me to it.'

'You're sleeping in the lounge, aren't you?' Oh gosh, I shouldn't be mentioning where he's *sleeping*. He could think I have ulterior motives.

'Yep.' He kicks off his flip-flops and climbs the steps without asking if it's OK if he joins me. He lowers himself into the bubbles, sitting opposite me, his eyes on me the whole time. 'You didn't even flinch when I walked across from the lodge. You must've been somewhere deep in that head of yours.' He laughs.

A strange twist of unease spirals in my stomach. 'I didn't realise anyone was around.'

'You should be more aware of your surroundings.' He says it lightly, but there's something pointed in his words. 'But don't worry, you're safe with me.' He smiles.

I tuck a strand of hair behind my ear, conscious of every inch of exposed skin. My underwear clings to me. I'm trapped here until he leaves.

'Just for the record,' he says, 'you've done well today.'

'Have I?' My throat feels tight.

'Some of the guests are saying how attentive you are. My mum doesn't think anyone's good enough, but even she admitted you're *trying harder than most*. So I'd ignore any unpleasantness... even if one of those causing it happens to be my girlfriend.'

A flush crawls up my neck, but Vince hopefully won't see it in the darkness. I don't know how to respond.

'I'm... um... doing my best.'

His gaze stays on me, too long, and too steady. 'I'm sure you are.'

A ripple of silence stretches between us. I scramble for something witty or interesting to say, anything to break the tension.

'Are you and your mum close? It must be nice working here together?'

He gives a low chuckle that doesn't actually sound like amusement. 'Yeah, apart from she forgets I'm not a kid anymore and still tries to tell me who I should be with. Who's worthy enough.'

The way he says *be with* sends a shiver down my spine. 'Tracy seems... keen.'

He laughs again, but more softly this time, his eyes flicking towards the building. 'Tracy's more keen on herself than me. My mum saw that as soon as they were introduced. She always knows a person's true character. Nothing gets past her.'

I glance toward the darkness beyond the hot tub, my breath shallow. I really want to get out. To get away from Vince's intense gaze and the heat beneath his calm tone. He seems different now that we're alone.

But even if I were wearing proper swimwear, I would be too shy to get out before him. No one's clapped eyes on my skinny body since George, and for now, that's the way it's going to stay.

'It's not a good look,' my ex remarked as he caught me one night getting dried after my shower.

'What isn't?'

'You look emaciated, love.'

'Well, perhaps if I weren't so stressed thinking you're messing about behind my back all the time, I might have an appetite.'

He sighed. 'Not this again. Honestly, Aneka, you'll drive yourself demented. I'm still here, aren't I?'

'I sometimes think you're only here for the kids.' It was on the edge of my lips to add that I couldn't have replicated a pattern from my childhood any more than I have. I'd married someone who was as emotionally unavailable as my mother. Just as I'd always known with her, I could never quite meet George's impossibly high standards.

'What the hell are you doing?' Both Vince and I jump at the screech of Nova's voice. '*You* shouldn't be in here.'

'Why not?' Vince tilts his head to the side as his mother arrives at the hot tub. It's the first time I've seen her without her Wellness with Sienna apron. She's wearing a thick black sweater, looking like she has no neck as the top of its polo neck meets the bottom of her bobbed hair.

'Your *girlfriend* wouldn't be too happy.'

'Tracy's gone to bed, but it's not as if Aneka and I are doing anything wrong. We're simply having a chat, Mum.'

'She's here to work, not to bask in hot tubs.'

'I've finished work, Nova.' I inject as much pleasantness as I can into my voice. As the hours wear on, I'm disliking this woman more and more, but I can't let her hostility grind me down. 'Sienna dismissed me for the day, and I assumed my free time was my own.'

'You're supposed to be in the chapel.' She wags her finger in the direction of its darkened windows. 'Not cavorting with my son.'

'Carvorting.' Vince snorts. 'Have you heard yourself, Mum?'

'Come on, out of there,' Nova demands, beckoning my exit from the water. 'Now.'

I glance up to see where I left my towel. It's too far for me to grab it and hurriedly wrap it around myself before she and Vince can see what I'm wearing. Or more to the point, not wearing.

'Mum, leave Aneka alone. I mean it.'

'This facility is for the use of paying guests. Not that you've been doing a great deal to help, from what I've heard. Come on out.'

I've got two choices here. I either stand up to the woman and tell her where she can shove her orders, or I make out like I'm too self-conscious to stand up and would prefer to wait until after Vince has gone back inside.

Either way, I don't know who the hell she thinks she is – speaking to me like I'm nothing.

22

I TAKE A DEEP BREATH. It's got to be the former option. I've only just decided that rock bottom has been reached and the only way is up. The 'new' me resolved only moments before Vince joined me in the hot tub that I was going to do whatever is in my power to improve the situation for me and my kids.

So this new version of me can't allow herself to be victimised.

'Haven't you caused enough trouble for one day?'

Nova's not going to let up until I've left this hot tub and got myself well away from her precious son. I'm not sure exactly what she thinks I might be capable of. 'I might take orders from you in the kitchen, Nova,' I begin – again, keeping my voice as pleasant as I can muster. 'But that's as far as it goes.'

'I won't be spoken to like this.' Her face darkens. 'I'm going to find Sienna.'

'And what's Sienna going to do?' Vince shakes his head. 'You're making a right show of yourself, Mum.'

'I'm sitting in this tub, minding my own business.' I lock eyes with her, and I won't be the first to look away. 'I'm not doing you or anyone else any harm.'

'You shouldn't even be at this retreat.' She's the first to break eye contact as her gaze flits over to the darkened building. 'You're not necessary. Nor are you even equipped to do what you're being paid for. You've arrived here with no proper references and without any proof of your so-called credentials.'

'Come on, Mum.' Vince raises himself from the water and grabs for the exit bar, the muscles on his arm rippling. I look away, focusing on the trees in the distance. 'Sienna will be in bed by now, so why don't I walk you back to your room? There's no need for you to be causing trouble for Aneka.'

'Cover yourself up for goodness' sake.' She grabs a towel from the hook and thrusts it at him.

He winks at me. 'Sleep tight, Aneka. I'll catch you in the morning.'

They walk away, still bickering. Why the hell has Nova got it in for me so badly? The door into the building closes.

I glance back at the towel hooks. Shit. She handed him the only towel. Mine. Vince must have come out here without bringing his own. They've left me out here with nothing to cover myself with. All my clothes are in the chapel.

Just as I'm considering what to do, the door that Nova and Vince disappeared through swings open again, this time with Alexander sauntering through it. He's heading over.

No! I've now got to sit in here with my boss's creepy husband. That's if I don't just dissolve into the bubbles. I've lost track of how long I've been sitting in the water. I hold my fingers in front of myself. Yes, they look like shrivelled prunes.

'Fancy seeing you in here.' Alexander slips into the tub. 'Oooh, this is just what the doctor ordered.' He manoeuvres himself into a corner, his face relaxing. 'Now all I need is you crouched behind me again with those magic fingers of yours, kneading at my head.'

My laugh echoes into the falling snowflakes, but it's a sound filled with nervous energy.

'I'm being serious. You're really good. So if you'd like some more practice, perhaps we can do a deal – I could give you a free Reiki treatment.'

Whatever this Reiki is, I'd love to try it, but absolutely not with Alexander. I don't want to be anywhere near him. If Sienna were to hear one of his inappropriate comments, it could put either my payment for this weekend or my prospects of future employment with her in jeopardy.

'No, you're alright, thanks all the same.'

'Oooh, you're turning me down.' He sounds surprised.

I smile back. I really don't know what to do or say.

'Bit of a cocktease, aren't you, Aneka?'

At first, I think I've misheard him. 'I'm a *what*?'

Oh my God, as if he's just used that word. In any other work environment, he'd be hauled over the coals for sexual harassment, but I can hardly report him to Sienna. It would be my word against his, and I'm certain she'd choose to believe her husband over her newly-hired help. I should jump out of this water and get away from him immediately, but with what I'm wearing and no towel to cover myself with, I'm stuck here until after he gets out.

'I've seen how you look at me, Aneka. And to be fair, you look like someone hungry for some action if you know what I mean.'

The trouble is, I know exactly what he means. What I don't know is how I'm going to free myself from this situation.

'I'm sorry if I've given you the wrong impression, Alexander.' I look him squarely in the eye. 'But I'm just here to work, earn my money and get home to my kids for Christmas.'

'Rubbish. Fate has placed us here, alone, in this hot tub together while everyone else has gone to bed.'

'I don't think so.' Shit, shit, shit. Because I'm not getting out of here and away from him, I bet he just thinks I'm flirting. Playing hard to get.

'Just because you're *working*,' he draws air quotes around the word, 'doesn't mean you shouldn't have a little fun.'

'I'm fine, thanks. I've just come out here for some peace.'

Leave me alone. Leave me alone. Leave me alone. I push my hair out of my eyes. It needs a good cut, but I haven't been able to afford to visit a salon. It's so cold out here that my hair's starting to freeze.

'Sienna would only have herself to blame if me and you, well, you know. She barely notices I exist these days.' He rolls his eyes towards the snowy sky.

So he's one of these cliche *my wife doesn't understand me* sort of creeps.

'It's a bit chilly to be sleeping in the chapel on your own.' He rubs his hands against his shoulders as if he's demonstrating the cold. I can't believe he's persisting. 'A skinny thing like you should have someone keeping her warm.'

I've got to defend myself. 'You are joking, aren't you, Alexander?'

'Maybe, maybe not.' He pulls a face as if to say, *try me.*

'Is this some sort of test? Because if it is, it's not funny.' I spot the door of the sauna. I should just jump out of the tub and wait in there until he goes back inside. It's a hop and a jump to the door – not as far to be parading myself in front of him in my underwear. I could get warm and dry in there and then rush back to the building as soon as the coast is clear when he's gone.

'Sienna and I have an understanding, if you know what I'm saying.' He's looking at me intently. 'What we do, what the other doesn't find out about and all that.'

'I'm really not interested, Alexander.'

'You're turning me down.'

'Of course I am.'

'All I have to do is tell Sienna about you coming on to me.

Following me out to the hot tub in your skimpy bra and panties.'

'I was out here first. Even Nova saw me.'

'Good luck with getting her to vouch for you.' He laughs.

'Vince will.'

'Then, inviting me back to the chapel to keep you warm.' Alexander goes on, seemingly undeterred.

'I'll make sure Sienna believes *me*.'

'Good luck with that too.' He smirks.

'You're really trying to blackmail me, aren't you?' What a dreadful man. I was right to try and stay well away from him.

'Like I said, you're nothing but a cocktease. You've given me the eye all day, and now, when push comes to shove, you're turning me down flat.'

'We women should stick together, not be jumping into bed with one another's husbands. I had it done to me and it's awful.'

'You stick to your morals, love. From what I've seen on your Facebook profile, they're about all you possess.'

I can't believe he's been looking at my Facebook profile. I need to get away from him sharpish.

'It's funny,' I hoik myself from the water, no longer caring about what he sees. 'I'd far prefer to have my morals than what you've got.' I look him up and down. 'Which is very little as far as I can see.' I storm across to the sauna, pulling the door behind me. I don't know whether to feel proud of my behaviour. Or very, very scared. After all, he could come after me. He could do anything, and I'd be no match for him.

I came out here for a lovely relax in the bubbles, and look what I got instead.

All I can do is hope that he leaves me alone.

23

My body is starting to warm back up after its exposure to the freezing air as I lurched from the hot tub to the sauna. But Alexander is still outside. I won't breathe easy until he's back inside the lodge, and never again will I put myself in this kind of vulnerable situation.

As the door is wrenched open, I jump. 'I'm warning you to leave me alone.' My eyes dart to the hot coals and the scoop used to pour water to make them steam. Either one of these things will have to be weaponised if Alexander comes a step closer. 'Just go back to your wife. I'm not interested.'

He could do anything to me out here, while it's just me and him. I'll fight tooth and nail, but I'm praying he'll back off before we get to that point.

Alexander's eyes are wild with fury – he's obviously unaccustomed to being rejected. 'Like I said before, if you think there's anything to be gained by repeating a murmur of this, it'll be your word against mine, Aneka. And you don't need me to tell you who Sienna will believe.'

I know who I'd believe in these circumstances, but I stay quiet. He's sounding as if he's shortly going to leave me alone.

I'm desperate for a drink of water, having been in the heat for so long. As soon as I know he's inside and away from me, I'll be scarpering.

The door to the sauna falls closed more softly than it was opened. I breathe in the woody scent, suddenly feeling light-headed. I didn't sleep well last night. Instead, I saw every corner of every hour while I lay awake, worrying about leaving the kids. I was stressed throughout my drive to get here, wondering whether there'd be enough petrol in the car. And now I'm anxious about how long we might be trapped here at the lodge. Also in the mix is that I haven't really eaten enough today.

A door in the distance bangs, signalling that Alexander has gone inside. I need to get myself out of here before I faint.

I'll give him a moment to return to his rightful spot at Sienna's side in the snug. The poor woman. To think I've watched her at the front of the chapel, coveting her way of being and hoping for some of her magic to rub off. I'd rather be single forever than married to a man like Alexander.

It's as if I emit some invisible frequency that attracts the takers and the tyrants. My past is littered with people who fed on my quietness, my willingness to please, people who grew stronger the more I shrivelled. My own mother. Friends who smiled in my face while slowly hollowing me out. And then George.

They didn't just hurt me. They took me apart. Piece by piece.

Something shifts inside me, a hardening. I'm done being the easy target. Those days are over.

With this new strength continuing to take root, I rise from the wooden bench. Though I've warmed up and my skin is nearly dry, my underwear is still soaked, and I desperately need to get out of the heat.

I gasp as the freezing air envelops me and run on tiptoes

towards the door into the main building. Hopefully, no one will see me as I slip in and get to my things in the chapel.

I tug at the wooden handle. The door doesn't budge.

Oh no.

The bastard has locked me out in the snow.

I bang on the door with all my might. 'Alexander, let me in – *now*.' He's probably standing right behind it, sniggering.

A few moments pass. The heat I gained from the sauna has quickly left me, and I'm already becoming numb from the cold.

A few more moments pass. If I don't get in there, I'm going to freeze to death. He's not coming back. He's done this on purpose – that much is obvious. It's his way of getting back at me for rejecting him. My teeth are chattering. I bang my fist against the door again. Someone has to hear me.

'Somebody, please, let me in.' I slap the door with my palm, but still, nobody responds. The only thing that feels warm is the heat of my tears.

I run around the perimeter of the lodge, banging on every door and window, ringing the doorbell in the main porch. Still, nobody hears. What if I'm out here all night? I'll be forced to melt some snow to get a drink. I'll have to alternate between the freezing air out here and the heat of the sauna to stay alive. But what good will that do me for an entire night? Plus, I won't get a wink of sleep, and I've got to work all day tomorrow.

It's no good. I rush back to the sauna to get warm, shaking off the snowflakes as I arrive. Every inch of me is trembling with the cold. What the hell am I going to do? Then, as I stare out of the window, I spot the answer to my predicament.

24

THE BIG RED button situated just above the hot tub is my only chance of getting back inside the lodge. An emergency alarm, which will hopefully sound inside the building. Once that's going off, I'll just keep banging on the window until someone realises I'm locked out in the cold.

I lurch back out of the sauna and towards the button, slamming the heel of my hand onto it. Instantly, the siren wails.

Shivering, I hurtle back to the door which Alexander so callously locked behind himself.

'Help!' I bang against the wood. Then, remembering something I once heard about alerting others to a problem more quickly, I yell, 'Fire.' And again 'Fire.' If anyone can hear me, even if my voice is muffled, that should rouse them all from their comfy beds. 'Please, someone, there's a fire.' Adrenaline floods my system, but it's useless against the cold convulsing through my limbs. That bastard Alexander. Somehow, I'll get even with him for this, that's for sure.

'What the hell?' Nova pokes her head through the door, looking at me as if I'm vermin.

'Just let me in.' I charge past her, knocking her into the

doorframe in my desperation to get back into the warmth of the lodge.

'What on earth's going on?' Sienna appears in the corridor, rubbing her eyes.

'Turn that bloody thing off.' It's Madison's whinging voice, giving the wail of the alarm a run for its money. 'I was fast asleep.'

'So was I.' Katina comes up behind Sienna in her skimpy pyjamas. Alexander, who's now also dared to show his face, is staring at what's visible of Katina's breasts above the neckline of her cami top, his eyes out on stalks.

'What's with the undies?' Tracy's eyes travel from my shoulders to my knees, her expression veering between disgust and amusement.

'What's going on?' Olive wraps her dressing gown around herself as she glides down the stairs with Brittany close behind. 'I thought this was supposed to be a relaxing retreat.'

'Thank goodness for that.' Another voice calls from the landing as the alarm is silenced.

'The alarm kill button is in the utility room if anyone needs to know for future reference.' Vince shrugs out of his dressing gown and wraps it around my shivering shoulders. 'How the hell did you end up locked outside?'

'It was *his* fault.' I glare at Alexander.

'I didn't even know you were out there.' Sienna narrows her eyes at her husband.

'Just for a few moments,' he replies. 'Aneka must have been in the sauna or steam room when I locked the door. I didn't know she was still—'

'Yes, you did. You know you did, you—'

I want to shout the word *pervert* into his face. I want to oust him here and now, before hanging him out to dry.

'You were clearly frightened, Aneka.' Sienna places a hand on my shoulder. 'I get that, But—'

'Look, forget it – I'm OK, I'll just get myself dried.'

By rights, everyone who's gathered here should know how he tried to blackmail me into sex. How he then callously locked me out in the snow when I wouldn't allow his bullying. Just because I'm the hired help around here and way below Alexander in terms of wealth, doesn't mean I'm way below him by any other standard. But he'll keep. As the saying goes, revenge is a dish best served cold.

'Go and get a hot shower,' Vince says. 'You can return my dressing gown in the morning.' If he notices the approving gazes of Katina and the hen sisters as he stands in his boxer shorts, he does nothing to acknowledge them.

'What have you given her *your* robe for?' Tracy looks daggers at her boyfriend. 'It's just as well I turned up on this retreat.'

'Now it's *you* parading yourself for all to see.' Nova's tone is brittle as she also glares at her son.

'He didn't inherit the milk of human kindness from his mother, that's for sure,' Sienna mutters under her breath.

'What did you say?' Nova snaps, seemingly forgetting that she's speaking to her boss.

'Go up to the main bathroom, Aneka.' Sienna points up the stairs. 'As you know, there should be some warm towels in the airing cupboard.'

'Thanks.' I shoot her a grateful look.

'There are.' Nova's face is still set in a firm, hard line as she continues to stare at me.

Only Sienna and Vince have offered me any kindness since I managed to get back in here. Everyone else is unamused that I've woken the entire lodge before bursting through the door in my underwear.

'Right, everyone, back to bed,' Alexander waves his hands around, ushering people back up the stairs, probably before I decide to elaborate on his behaviour. 'At least it was nothing more serious.'

Oh, but it could be. I stare at him.

If you come within spitting distance of me over the next two days, things could get very serious.

I head towards the stairs.

25

THEN

'I'M sorry there's nothing else I can add.' I stare mournfully at the officer to whom I've just given a statement. 'It seemed to be over in seconds.'

'I think our greatest chance is to get you into the public's minds and hearts,' he says. 'As quickly as we can. The crew are just setting up in the staff room, and then we'll be ready to go live.'

'OK.' Normally, I'd be terrified at the prospect of being on TV, but all I want to do is catch whoever put my little girl inside an operating theatre. She's fighting for her life while he or she will be at home, sitting by their Christmas tree, and acting like they haven't changed our lives forever.

I retake my seat beside my husband in the waiting room, staring at the floor, unable to meet his eye after what I've done to our family. I shouldn't have let her ride her scooter; I should have made her hold my hand. It should have been me the car hit. Not my baby girl.

'Are you sure you're up to what they're asking?'

'I need to be doing something, anything to help,' I reply. 'I feel useless, just sitting here, waiting for news.'

He reaches for my hand.

'Thanks for not blaming me.' Fresh tears roll down my cheeks. I didn't imagine I could have any tears left to cry after the last few hours.

'It wasn't your fault, love. It was his.' He spits the word 'his' out like it's a piece of rancid meat. My husband's convinced it must have been a man. 'How anyone could mow a four-year-old girl down with their car and then drive off like that beggars belief. I just hope they get the bastard.'

I'm almost shocked to hear him swear. We made a pact when we became parents not to swear, so that we'd never slip up in front of our daughter. Being her mum and dad is the most precious and important thing we've ever done.

And what if it's going to be all snatched away?

26

FINALLY, I'm lying, showered and safe, or at least I hope I'm safe, in my sleeping bag. There are three people here who threaten my safety, the main one being Alexander, for obvious reasons. But to a lesser extent, there are two other people I wouldn't trust as far as I could throw them – Katina and Tracy.

There are no blinds or curtains at the windows of the chapel, so the white of the world outside is still visible, along with branches swaying in the wintry wind. I should be exhausted after the day I've had, but it's making me jumpy rather than sleepy.

The dim light casts shapes over the room. Yoga mats are still laid in their rows, blankets and pillows folded on top. The last time I was in here, I just wanted to lie down on one of them and sleep. And now I finally have the opportunity, I couldn't feel more wired.

I've pumped my airbed up the best I can with the crappy footpump, but really, I'd probably be more comfortable lying on a yoga mat.

I wrap my arms around myself, spreading my fingers against my shoulders. I really can't get warm. Being forced to stand out in the snow, my underwear still wet from the hot tub as I fought to get inside, has left me chilled to the bone.

No doubt Alexander will have just fallen asleep without conscience after locking me outside. And if there hadn't been that emergency alarm, perhaps no one would have known he'd locked me out there until morning. Would I have been able to keep myself going by swapping between the extremes of sauna heat and freezing winter air?

I can't forgive Alexander for leaving me in that sort of predicament. He's a man who's clearly unaccustomed to being turned down, but now that I have, he'll either make my life a misery or just move on to someone else.

It's strange how Nova softens in Alexander's presence in a similar way to how she does around her son, and even Katina seems unable to take her eyes off him. To say she's supposed to be so madly in love with my ex-husband, this has come as a surprise. But hers and George's relationship is hardly built on a bedrock of trust. I don't know how long they were sleeping together before I found out, but if he can do it once, he's capable of doing it again. And she clearly also doesn't place fidelity high on her list of values.

I tilt my phone towards my face. It's well after midnight, and there is still zero service on my phone. I imagine Barnaby in his bed, surrounded by his bears, and just pray he's fast asleep. Hallie too. She'll no doubt be worrying because I haven't called. However, at least she knows I got here safely from our brief conversation yesterday afternoon.

Sometimes I can't believe I'm already the mother of a sixteen-year-old. Hallie's the same age I was when I was pregnant for the first time, and the idea of her being in the situation I was in is unthinkable.

'What would you say if I came home expecting a baby, Mum?' She asked me not so long ago.

'Well, I couldn't exactly have a pop at you, could I?' I'd

laughed. 'But really, on a serious note, I want you to have a better chance at life than constantly working and worrying about making ends meet. I want you to enjoy travelling, to have a career, and everything else. There's plenty of time for babies.'

'Do you regret any of it, Mum?'

'Oh my God, of course not.' I pulled her towards me. We might have often been short of money in our house, but there was never any shortage of hugs. 'My kids are the best things that ever happened to me.'

I swore long ago that I would be nothing like my mother. Where she withheld love, I would give it freely, fiercely and without condition.

And the moment I gave birth at sixteen years old, I was terrified and exhausted, but I knew I hadn't just become a mother. I had found my purpose.

The midwife, still in her scrubs, had glanced at the clock and then at me with thinly veiled disdain. She laid my daughter back in the cot with a sigh.

'That's me done,' she said. 'Time to go home, get my gladrags on and hit the town. I'd hate to be where you are. Saddled with a baby at sixteen. What a waste.'

Her words should have hurt me. That was probably her intention. But the moment my fingers brushed the soft, perfect curve of my daughter's cheek, something ignited in my belly. A strength I didn't know I had.

'I'd hate to be where *you* are, actually,' I said quietly. 'Because me and this little girl? We're going to have the time of our lives. I've already got everything I need.'

She raised an eyebrow, but I didn't look away from her sneering face.

For the first time in my life, I wasn't somebody's burden or disappointment. I was somebody's world. And I finally had my own family.

I slam my head into my pillow. I really can't sleep. I mean, who could in a room like this? It's one thing when you've got gong vibrations thrumming through your chest and you're getting essential oil massaged into your temples, but this is totally different.

I keep imagining the rows of corpses lying in place of the yoga mats. The souls of the workers who fell to their deaths as they built the nearby viaduct. Young men who won't have been much older than Hallie. I wonder where they're buried.

I tug my sleeping bag tighter around myself, recalling the warmth of Vince's dressing gown as he draped it onto my shoulders. Tracy doesn't know how lucky she is to have him as her boyfriend. I don't know if he's friendly and kind to *all* women, but along wth Carley, he's certainly made my time here more bearable.

Who are you trying to kid? My mother's voice is so tangible in the darkness, I squint and stare around at the shadows, half expecting her to be kneeling beside my airbed. *Nobody else will ever want you.*

Tears pool in my eyes.

You're lucky I haven't left. George's words when he was once drunk have etched themselves into the fibre of my being. It wasn't long after I'd had Barnaby that I was struck with post-natal depression. *Not many men would have stuck around.*

Tears roll from each eye and pool in my ears. George was awful to me around that time. When I most needed his love and support was when he was at his most distant. And all the time, I was terrified that history was repeating itself. Mum had been severely ill for several years with postnatal depression after having me, and I was terrified I was heading the same way.

But I got help. I got it early, and bit by bit, I recovered. George came back around. Until he left again.

Your mum was right. You do give off a bad vibe. Lots of people agree with me.

It was one of George's excuses for sleeping with Katina. It was *my* fault. Even after indulging in the most hurtful betrayal a man can ever do to his wife, he still heaped the blame onto me.

I turn onto my side, the airbed wobbling beneath my weight. I probably haven't pumped it with enough air. But I'm too tired to move. At least my body's too tired. If only my mind would follow suit.

George is now happy with Katina, driving around in her posh car and ignoring the existence of his two kids, whilst I, who thought I'd be happier once we'd divorced, am lying alone in a spooky room without a penny to my name, wondering if I'll be able to give my children anything for Christmas. Or even, I glance out at the relentless snowfall, wondering whether I'll be able to get back home. My earlier resolve to turn things around, for now, seems to have evaporated.

Being locked out like that made me feel vulnerable. Not to mention, utterly hopeless.

27

'You need to move.' I open one eye in the semi-darkness. It's only illuminated by the rectangle of light emitting from the far end of the room.

What a vision to wake up to. Nova's looming shadow.

'But it's the middle of the night.'

'It's six in the morning.' Her voice is sharp. 'Sienna wants to get this room warmed up before everyone comes in at 7:15.'

I sit up, rubbing my eyes. At some point, I *must* have fallen asleep, even if it feels like I've only been sleeping for five minutes.

'And I'd thank you to get yourself fully dressed before you leave this room.' Nova turns on her heel. 'Especially after the eyeful you gave everyone last night.' She heads in the direction of the rectangle of light.

If I were waking someone this early, I'd gently touch their shoulder. I'd have made them a mug of hot coffee, and at the very least, I'd say good morning and ask if they slept well. But the only people Nova seems capable of extending these niceties to are Vince and Alexander. Vince, because he's her son, and Alexander, well, she must have her reasons.

I dress quickly before rolling up the sleeping bag and airbed, then I stack both in the corner of the room. This is the story of my life, taking up as little space as possible. I desperately want to be like the other guests. I glance through the window at the three hen sisters basking in the heat of the hot tub with steaming mugs balancing on the edge. I want to have the money to spend on luxuries and weekend breaks with my children. But mostly, I want at least a little time when I don't have to jump to my feet and constantly have to serve other people.

As I head to the door into the kitchen, raised voices echo from behind it as mugs and pans clatter. It's Sienna and Nova. At first, their voices are muffled, but as I get nearer, I can hear them word for word.

'She's bloody useless,' Nova snaps. 'If you're so intent on undermining me in this way, at least bring in someone decent.'

'You're forgetting yourself, as usual.' Sienna's voice is softer than Nova's. 'This is my retreat and I call the shots.'

'I thought I was in charge of the kitchen. And her.'

'*Her* has a name. Why do you have to be so damn unkind apart from to those you choose?' Ah, so Sienna's noticed how Nova's only kind to her chosen ones.

I push the door into the kitchen and plaster a bright smile across my face. 'Good morning.' I breeze in and unhook my apron from the back of the door. 'Where would you like me to start?'

'You could start by telling me how you came to be locked out last night in your bra and knickers,' Sienna frowns. 'Before blaming Alexander – why?'

'Because he was outside for a short time too.'

'Are you saying he was in the hot tub while you were in the steam room or sauna?'

She's asking a leading question. Probably because she suspects how he might have behaved and is secretly scared of my confirming it. 'Possibly.' I'd better err on the side of caution.

'Hmmm.' She looks thoughtful as she twirls her thumbs around and around each other. 'We probably need a system for tonight to make sure it doesn't happen again.'

'Why don't you say no one in the hot tub or sauna after 10 pm?'

'Why don't you remember why you're here and get on with helping me to prepare breakfast?' Nova wags her finger towards the corner of the kitchen. 'Start chopping fruit. Hopefully you can manage that without incident.'

Sienna raises an eyebrow. 'I'll leave you both to get on. Go easy, please, Nova. I need to get ready for the stretch session before breakfast.'

'Do you need me for the shoulder and oil thing this morning?' I hope not – not after the two occasions when Katina accused me of hurting her yesterday.

At least Sienna has offered to take charge of Katina from now on. However, I don't particularly want to put my hands on Alexander either. I might just end up wrapping them around his scrawny throat. The same with the self-obsessed Tracy. Or moaning Madison. Oh dear, perhaps there wouldn't be too many people left on this retreat if I had my way.

'No, we'll save the final offering for our lunchtime meditation, after our midday yoga vinyasa,' Sienna replies. 'You just crack on with breakfast and make sure there's plenty of fresh coffee available for 8:30. Once you've finished with breakfast, I'd like you to go around the rooms – make everyone's beds and ensure all guests have fresh towels and plenty of toiletries.'

'Right you are.' I glance through the open door at Olive and Brittany passing by in their comfy-looking clothes, all ready to go and lie on their yoga mats. I wish I could just lie down and do morning stretches. I wish someone would serve me coffee, fruit salad, warm pastries and a freshly-cooked omelette. And I want someone to make my bed, that's if I had one, and leave me fresh towels.

Will it ever be my turn in life? Will anyone ever look after me?

28

THE SISTERS and the mother and daughter are first into the dining room to be served their coffee after their stretching.

'Are you OK after last night?' Olive asks.

'Yes. Thanks for asking.'

'What happened?' Brittany goes on. 'Being locked out must have been scary.'

'I'm not sure.' My eyes meet Alexander's across the room, and I hope I'm conveying what's running through my mind. *I'll get you when you're least prepared.* Though I really don't know how.

'I don't blame you for setting the alarm off,' one of the sisters says. 'You must have been terrified.'

It's a pleasure to serve these ladies. At least they all say please and thank you and smile at me like I'm a person. Instead of a commodity.

'This better be decaf.' Madison curls her lip as I fill her mug. The not-so-nice 'ladies' have now entered the room.

'You never asked for decaf.' But I stop pouring. As Sienna said, *the customer is always right.* 'I offered tea or coffee and you just said coffee.'

'Decaf's on my form. Didn't you read it?'

Without responding, I take the mug from her and place it in front of Tracy. 'There you go. Coffee.'

'What's with the tone? I think you need a lesson in customer service. I'll be sure to let Sienna know.'

'Listen, no. I'm sorry. Look, would you like milk? Cream?' It's an effort to keep the sarcasm from my voice. I'm absolutely shattered after barely any sleep, and there's nothing I like about this woman. She causes the hairs to stand up on the back of my neck.

'I'd like my coffee to be served by someone else.' She turns to Katina. 'Blimey.' She pulls a face. 'I'm really seeing what you mean.'

'Is breakfast on its way?' Katina seems to be looking right through me. 'I'm starving.'

I gesture to the fruit salad and the pastries on the sideboard. I hope there'll be plenty of them left, as I'm also hungry.

I was bollocked by Nova for picking at grapes while making the fruit salad. 'Do you think our guests want their breakfasts contaminated?'

'Is that all there is for breakfast?' Katina pulls a face. 'Fruit salad and croissants? Is that why we've paid all this money?'

'Where's my decaf?' Madison calls from across the room.

'Leave her alone for pity's sake.' Olive rests her book down and frowns.

Brittany's filming us again, no doubt for her blog. I'm sure it will make interesting reading.

'Tell your daughter to stop filming,' Tracy demands. 'I haven't given permission for anyone to record my face.'

Brittany rests her phone on the table, but I've no doubt she'll be filming again when everyone's distracted. 'Perhaps we should stay out of it, Mum.' She nudges Olive.

'I can't just sit here and watch this poor lass running around the room and taking grief from three spoiled women who can get up off their own fat arses.'

'I think you'll find,' – Katina stands from her seat and wiggles, – 'that my arse is in no way fat. You, however, need to take a closer look at your own backside.'

'Ladies, for goodness sake.' Sienna flies into the room. 'We're here to relax in an ambience of calm.' She shakes her head. 'Aneka, see who wants omelettes and take care of those for me, please.'

'You'll want one, won't you love?' Vince calls over as he fills himself a mug of coffee. It's the first time I've heard him use any kind of term of endearment towards Tracy, and she looks rather pleased. Sienna, on the other hand, is bearing an expression I can't decipher.

'Oooh, yes. With plenty of mushrooms,' Tracy replies.

'Same,' says Alexander.

'I hope they choke on them,' I mutter to myself as I head back to the kitchen.

'What are you doing now?' Nova glares at me.

'Two people want an omelette.'

'Can't you see I'm busy?' Nova's angry expression changes, but then a smile suddenly crosses her face. I glance behind me to see who it could be. Alexander.

'Morning Aneka.'

'I'll have an omelette as well,' Sienna appears behind him. 'But I only want cheese and onion, no mushrooms.'

'Can Brittany have one too?' Olive calls from the doorway. 'Just with cheese. She'd love one made properly, as she says mine are more like scrambled eggs.'

'Right you are,' I call back.

Vince is also hanging around in the kitchen.

'If you want one, you'll have to wait,' I tell him. 'There are only four burners on the stove.'

'Why don't you sit?' he tells me. 'And I'll cook *you* an omelette. You've been running around since you got out of bed.'

'That's what she's being paid for.' Nova says drily.

'She's right.' I shrug. 'I'm happy to wait for my breakfast.'

'I'd better give you a hand,' Sienna says as Nova adds ingredients to a bowl. I'm unsure what she's doing, but it doesn't look to be anything to do with breakfast. 'There are some onions already chopped in the fridge – I'll start frying them off while you sort the cheese and whisk the eggs. Three per omelette.' She nods to where some jugs are stacked beside the pans.

Vince is also buzzing around, passing things, clearly keen to make himself useful so the rest of us can also sit down sooner.

'Vince, we're supposed to be eating breakfast together,' Tracy hollers from the dining room.

'Go and sit down,' Nova says. 'Have you never heard the saying about too many cooks?'

There's a sizzle as Sienna slings mushrooms and onions into the pans she's assembled on all four burners. 'Don't be long with those eggs,' she says, shaking each pan in turn.

'I'd have never thought to do them all at once.' I head over to her with a jug of whisked eggs in each hand.

Nova sniggers at something that Alexander says, and Sienna turns up the music. 'We'll need the cheese in just a minute,' she says as I rummage around in the fridge for the bag of ready-grated cheese. It wouldn't do to serve them cold omelettes. 'Then if you take charge of these two pans, I'll watch these two.'

Sienna and I would make a much better team than me and Nova. Hopefully, after Nova's enforced retirement, this is exactly how things will be.

The smell of onions is nauseating at this early hour after so little sleep, and the stench of mushrooms as Sienna stirs three of the four pans with them in is even worse. I've never been able to eat mushrooms. The look, smell, texture and taste are enough to make me retch.

I sprinkle grated cheese over each omelette before picking each of my designated two pans up by the handle and flicking the omelettes around. Then I slide the contents onto two plates, and Sienna does the same.

'About time too.' Tracy doesn't make any effort to move her crumb-covered plate from in front of her to make way for the omelette. Instead, it's down to me to make a space. I set the plate before her without a word of thanks.

Instead of getting on with her breakfast, Tracy continues with whatever story she was telling. I'm not quite sure who she's talking to, but it could be the hen sisters. One of them looks slightly interested. But only slightly. This time, she's going on about a time when she was wild swimming and felt so cold she was unsure whether she'd make it back to shore without her heart stopping. She's on about finding her way through the surrounding woodland and taking an icy dip in the lake. While I wouldn't try to stop her, I'm certain that Sienna would, if only for insurance purposes.

'Don't you ever get sick of the sound of your own voice?' Madison screws the lid back on the jam and pushes it away so it slides towards the centre of the table.

'Are you talking to me?' Tracy wrenches her knife and fork from either side of her plate. 'Because if you are, it's only because you're jealous.'

'Of what?' Madison laughs. Honestly, what's wrong with these women? She, Tracy, Katina and Nova could form their own coven of witches. All they'd have to do is join forces in that kitchen, and they could come up with a potion that would wipe the rest of us out by lunchtime. Apart from Alexander and Vince. I'm sure Nova wouldn't want to do them any damage.

'Like Sienna said, this is supposed to be a time for us to relax and be, not to listen to the Tracy show.' Madison scowls. In fact, I don't think I've seen her smile since she arrived.

The hen sisters giggle into their cornflakes while Olive watches on with nerves etching her face. Brittany's looking at her phone, clearly, there's no signal, so she must be recording again, albeit much more inconspicuously this time.

'At least I have something worth talking about.' Tracy spreads a napkin across her lap. 'Meanwhile, I don't think I've heard you do anything other than complain.'

'Don't ever apply to come on one of my retreats, will you, Madison?' Katina edges her chair closer to Tracy, possibly in solidarity.

'Ooh, you'll have to tell me more about what you'll be offering.' Tracy pulls an excited face.

'Why don't you just eat your omelettes before they go cold?' Sienna's voice is the snappiest I've ever heard it. I don't blame her. I've already gathered that Katina's in the wellness industry, but that doesn't give her the right to peddle her wares at someone else's retreat.

We're barely into day two, and trying to appease everyone is proving to be an almost full-time job. I can't wait to tell Hallie all about her father's new girlfriend.

Once she learns how spoiled, whiny and nasty Katina is, Hallie will realise that it's only a matter of time before her father sees his girlfriend for who she really is.

What goes around always has to come around.

29

'DID YOU ALL ENJOY A GOOD BREAKFAST?' Sienna stands at the doorway to the dining room, her hair plaited to one side, wearing purple baggy trousers and a loose, flowing white top. I'd love to have her style. I'd love to have *any* style.

She shoots me a smile as I pause my gathering of plates to allow her to speak. She's already reminded me this morning that she's still looking for a new wingwoman to replace Nova once she takes her long-overdue retirement. So no more getting locked out of the lodge in my underwear. She looked at me with amusement when she said that, so clearly she isn't feeling any animosity.

'Yes, thank you,' the hen sisters and mother and daughter chorus.

Alexander pats his belly. 'I couldn't eat another morsel.'

Carley squeezes around the side of Sienna and does a mock tiptoe thing back to her seat so as not to disturb our leader.

Outside the window is a blanket of white as far as the eye can see. The snow is still falling, but not quite as heavily as last night. Perhaps it's easing. Maybe we won't be cut off for Christmas. I really hope everything is going to be alright.

I think of my kids, once again lamenting the fact that I can't speak to them. Perhaps Hallie will have worked out that the phone lines might be down with the weather.

'This morning is your free time,' Sienna continues.

'We could have had that at home.' Madison sinks into her chair, and I shoot her a look.

'We were supposed to have the hike this morning.' Sienna continues talking without acknowledging Madison. 'Clearly, the weather has put a lid on our programmed activities, so if you still want to get outside, there's the sauna, steam room and hot tub, which are all looking particularly inviting this morning. Then I have a couple more options for you since there's no hike. Oh, what was that?' The lights flicker off and then back on again.

'Oh great, the power's going to be off next.' Madison shakes her head.

Sienna and Vince exchange an uneasy glance.

'We're waiting for these options.' Tracy drums her fingers against the table. She really is one of the rudest people I've ever encountered. It's little wonder she and Katina have so easily made friends.

'I've cleared the snug of all our sleeping paraphernalia and we're going to have a movie morning,' Sienna announces. 'We have snacks, beanbags, fleeces and Eat, Pray, Love.'

'No, thank you very much.' Tracy pulls a face as though she's never heard of anything more beneath her.

Katina hisses something into her ear, but I only catch the words, *my retreat.*

'There are shelves filled with books.' Sienna points at the bookcase behind where I'm standing, 'and Alexander's going to light a fire in the main lounge before his first appointment at ten if you want to cosy up with a book. Plus, there are games in the games room.' She points in the direction of the room off the corridor, which leads to the chapel. 'Card games, board games, puzzles. Or you can just find a quiet space and have a snooze.'

If only I could do just that. At least, I've managed to eat this morning - some fruit and a pastry while Nova was distracted by whatever she and Alexander were discussing. Vince once again offered to cook me something and fix me a drink, but as people keep reminding me, I'm here to work.

But I've gone really weary, especially after such a broken night's sleep in the chilly chapel. However, I've still got the bedrooms to get around, plus I've to assist Nova with the lunch prep.

'We'll reconvene at noon in the chapel for vinyasa yoga, followed by lunch at one thirty.'

'Is there any sign of the internet being restored?'

I'm grateful Madison's asked this question, as it's one I also need answering.

Sienna looks apologetic. 'It's unlikely to be put back on over the weekend,' she replies. 'But we can still live in hope.'

There are several groans around the room. I'm not bothered in the slightest about the internet. My only concern is whether everything's OK at home.

'What's happening this afternoon?' Katina stifles a yawn, sounding bored. Tracy smiles.

'That will be the time to have your pre-booked treatments with Alexander, Carley and Vince.' She gestures to them in turn. 'Those not in a treatment can return to the activities, and we'll vote on a different film before our late afternoon meditation. How does that sound?'

There are several mutterings, but nobody, not even Madison, complains again. Instead, people stretch in their seats and begin making their way from the room, leaving me and Nova to clear up after breakfast.

I don't know how anyone can moan. It's such a beautiful place that to be busy doing nothing sounds like a luxury.

As I spend the morning completing my tasks, I notice Katina and Tracy in their perfect two-pieces as they venture outside with a glass of fizz in hand. Within minutes, Alexander follows them out there like a lap dog. I can't imagine Sienna being too pleased if she can see them from the window of the snug, where she's beginning her film with the hen sisters.

'You don't need to do anything in *my* room.' Carley appears in the doorway as I make her bed. 'Have a sit-down for ten minutes instead. I'll bring you a cuppa.'

'Are you sure?'

'I wouldn't offer if I wasn't.'

As the door closes behind her, I flop down in the easy chair by her window, staring out at the beautiful snowscape before closing my eyes. All I can see are the pink faces and bobble hats of my children when they were younger, beyond excited to be out on sledges before I took them home for hot chocolate with marshmallows. Sometimes I would envisage life when they were grown up, and my life would become my own again. But now Hallie's sixteen, there isn't much I wouldn't give to have our time over. And not just with her.

You don't know what you've got until it's gone.

'You wouldn't think it was Christmas in six days, would you?' Carley thrusts a steaming mug at me.

'I know what you mean. The snow's quite festive, but other than that...'

'That's the appeal of these solstice retreats,' Carley continues. 'They get people away from the chaos and commercialism of Christmas. Sienna likes to think of them as an oasis from reality.'

'I can't imagine being here beyond Monday.' I take a welcome sip from my mug. 'It's good to be busy while I'm here, but I think I'll have severe cabin fever by then.'

'Me too. Everyone's booked a massage, so that's quite a few hours taken up, as everyone's booked either seventy-five or ninety minutes. However, I can see why there was some disgruntlement this morning. Without the outdoor activities that were planned, it's going to be a loooong weekend for some of them who are used to being more occupied.'

'Some people have to *do* rather than *be*, don't they? It's as if they stop, they'll be suddenly forced to take a long, hard look at themselves.' I sip from my cup. 'You make a good brew.'

As Carley nods, I realise I'm talking about myself. But I don't mind turning inward even if it feels weird and scary. I've never given myself the space to improve, but more than ever before, I want to change. I want to be the someone I've never had the chance or even the volition to be until this weekend.

'You OK, Aneka?'

I wish I could confide in her about what happened in the hot tub last night with Alexander. I want to tell her about the filthy remarks he keeps slinging in my direction, and about him locking me out in the snow. But I'm scared I won't be believed. He's one of the therapists here, like Carley, and they've clearly worked together before.

I'm the newbie, the outsider, and no one's ever going to believe me over the boss's husband.

30

THEN

'Earlier this evening, I set out to the park with my little girl so she could play on the swings before tea–time,' I begin, my voice shaking.

'She was only feet in front of me, riding her scooter, when I heard a car being driven erratically. Moments later, it swerved and mounted the kerb. She didn't stand a chance of getting out of its way.'

It's a struggle to speak; I'm trying so hard not to break down. It doesn't help that my husband's sitting in a seat directly opposite with tears rolling down his cheeks. Tears for my pain, for his own, and for our beautiful daughter whose life now lies in the hands of the surgeon.

'The driver didn't stop,' I continue. 'They knew what they'd done, yet just turned the car around and drove away, leaving my daughter for dead.'

Come on, come on, hold it together. You're doing this for her.

'Tonight I'm making this appeal directly to the driver. Our little girl was counting the days down until Father Christmas came down our chimney. She loves princesses, the dressing up box and baking biscuits. She's so full of life –one she's now fighting to keep living.'

The room is silent apart from the click of cameras.

'I'm asking you to do the right thing. Own up to what you've caused. *Come forward to the police so that we and our daughter might get justice for what you've done to our family today.'*

I squint as a flash goes off straight in front of my eyes.

'Your car will be damaged. The police are already starting to put together a picture of your vehicle. Perhaps you'll be acting with guilt, and your own family will be wondering what's wrong with you.' My voice is becoming stronger.

'To this end, I implore everyone out there to be vigilant to signs of front-end car damage. To signs of a family member carrying the shame of the cowardice they've shown today.

Please, please help the police catch up with the person who's done this to us. And please, please pray that our little girl doesn't die.'

31

Tracy and Katina's room looks like it's inhabited by teenagers instead of two thirty-something women.

Clothes and towels are strewn all over the place, the curtains are still closed, and their beds are unmade. The dresser is littered with cosmetics and hair products, and their now-not-necessary walking gear is piled in the far corner. They look like they're staying here for a fortnight rather than three nights.

Sighing, I pull back the curtains, first looking over the snow-carpeted grounds, before my gaze rests on the area I was locked out in last night. Tracy's sitting at one side of the hot tub, her arms spread out to either side like goalposts, her dark hair piled in a bun on the top of her head. Katina's perched on the edge with just her legs dangling into the pool while the overhead jet showers water onto her shoulders.

I resist the urge to rub some of the expensive-looking moisturiser into my parched skin or spray myself with some of the lovely perfume I can smell. But I'd better get on with what I'm supposed to be doing.

I straighten the sheets on the twin beds before smoothing

the duvet and over-blanket across each one. I plump up the pillows and look around once more. Should I fold and stack their clothes, or do I risk inviting trouble if I touch them?

I should probably leave them alone. I move to the ensuite, squirt some bleach around the toilet bowl and then sidestep to the sink. It's just as cluttered in here as it is in the bedroom. Bottles of shampoo, facial scrubs and cleansers, shower gels, and... what's that poking from the toiletry bag?

A pregnancy testing kit.

I pluck it from the bag. One test has been used, and the other is still intact inside the box. I step on the lid of the small chrome bin by the sink and peer inside. There it is, the only item in the bin. I look for the line in the 'pregnant' window. It's bold and pink, so there can be no doubt about that result.

Either Tracy or Katina is pregnant.

I rummage through the rest of the toiletry bag, pulling out a face mask, a facial hair remover and then a pharmacy-dispensed box of what looks like iron tablets. *Katina Hendersen*, the label reads. *Take one tablet a day.*

I shove everything back in the bag and stagger backwards out of the bathroom. Katina's expecting a baby. Hallie and Barnaby are going to have a younger brother or sister.

I perch on the edge of one of the beds and drop my head into my hands. I wonder when she took the test. She was trying to tell me something that would 'shut me up' last night. No wonder she feels she can speak to me with such superiority. I wonder if they'll marry and if my two kids will be cast out of George's life even more than they already are.

However, there's a part of me who still loves George. The part which is torn between desperate sadness and venomous rage. And I'm not sure which one will win out the next time I'm forced into Katina's toxic presence.

I don't know how long I've been sitting here, numb with disbelief, my mind looping the same awful truth over and over until the room finally swims back into focus. That's when I see it – a bulging purse, half-spilling out of a handbag shoved under the other bed.

A thick wad of cash. Twenties, tens – *easily* five hundred pounds.

Who carries that much cash these days? I pull the bag toward me, my heart thudding, and my fingers trembling with a mixture of nerves and something darker. Power? Temptation? Self-preservation?

Katina's face flashes in my mind. George's too. The money he owes me in child support – money he's probably using to fund this luxury retreat for her. My children go without, while she reclines in hot tubs and drinks prosecco.

That's *my* money. *Our* money.

For a heartbeat, the thought is intoxicating. I could just take fifty pounds. Or even a hundred. She'd never notice. It wouldn't even be stealing, not really. More like restoring the balance.

But then another thought intrudes into my mind. *What if it's not hers?* What if it's Tracy's? My hand hovers over the notes. Then, the door bursts open.

Kicking the bag back under the bed, I jump to my feet and grab one of the pillows in an effort to look like I'm plumping it.

'What were *you* doing?' Tracy stands, just a bedlength from me, her hands on her hips as she surveys me with her usual level of distaste.

'Nothing.' But I can feel my face burning, so no doubt she can see that I've turned the shade of a tomato.

'You're a liar,' she shouts, reminding me of how my mother used to shout at me when she caught me red-handed as a child.

'We don't want you in our room.' Katina tightens the belt on her robe as she comes up behind Tracy. 'We'll keep it clean and tidy ourselves.'

'Yeah, and so far you're doing an amazing job.'

'What did you take from my purse?' Tracy lunges at me and thrusts her hand into the kangaroo pocket of my apron.

'Get the hell away from me. I didn't take anything.'

'Turn out the pockets of your jeans.' Tracy tugs the turban-wrapped towel from her head and throws it on one of the beds. 'Now.'

'No chance.'

'We need to get Sienna.'

'I haven't done anything.'

'Keep her in this room.' Tracy touches Katina's arm as she passes. 'I'm off to fetch Sienna.'

'There's absolutely no need to involve—'

But the door has already banged. Great. I head after her, but Katina steps to the side so she's blocking my exit.

'Let me out.'

'No chance. If you've got any of her money stuffed down your scabby grey bra, I want Sienna to find it there.'

'You won't find a thing.' I'm panting, anxious to get out of this room and to be able to carry on with my jobs. But then a red mist descends. 'Not like what I've just found in your bathroom.'

'What are you talking about?'

'You know exactly what I'm talking about. In your bin. You must have known I'd be cleaning the ensuite. You must have *wanted* me to find it.'

She looks startled for a second. 'Oh, that. Well, I only took the test yesterday.' Her tone has calmed somewhat. 'I haven't gotten my head around it yet.'

'Does George know?' I'm gutted, absolutely gutted, but I won't let on to Katina.

'How could he? We've got no signal to call or text anyone.'

So I know about George's third child even before he does.

'He'll be just as useless as he's been with my two, you know.'

He never changed either of their nappies when they were babies. And now, well, as you know, he can't even stump up the maintenance he agreed to pay. If you think he'll be any different—'

'You're only jealous, Aneka.'

'Not jealous. Just furious, as it happens. At how he's treated our children, mostly. And he won't get away with it. Like I've told him, I'm filing a claim with the Child Maintenance Service. They'll apply for an attachment of earnings order.'

'Why don't you just let him go?' She folds her arms across her ample chest as she steps even closer to me. 'Can't you see how happy he is with me now?'

'He'll do to you what he's done to me eventually.' Our faces are so close that one of us could either kiss or headbutt the other. I know which of those two options I'd select. 'Just as soon as he gets bored. Which is coming, you'll see.'

'You know nothing about our relationship,' she shouts into my face.

'Enough now,' barks a voice from the doorway.

Great. Sienna must have sent Alexander in her place. This is all I need.

32

THE HUGE GONG reverberates from the chapel, signalling the time for vinyasa yoga. I don't know a yin from a yang in yoga speak, but I'd love to learn. Sienna seems so at one with herself, so serene and joyful that I wouldn't mind some of that in my own life.

I've managed to pull myself together after the earlier altercation in Tracy and Katina's room. Alexander forced me to turn out my pockets until the three of them were satisfied I hadn't been stealing. Tracy, after counting her money, was forced to admit that everything was intact.

'Sienna wants you in at the end of her session.' Nova doesn't look up from where she's kneading bread as I enter the kitchen with an armful of freshly ironed tea towels. I mean, who irons bloody tea-towels? But I'm here to do as Nova instructs, get my six hundred quid at the end, and get home to Hallie and Barnaby.

'What shall I do in the meantime?' I press the towels into a drawer.

'Do you really need instruction at every turn? Honestly, you're more of a hindrance than a help.' Nova won't even look in my direction. 'At least when I had Nancy working with me, she could use her initiative.'

'You're really not being fair.' Suddenly emboldened, I stride across the kitchen and position myself in Nova's way so she has to look at me. 'I'm just trying to earn some extra money for my kids at Christmas, and you've made my life a misery since the moment I walked through the door.'

'You're after my job.' She rounds on me. 'And my son.'

'If Sienna wants to offer me more work after this, I'm not in a position to turn it down,' I reply. 'As for your son, he's a nice man. But that doesn't mean I'm *after* him. It simply means I think he's a nice man.'

Something in her face softens. I'll crack this woman before I leave this place.

Or I'll die trying.

'The truth is that the ink is barely dry on my decree absolute. So right now, I'm completely off men.'

'I'm not paid to listen to your sob stories.' Nova turns back to her kneading. 'There's a dishwasher over there which you can unload, and cream that needs whisking for the cheesecake.' She waves me away with a flick of her wrist.

I slip back into the chapel at one o'clock as Sienna requested. Lunch is due to be served at half past, after the retreat attendees have finished their relaxation and have had a chance for a comfort break. The time is dragging yet speeding by all at the same time. I'd feel far better if I could reach my kids by message or on the telephone, but there's no point in getting upset about something completely out of my control.

Sienna nods at me to begin at the far end of the room. Olive sinks into her mat in anticipation as I rub my hands in the essential oil next to her head. She's probably the most chilled out member on this retreat, but then I suppose she's got her daughter in tow, while I'm just riddled with guilt over my two. Monday can't come soon enough.

I'm closing in on where Katina's lying, so I try to catch Sienna's eye, as she'll be the one, as agreed, to administer Katina's relaxation. My husband's lovely new girlfriend has categorically stated that she doesn't want me anywhere near her. But Sienna's focus is a hundred per cent on the scene she's reading to the group, on the ebb and flow of the tide to which she's transported them.

Tracy, as I approach her mat, doesn't seem entrenched in any ebb and flow. Instead, she's rocking from side to side, her knees drawn up to her chest with pain etched across her face.

'You OK?' Katina whispers as she props herself onto her elbow to study her new-found friend.

In response, Tracy uses the curve of her back to rock forwards to her feet, and with her hand clasped over her mouth, she hurtles across the room towards the kitchen.

'You can't do that in the sink,' Nova shrieks.

Sienna stops reading her relaxation script as everyone looks towards the kitchen. All that can be heard are the vile sounds of Tracy's retching and burping.

'Ugh.' Alexis, one of the hen sisters, stuffs her fingers inside her ears while Brittany, who was on the mat in front of Tracy, leaps up and dashes across the room towards the fire exit.

'She's an emetophobe,' Olive explains. 'She can't bear to be anywhere near someone who's being sick.'

'Neither can anyone else.' Madison looks appalled. 'Were the two of you drinking last night? Is she hungover?'

'Maybe it's a bug,' Katina says as she taps her own belly. 'I haven't been feeling a hundred per cent this morning.'

Yeah, but we know what the cause is with you. I couldn't be any more bitter about Katina's pregnancy.

Alexis, who's been lying beside Tracy, shuffles sideways until she reaches the mat of one of her sisters. Meanwhile, Olive has gone after her daughter.

'I want you out of my kitchen.' Nova shrieks at Tracy. I glance over at Sienna, expecting her to take charge of the situation, but she seems rooted to the spot.

'I'll go and calm Mum down.' Vince pushes his blanket to the bottom of his mat. 'Can you take charge of Tracy?' He cocks his head to one side as he addresses Carley.

'I'll help her to her room, but I'm not cleaning any mess.' Carley gets to her feet.

'Won't that be Aneka's job?' Despite being *under the weather*, Katina looks almost gleeful at this prospect.

'If it's a bug, perhaps you'll be next.' I give her my hardest stare. 'With the two of you sharing a room.'

Her face drops, but at least the disgusting sounds from the kitchen seem to have subsided. All that can be heard is the disapproving clucks from Nova, and Carley's calm tones as she cajoles Tracy out of the kitchen.

'What's happening about lunch?' Alexander raises an eyebrow in Sienna's direction. 'Will it still be OK after that little performance?' I'm so glad I never made it to his mat to administer the oils. His neck is one I'd certainly enjoy wringing.

'It's soup in an urn, so that will be OK,' Sienna replies. 'Hopefully, the sourdough rolls were well out of Tracy's way. But I'll double check.'

Everyone stays quiet. Why did she have to go and puke in the place where food is prepared? Is it better for her to have rushed in there or for it to have happened in the room where I've got to sleep tonight?

'Can you get in here and bleach this sink, Aneka?' Nova's standing at the door.

Everyone looks at me through the semi-darkness of the candlelit room, sympathy etched across their faces. That is apart from Katina, Madison and Alexander. The latter two look amused. Katina, however, appears troubled.

'I'll be back shortly,' she announces as she rises unsteadily from her mat. Like Brittany, she heads out of the fire escape door.

'Is she alright?' Ana, one of the other sisters, looks quizzically at Sienna. 'I hope this isn't going to be like one of those cruise ships where a nasty stomach virus rips through everyone.'

'She'll be going to make sure Tracy's OK,' Ashleigh suggests.

'I'll be after a refund if I get sick,' Madison says.

Sienna frowns as Madison's comment evidently brings her into the moment. 'Aneka, if you wouldn't mind doing as Nova asked,' she begins. 'And bleach wherever Tracy's been this morning. As for everyone else, I apologise your relaxation was brought to an end so abruptly, and if you'd like to convene in the dining room, lunch will be served as soon as possible.'

'You'd better double and triple check there's no risk of contamination.' Madison nods towards the kitchen.

'There is nothing of greater importance right now than the safety and comfort of my retreat guests.' Sienna pulls a face as if she can hardly believe Madison would suggest otherwise.

'Leave that. I'll sort it.' Vince appears in the kitchen doorway. 'Katina and Carley are up there with her. I've left them to it.'

'Cleaning the sink is not your job.' Nova bends to the oven.

'We're a team, aren't we?' Ignoring his mother, he strides to the sink and opens the cupboard beneath it. 'Do we have some rubber gloves?'

'You're an absolute angel.' I won't look in his direction as I don't want to look into the sink. After hearing Tracy throwing up, I'm also feeling slightly ropey. But I'll be fine. I'm never sick. I haven't got time for illness.

'When you've finished flirting with my son, you can lay the dining room for lunch.' Nova points in its direction, her voice trailing off as Alexander sidles up beside her.

'What soup is it?' He looks at her in a similar way to how he looked at me across the hot tub last night. Perhaps he's like this with all women. A creep.

'Winter vegetable.' She smiles. 'Made by my own fair hands.'

'Then it will be delicious,' he replies. 'But with the two Reiki appointments I'm doing this afternoon, and with yours as an unscheduled extra,' he winks at her. 'I'll need a little more energy than what soup and sourdough can offer.'

She whispers something in his ear as she nods towards the cooling tray laden with what looks like freshly baked flapjack.

'Now you're talking,' he laughs, and then she whispers something else.

'What's going on?' The sharpness of Sienna's tone brings me up short as I lift a stack of soup bowls from the cupboard.

'I'm just securing myself an appetiser before lunch.' Alexander heads towards his wife and fondles her backside as he gets to her. She seems to be uncomfortable as she shimmies out of his reach. Probably because of the presence of her staff. 'Like you suggested.'

'Well, there's no need to whisper in corners,' She frowns. 'Anyway, the guests are asking for drinks. Aneka, what are you currently on with?'

'Nova's asked me to lay the table.'

'Leave that. Make a pot of coffee instead. And don't, whatever you do, forget to make a pot of decaf, or we'll never hear the end of it.' She doesn't need to remind me who she's referring to.

33

'How come *she* gets those?' Madison looks enviously at Katina's extra dish.

'They were left over from breakfast,' Katina replies, 'and I've been dreaming about these since I saw a couple of others eating them earlier.'

I fought not to gag at the smell as I was frying them. I tried to refuse, but Nova said she was busy. Garlic mushrooms in butter – what a sickening pregnancy craving to have.

'They stink.' Ana pulls a face.

'It's the garlic I'm more bothered about.' Olive wrinkles her nose. 'You'd better move your mat well away from mine this afternoon.'

Katina has nearly eaten the contents of her bowl. If she was feeling peaky before, she seems to have fully recovered.

Nova rests the urn onto the sideboard in the corner of the dining room. 'If you'd all like to help yourselves to soup, Aneka will come around with bread and black pepper.'

'How's Tracy?' Olive settles down at her table where she's facing Brittanny.

'Not too great,' Carley replies.

'Which is why we've left her to sleep,' Katina adds.

'It's nice to see how friendly the two of you've become since yesterday's arrival,' Sienna says.

I can hardly believe it was only yesterday, less than twenty-four hours ago, that we've all been stuck indoors because of the snow. It feels like a hundred years.

'When everyone's got their lunch, can you go up and check on her, Aneka, for me, please?'

At least Sienna says please, unlike her bloody cook, but still, I almost feel like stamping my foot in grievance at not being permitted the luxury of sitting down and getting some lunch with everyone else. Breakfast consisted of a gobbled-down croissant and a piece of fruit, and I only got a hot drink because Carley made me one. I suspect lunch is going to be no different. Nor do I particularly want to go upstairs to check on Tracy. However, I still want Sienna to offer me further work, so I'll continue to do as I'm told.

The disgusting sound of retching is evident before I'm more than halfway up the wooden staircase. At least Tracy's got a room to escape to. However, I wouldn't swap places with her for all the tea in China, from what I can hear. Ugh.

I trudge across the thick carpet on the landing to the door, saying *Katina and Tracy*, and knock. Gingerly.

'What?' A low moan rises from within.

Gently, I push the door ajar and poke my head around it. It's like something from a horror film. The bed, the floor, all covered in vomit. Tracy's bent double over a bucket. I slam the door behind me and bolt back downstairs.

There's a lull in the conversation as I burst into the dining room. Sienna frowns as if to say, *not in front of the guests*. I jerk my head towards the kitchen, where we can speak privately. Well, also with Nova eavesdropping.

'She's still puking,' I whisper as Sienna stands before me by the pantry. 'She doesn't look like she'll be moving from her bed for the rest of the day.'

Carley comes up behind her, her hand splayed across her stomach. 'I bloody hope it's not something contagious. And you were in their room this morning.' She points at me.

'I know.'

'Like Madison suggested earlier.' Alexander is standing by the door. 'Tracy was on the fizz last night. It could even be something she's eaten.'

'What *has* she eaten?' Madison's voice echoes from the dining room.

'Thanks.' Sienna glares at her husband. 'I was trying to keep this conversation between us staff, then you open the door so everyone can hear.'

'Sorr-ee.' He pulls a face.

'We might as well go back in.' Sienna continues to glare at Alexander as she strides past him back towards the dining room. Nova gives me a look which I struggle to make out. Is it one of solidarity, being that we're both responsible for the food these guests are eating, or is it one of condescension, like she knows something?

'So what has Tracy eaten that could be dodgy since she's arrived?' Brittany reiterates Madison's question. If, as her mother said, she has a sickness phobia, she'll be trying to rule herself out of potential food poisoning. She probably won't relax now for the rest of the trip, constantly analysing herself for signs of illness.

'Did she have the quiche option last night?'

'She could have done.' Sienna screws her face up as if trying to remember. 'But without asking, I'm not sure.'

'Lots of people ate quiche,' Alexander says.

'She had an omelette this morning,' Nova goes on. 'Which Aneka cooked.' All eyes in the room turn to me.

'Oh my God, so did I.' Brittany's clearly tearing herself inside out. 'Did you make sure the eggs were in date?'

'I hope you're not suggesting—' My voice trails off. Sienna hasn't jumped to my defence like I'd expect her to.

'I hope there isn't anything wrong with the eggs. I ate them too.'

'Even if there was, it wouldn't be Aneka's fault,' Carley pipes up from where she's sitting in the corner. She rests her spoon against the edge of her bowl. 'She's not responsible for the ordering and checking of food.'

All eyes turn to Nova.

'Those eggs are as fresh as the snow out there.' She wags her finger in the direction of the picturesque view beyond the window, the most festive thing about this lodge.

I keep forgetting how close we are to Christmas. By now, Barnaby's usually beside himself with excitement. I hope that joy is still living within him, even despite his anxiety that something bad's going to happen. His face emerges in my mind, and I find myself wishing for the millionth time that I was warm and comfy at home. If George had only paid what he owed, I would never have needed to be part of this retreat.

'If it isn't eggs, the only other explanation is poor hygiene. I've seen how quickly Aneka visits the toilet and then leaves,' Madison goes on. 'I've been in straight after her. There's no sign of water around the sink, or even the soap having been moved.'

Right now, I'd love to shove a bar of soap straight down her nasty throat. 'That's absolute rubbish.' And even though it is, I still flush to the roots of my hair. I can't bear her saying this stuff in front of everyone.

'Have you even got a food hygiene certificate?' Madison pushes her soup bowl away. 'I don't know if I want to eat food that you've been anywhere near.'

'Now come on.' Carley jumps to my defence. 'Tracy's sick, yes – but it's probably only a virus.'

'But did you check the dates of the eggs?' Brittany points an accusing finger at Nova. 'I need to know.'

'We need to let this go.' Sienna jumps to her feet. 'Yes, so we've unfortunately got one of our group down with something, but if we're meticulous about keeping her separate from everyone, no one else has to get ill. So we'll go on with our programme this afternoon. The therapists have got two bookings each and we're repeating this morning's offerings in terms of the games, film and another reconvening in the chapel. Of course, it will be a different film.'

'I can't have food poisoning right before my wedding.' Ashleigh looks at her sisters and then back to Nova. 'My dress already needs to be taken in.'

'Like Sienna said, it's only a virus,' Alexander reaffirms. 'And the rest of us are still well.'

34

'HOW WAS YOUR TREATMENT?' Brittany glances up at her mother from where she's curled up with a book in the corner of the sofa. She reminds me of a pampered cat, buried in fluffy cushions, the firelight flickering softly over her perfect skin. Outside, the snow has thickened some more, and the fading light has turned the windows into mirrors.

Dusk is also falling, though it feels like it hasn't gotten properly light today. I'd give my right arm to swap places with Brittany. Her only care in the world is observing herself for signs of illness. I'll linger for as long as possible where it's toasty warm, under the guise of refuelling and stoking the fire.

'You're back earlier than I thought.'

'I'm concerned, as it happens,' Olive flings herself into the armchair facing her daughter. 'Alexander cut my treatment short and looked a little green as he shot out of the room.'

'Oh God.' Brittany clutches her belly. 'It's going to be me next.'

Other than Katina, I can't think of two people I'd have chosen instead of Tracy and Alexander to be down with this sickness, but clearly, I'm not going to put my sentiments into words. I've already had one or two people trying to lay the blame at my feet.

'Has anyone checked on Tracy this afternoon?' Olive slides the footstool towards herself and rests her feet on the top.

'I've been asked to, but I'm stalling.' I rock back onto my heels. 'It wasn't the nicest of sights.'

'I don't even want to imagine.' Brittany shudders.

'Perhaps someone should check on Alexander.' Olive says with a yawn. 'And you need to tell Sienna. I just hope to goodness he hasn't passed anything onto me during that Reiki treatment.'

'To be honest, Mum.' Brittany lays her book face down on the arm of the sofa. 'I want to go home. Away from all this illness and back to where I feel safe. You said this retreat would do me good, but it's raised my anxiety more than ever.'

'No one's going anywhere until it completely stops snowing and starts to thaw.' Olive points at the window. 'Can you imagine driving?'

'But this is awful. Not even being able to message anyone or get online. It's the worst weekend of my life.'

'I know, love.' Olive reaches across and touches her daughter's hand in a way which causes a pang in me. My mother never used to touch me unless it was in anger.

'That's two people down.' Sienna wrings her hands as she sits at the foot of the stairs. 'I might be sleeping in that chapel with you tonight, Aneka. I can't stay in the snug.' She jerks her head in the direction of the door, where more disgusting noises are emanating. 'It's gone very quiet upstairs,' she goes on.

'Perhaps Tracy's sleeping,' I reply.

'Where's everyone else?

'Vince is doing a reflexology treatment for one of the

sisters,' I tell her, 'and Carley is doing a massage. I believe the third sister is out in the hot tub. But I haven't a clue about Madison. She might be in the sauna or steam room.'

'OK, well, if you could check on Tracy, find out where Katina is, and I'll go and get set up for the next session in the chapel. The show must continue.'

I must loiter for longer than she'd like me to, for Sienna's face bears the ghost of a frown, even though she's still holding her smile in place. 'You'll be used to dealing with this sort of thing, won't you?'

'What sort of thing?'

'People being ill.'

'Sometimes,' I reply. 'Well, perhaps not a stomach virus sweeping through lots of people but—'

'I just meant that you've got two kids,' she goes on. 'You're probably more nurturing than me.'

'Ooh, I don't think so.' I want to tell her that she seems like one of the most nurturing people I've met, but that would be too gushy.

Nurturing is one thing, I think to myself as I trudge up the stairs. Acting with sympathy to the two people who've been unpleasant to me since the moment they arrived here is something else entirely.

I pause on the landing for several minutes. I've been in that room once, and I'm not going in again. No way. And nobody ever needs to know.

'Has anyone seen Aneka?' I jump as Nova's voice echoes from the bottom of the stairs.

'I'm up here. What is it?' I shoot back along the landing to the top of the stairs, avoiding her eye as if I'll somehow give myself away. I can't have her finding out that I haven't done as I was asked.

'There's a pile of veg which needs chopping for this

evening's moussaka.' She gestures to the kitchen. 'And you can take charge of buttering bread for afternoon tea.'

'Are they for...' My gaze roams to the plate of biscuits and the jug of iced water in her hands.

'Never you mind,' she replies. 'Just do as I ask.'

They're not for Tracy. I'll bet she's heading to the snug to see Alexander. If Sienna finds out she's in there, I wouldn't like to be in her shoes. Maybe I should drop her in it. After all, she'd have no qualms about doing the same thing to me. But no, I won't come down to her level. Not this time.

The next couple of hours pass in a blur of chores as the world outside turns pitch black. Sienna hasn't requested my assistance in the chapel during the meditation, so I'm quite happy to be left alone. I've no idea where Nova is, and can only assume that because she's tasked me with just about everything else, she's having some free time. She's probably taking part in whatever's going on in the chapel.

'Did you enjoy the meditation?' I don't know why I keep trying to forge a conversation with Nova after she's made it clear that she doesn't like me, doesn't trust me and doesn't want me around.

'What do you mean?' Sienna takes two plates of the film-wrapped sandwiches I made from the fridge as she waits for one of us to reply.

'Sorry, I just thought...'

'Nova wasn't in there.' Sienna looks puzzled.

'Perhaps *I'm* also feeling under the weather.' But Nova doesn't look remotely under the weather. Instead, her face is burning an interesting shade of scarlet. Evidently, she's been up to something.

Which begs the question, if she wasn't in here with me, or in the chapel with the others, then what *has* she been up to?

35

THEN

IT'S BEEN *five days since my life ended. More to the point, since my daughter's life ended. I try to take comfort in the fact that her organs have been donated to give several other people the chance at life, but it isn't working. Nothing's working.*

Perhaps it wouldn't be so bad if the person driving wasn't still walking free.

My little girl looked like a sleeping angel as they switched off her life support. It's an image I'll never erase from my mind. I see it every time I close my eyes, and without the sleeping pills that offer oblivion each night, it would be all I'd ever see.

Which is where I am now. Picking up another, more potent dose of sleeping tablets.

As I wait to enter the pharmacy, a woman is dragging her wailing toddler out.

'I've had just about enough of you.'

I don't know who's more purple in the face, the mother or the daughter, but I want to shake the mother and tell her she doesn't know how lucky she is to still have her little girl.

Watching them is clearly doing me no favours, but I can't tear my gaze away. Gripping the toddler's arm, the mother swings her off her feet and roughly dumps her in her car restraint. But the car — it looks just the same shape, size and colour as the car that...

'Keep still and let me fasten you in.'

Then I notice the cracked number plate, the smashed headlight and the dented bumper. But most importantly, it's the paint colour. Metallic red, just as the police identified on my daughter's mangled scooter.

'You're straight into your bed when we get home.'

As the woman slams herself into the driver's seat, I march across the pavement to her door and repeatedly ram my fist against her window.

'What the hell?' She winds down her window, probably expecting me to comment on how badly she's treating her child.

'What happened to your car?' I demand.

A flicker of recognition crosses her face as she crunches the gearstick and revs the engine. I've never seen anyone look more panic-stricken.

Either she or someone she allowed to drive killed my daughter. One of them is the driver from six days ago, I'm absolutely convinced.

And as the woman speeds off along the street, although my hands are shaking, I manage to get my phone out in time to capture her registration plate.

36

'Katina's been sick.'

'Has she gone to bed?' Vince's gaze darts towards the staircase.

Brittany's chewing on her lip so hard it's turning white. 'That's three of them,' she whispers. 'This is a nightmare.'

'It *has* to be a stomach virus.' Sienna sweeps her gaze over everyone. 'They're common at this time of year. Give them a few hours' sleep and they'll all be right as rain.'

'I still think it's the eggs.'

'Katina hasn't eaten any eggs while she's been here,' Carley blurts as she paces around the dining room. She seems unable to keep still. 'I helped to serve the quiche last night. Katina didn't want any.'

'She could've crept down later for a slice,' Nova says from the doorway, her face unreadable.

'So any of *us* could go down with this?' Ana glances at her sisters with growing horror. 'This is mental. We should've gone clubbing like normal people instead of pretending Christmas doesn't exist.'

'Nobody *forced* you—' Nova begins.

But she's cut off as an ear-splitting scream slices through the air.

The room freezes. My heart misses a beat. Nobody screams like that without good reason.

Sienna's on her feet in an instant. Chairs screech back, and someone knocks a glass to the floor.

'Everyone – remain in here while I see what's happened.'

But I'm straight after her.

'Mum!' Brittany, too, bolts for the hallway before Vince gets in the way to block the door and prevent anyone else from leaving the room.

'Olive?' Sienna shouts up the stairs, her voice tight as the dining room door slams.

'Up here. Quickly!' Olive's tone is bordering on hysterical.

Brittany tries to sprint up the stairs, elbowing me in the ribs in her scramble to get past. 'Let me get to my mum.'

I stumble back. If I had a mother I loved, maybe I'd understand the madness in her eyes. But I don't. So I don't.

Olive appears at the top of the stairs, her face ashen, her mouth trembling, and her eyes full of horror. She clutches the bannister like she's trying to stop herself from fainting.

'I... I went to check on Tracy and Katina,' she says, her voice shaking. 'They weren't being monitored closely enough for my liking. If it were my girl—'

'And?' Brittany's fingers dig into her mother's arm.

Olive crumples to the top step. 'I've never seen a dead body before.'

'A *what?*' Brittany shrieks.

Sienna charges past them and heads towards the bedroom.

For a moment, all that can be heard are the anxious voices from the dining room and the muffled moan of wintry wind against the glass. The wait for news seems to last forever.

Then Sienna reappears, her face etched with a combination of fear and disbelief.

'She's dead,' she says. It's a sentence that cracks its way down the centre of us all.

'Who?' Something inside me is already rising, a terrible, shameful *hope* that it's Katina. This isn't like me at all. But I can't help it.

Time seems to slow. The snow outside falls harder, blurring the present into white silence.

'It's Tracy.' Sienna's words are just a breath. 'She's gone.'

A sound escapes Brittany, half gasp, half sob. 'But stomach viruses *don't kill people!*'

'This one has.' Sienna wraps her arms around herself, shaking. 'It looks like she choked on her vomit. It was... There was nothing I or anyone else could have done.'

'We need to call someone.'

'We can't get a signal.'

'We can't leave her there—'

'What about the others?'

'Who's going to tell Vince?'

'What if it's something worse than just a virus?'

This last question hangs in the air, unspoken, but *felt*. Like a shadow creeping along the landing.

And deep in my stomach, the dread I've been feeling since I arrived intensifies.

37

'Do you think we can do this between the four of us?' Carley asks. 'Really, we could do with Vince.'

'He wants to be left alone,' Nova replies. 'He's really struggling with the news of Tracy's death.'

'He's not the only one.' Carley says. 'But I have to say, moving her like this doesn't feel right.'

'We could be trapped here well into next week,' Sienna whispers as we stand outside the door. 'If Tracy remains in there for that length of time, I dread to imagine how foul this room will smell. It will seep through to the rooms on either side.'

'I imagine it smells bad enough already.'

'What do you mean, you *imagine*?' Nova gives me one of her nasty stares. 'I thought you'd been checking on them.'

'I just mean that the smell will get worse as more time passes, like Sienna just said.'

'It's not only that,' Sienna goes on. 'It's also that this room doesn't lock. We can't keep people out. But with the utility room, we can.'

'OK then,' Carley says. 'First, we cover our faces.' She hands us all a tea towel. 'Then we cover Tracy with a sheet. Next, we roll her onto a yoga mat.' She tugs it from beneath her arm, 'And lastly, we'll take her by the corners of her bed sheet to carry her down the stairs. I can't think of any other way of doing this.'

'As long as you don't expect me to do any of the heavy lifting.' Nova sniffs. 'As you keep pointing out, I'm not getting any younger.'

'All we need you to do is to hold doors open,' Sienna says.

'Where *is* Vince?' I pass my tea towel from one hand to another. 'We could really do with his help.'

'In the chapel, as far as I know,' Nova replies. 'We need to leave him be.'

I don't know if I can do this. We should have proper masks to have any chance at not breathing in the stench in there, not poxy tea towels.

'What if any of the guests see us moving Tracy?'

'They're under strict instructions not to leave the lounge,' Sienna replies. 'Until I say otherwise. They all know what we're being forced to do, but they certainly don't need to witness Tracy being moved.'

I can only imagine the reviews Sienna will be receiving on Tripadvisor after this weekend. *The host poisoned three guests, killing one. We were snowed in all weekend. It was a nightmare experience. The staff moved a body out of sight.*

I fold my tea towel in half and attempt to tie it around my head, but it's not long enough. At best, it might act as a muffler between my nose and the inevitable stench until I need both my hands for the heavy lifting.

'Ready, one two, three.' Sienna pushes the door open, and we all follow.

'Oh my God.' I press the towel as hard as I can against my face. 'This is horrendous. Can we open a window?'

It's like nothing I've ever encountered. Every kind of decay and body fluid mixed with the stench of sewage. They've clearly suffered from both ends. And Katina's continuing to do so.

'We can't touch the windows. *She* needs to keep warm.' Carley points towards Katina, who's sweaty and delirious, rolling around on her side as she faces away from us towards the wall. Her hair's matted, and she's moaning like a wounded animal.

'Sleep and plenty of water are the only things which will fix her.' Nova places a glass filled with water on her bedside table.

In spite of all previous thoughts, a wave of sympathy crashes over me. Katina might not be my favourite person, but I've got to let the others know of her predicament.

'Listen, I might be talking out of turn, but I've gathered from cleaning their room that Katina's in the early stages of pregnancy.'

'*What*?'

'How did you find out?'

'There was a positive test in the bathroom, and Katina confirmed it was hers.'

'To *you*?' I've never seen as much scepticism across someone's face as Nova's displaying.

'I think I caught her unawares.'

'There's nothing we can do other than keep a close eye on her.' Sienna's voice is muffled from behind her towel. 'Once we've moved Tracy, we'll then move Katina and Alexander into the lounge and take turns to sit with them.'

So we've two more people to move after this. People who could potentially throw up all over us while in transit. Excellent.

We pick our way across the carpet, avoiding the pools of mess the two of them have made. Then Carley uncoils the yoga mat on the double bed beside Tracy.

'We need to roll her onto it,' she instructs. Her eyes are watering. Either with grief or disgust at the smell.

'What *is* this bloody virus?' Sienna shakes her head as she presses her towel harder against her face. 'I thought I was made of tough stuff, but this is making me want to—.' She dry retches. 'We need to hurry and get out of this room.'

'Right, after three, we roll her over,' Carley commands. 'One two, three.'

With great effort, we manage to roll her over and onto it, albeit we have to watch what we're touching. The last thing I want is for my fingers to slide against the contents of this bed. And this feels like the easiest part of the proceedings. We haven't tried to carry her anywhere yet.

'Right, the two of you grab a corner of the sheet and get ready to lift her down to the floor. I'll get this end. That's right, gently does it.'

With even more effort, we slide her from the bed so she's resting on the carpet. Even Nova does her best to help. I can't be the only person who's wondering how the hell we're going to get her along the landing and all the way down the stairs and into the utility room. Dead bodies, after all, are notoriously heavy.

As I bend to raise my corner of the load into the air once more, Katina grabs at my arm.

'The baby,' she whispers with haunted eyes. 'I'm scared.'

It takes us forty minutes to reach our destination as we need to keep pausing to rest. Or one of the four of us becomes overtaken by disgust, especially when accidentally knocking her head into a wall or into one of the spindles on the stairs.

'Lower her down,' Sienna hisses as we finally reach the door into the utility room. 'Nova, get the door.'

I rest my head against the wall, cooling the heat of my sweating forehead against its coldness. My stomach's churning, my lungs feel ready to explode, and I'm beside myself with anxiety. I feel like I've somehow incriminated myself for telling them about Katina's pregnancy. The finger of suspicion will be pointing even more in my direction.

By the time we've managed to lay her body to rest on the wooden floor of the utility room, I feel as sick as a pig.

'Can someone fetch another sheet to drape over her body?' Sienna instructs no one in particular. 'Then we'll lock the door. It's just for a couple of days, until help arrives.'

I race off to the linen cupboard, glad of an excuse to get away. It's completely dark outside, but not nearly as dark as it feels in this lodge. And as I pass by the snug at the end of the hallway, I can hear Alexander moaning softly behind the door.

38

'How's Alexander doing?' I whisper to Sienna in the darkness. It's less creepy in this chapel at night with someone else in here, albeit my boss, who it feels weird to be sharing a sleeping space with. 'When did you last check?'

'Not so long ago,' she replies. 'I took them both some water and electrolytes. But there was no way I could sleep in the same room. Vince is keeping an eye on them overnight.' Sienna's been really calm throughout all this – almost too calm. Apart from earlier, when I witnessed her walking around the building with a stinky burner thing in her hands, chanting some Sharanam something or other. She told me she was burning sage and was going on about energy cleansing after what had happened to Tracy.

'How's Katina?' Hopefully, Sienna doesn't detect the edge to my voice.

'Much better,' she replies. 'She's even eaten half a Rich Tea biscuit. It's keeping up her fluids that's important over the next day or two. I've told her to keep sipping water.'

'Does she know what happened to Tracy?' The image of her

sprawled prostrate across her bed, her face crusted with vomit, will probably never leave me.

'Not yet. We'll wait until she's made more of an improvement.'

'At least no one else is showing signs of coming down with the virus.' I stare up at the pattern the beams make against the ceiling.

'We're all feeling queasy, but that's with the stress.'

I stay quiet. I don't know how I feel. It's hard to think straight when there's a dead body lying literally feet away.

'I bet you regret ever coming to work for me. It's turned into a complete and utter nightmare.'

My gaze shifts to the stained glass above the door. I haven't noticed it before, but the shapes look like watching eyes. I'm hardly going to say yes in reply to her question. Not when I want to be paid before Christmas.

'I'm more worried that everyone thinks I'm involved in what's happened.'

'Because you cooked Tracy's and Alexander's breakfast?'

'It was Tracy's last meal before she became ill.'

I want to discover whether Sienna agrees in any way with Madison's nasty speculation. There's also the common knowledge that things were pretty hostile between me and Tracy – and Alexander and Katina.

'I'll have to look at Tracy's registration form for the details of her emergency contact. As soon as we can get a call out of here, we'll have to let them know – or the police will.'

I wish I could see the expression on her face as she mentions the police. But if Sienna suspects me of something, surely, she'd just come out and accuse me. Or quiz me. At least I'd know then what I'm supposed to be defending.

'How long do you reckon we'll be cut off like this?'

'How long's a piece of string?' In the darkness, I see the outline of her arm as she gestures towards the window. 'It needs to stop snowing for us to have a chance. I had no idea it would be this bad this weekend.'

I look towards the huge window, the one she normally sits in front of when she's leading the group. Outside, branches sway in the low, moaning wind, casting ghostly shapes against the black sky. 'Do you think anyone else could have reported the wifi being out of action?'

'There aren't any other properties for a couple of miles.'

'So all we can do is play a waiting game?'

'I guess so. But, obviously, for any days you're here beyond the end of the retreat, I'll continue to pay you at our agreed rate of a hundred and fifty pounds for each day.'

She's back to business again.

'I really need to be home by Christmas Eve.' I shiver. The heating went off a couple of hours ago, and it's so chilly, it's almost like it was never on.

'Doesn't everybody?'

'I'll be honest with you, Sienna. As yet, I haven't even bought my two kids anything for Christmas.' Since she's brought up money, I'm going to go for it. 'I'm counting on the money I'm earning here to sort their presents out, and I need to be back at home. They haven't got anyone else.' Tears fill my eyes as their faces enter my mind.

'Let's just get some sleep.' Sienna nestles down in her sleeping bag on the air bed next to mine. 'Who knows what tomorrow might bring?'

That's what I'm scared of.

39

'SIENNA, IT'S NEARLY EIGHT O'CLOCK.'

'Um, yep, OK.' She rolls off her airbed while I huddle further inside my sleeping bag. I'm absolutely freezing. Tonight, I'll just sleep fully clothed and pinch some extra blankets from people's yoga mats.

Nova doesn't move from the illuminated doorway, her large and dark presence nearly filling the space. 'I've been calling you both for the last hour. What do I have to do to get some help?'

'Aneka, I thought you'd set an alarm.' Sienna hops around beside me, presumably looking for her clothes in the dim light.

Great, I'm getting blamed for us sleeping in – as well as for poor hygiene habits and for using bad eggs, which might have contributed to making people poorly.

'I erm.' I grapple around for my phone. It's dead. 'With me not using it for calls or texts, I've kind of forgotten to keep the battery charged. I'm sorry.'

'Alexander and Katina both seem much better this morning.' I can't see Nova's face, but I can hear the smile in her voice.

'Really?' Sienna sounds surprised, but in a good way. 'Well, that's great news. Has anyone told them what's happened to Tracy?'

God. Tracy. In my sleep-fuelled, morning haze, I'd momentarily forgotten about her, but now I've been reminded, the image of her body, laid out across the utility room with a sheet draped over and her pedicured toes poking out from underneath, poisons my mind. Today is the twenty-first of December, the shortest day of the year. It also feels like the darkest day.

Nova comes further into the chapel. 'Yes, to be honest, the others were falling over themselves to tell them. They're all waiting in the dining room for coffee.'

'Do they know where we've put her?'

Nova nods. 'They knew last night. But as I've told them, the door to the utility room will be staying locked. Everyone deserves a little dignity in death.'

Even Tracy, I stop myself from adding. Instead, I say, 'But the other two are alright? That's a relief.' I hope my words sound more genuine than I feel.

'Much better than yesterday. They're still laid out on the lounge sofas and won't be holding any yoga poses or eating much, if anything, today. But at least they've both stopped throwing up.'

'That's something.' Sienna pulls her baggy trousers over the woolly tights she's slept in and shrugs into her jumper. I don't feel comfortable dressing in front of her and will wait until they've both left the room.

'Where's Vince?' she asks.

'Now that they seem to be out of the woods, he's using my room to get some sleep,' she replies. 'He's said he'll be down in a couple of hours but doesn't feel up to doing any treatments today.'

'I wouldn't expect him to,' Sienna replies. 'I expect he'd feel guilty.'

'Guilty?' I can imagine Nova's raised eyebrows. 'Why would he feel guilty?'

'I just meant, if he were to carry on as normal. You know, after what's happened to Tracy.'

～

'Nobody's ordering eggs for breakfast.' One of the hen sisters giggles as I enter the gloom of the dining room.

'I hope you've washed your hands.' The look Madison throws my way is enough to turn me to stone. She still clearly thinks I'm to blame. 'I shall be writing all my observations from this weekend when I come to add my review.'

I glare back at her. She's a cow. And Brittany must be feeling less anxious today because she's back to her undercover, that's not so undercover, recording. This time, she seems to be filming Madison's little rant.

'Make sure my coffee is decaf,' Madison continues. 'And none of that instant rubbish.'

Gosh, she's on form this morning. As I march through to the kitchen to organise the coffee pots, I can't help but be peeved that Madison has been unaffected by yesterday's sickness. If she were to succumb, it would be richly deserved. *No, Aneka, stop thinking such thoughts. There's been more than enough destruction.*

'Take those through to the lounge.' Nova nods towards two pitchers of iced water and glasses. 'Make sure the water is right by their sides as they're still too weak to reach.'

'I thought they were on the mend.'

'They are. But they're both still struggling.'

Balancing the pitchers on a tray, I pass through the dining room and head down the hallway to the lounge.

The curtains are drawn across the huge window, and breakfast TV is talking to itself in the corner. It's probably only been switched on to drown out the oppressive silence which seems to have settled over the lodge. Neither patient seems to be watching it. The air is heavy with their misery.

Katina lifts her head from the cushion as I enter the room. 'Oh, it's you.' Her voice is wobbly, and I've never seen a face so white. Apart from Tracy's yesterday, that is.

'I've brought you both some water.' I try to keep my voice pleasant even though I can't stand either of them. I do have some humility and certainly wouldn't want to change places.

'What have you put in it, though?' Katina turns away, the movement clearly an effort. 'This is the question. I'm not accepting anything you offer.'

'Me neither.' Alexander looks terrible. His eyes are dark in his pasty face, and he has a day's beard growth, complete with splodges of dried vomit. I couldn't bear to look at him before, but I'm even less inclined to do so today.

'It's just water, for goodness sake.' I feel like tipping the lot over their heads. 'Nova asked me to bring it.'

'Just leave us alone. We don't want you in here.'

I march back to the kitchen and bang the tray onto the counter. 'They've sent me away.' The words are tumbling out before I've even made it through the door.

'I don't blame them,' Madison shouts from the dining room.

'I'll sort the water,' Nova says. 'If you could take the croissants and the porridge pot through to the guests.'

'Why's everyone blaming me for what happened?' Tears sting my eyes.

'Word has been spreading about your outside connection with Katina.' Nova is stifling a smile. 'She told Vince last night. And it was obvious you also had it in for Tracy and Alexander.'

'If that was the case, then you and Madison should also be rolling around clutching your stomachs.'

'That's enough, Aneka.' I don't know where Sienna has

suddenly sprung up from. I thought she was in the chapel, setting up for the remaining guests.

'Why didn't you let *me* know about your association with Katina?' Sienna's straight to the point, but from her softer expression, she seems calm.

'I didn't know she was going to be here until she actually arrived.'

'So you should have told me *then*.'

'I thought we could rise above it. I just wanted to make a good impression, to—'

'Oh, you've made an impression, alright.' Nova continues whisking something in a bowl.

'It's probably for the best if you keep away from the lounge while Katina and Alexander are recovering,' Sienna says. 'They're both demanding that I eject you from the retreat, but given the weather conditions...' Her voice trails off as she gestures to the kitchen window. It looks like the North Pole out there.

'Would you have ejected me if it *wasn't* snowing?'

'I just don't know, Aneka.' Sienna sighs, and I bite my lip. I only hope she's still going to pay me what I'm owed.

40

THEN

'Are you really sure you want to come?' My husband's straightening his tie in the mirror, his face lined and etched with misery. 'Only one of us needs to attend.'

'I want to face that bitch, even if it's just across the courtroom.'

I'll never forget her expression when she realised who was hammering on her car window outside the pharmacy.

'I want to hear from her evil mouth what was going through her evil brain when she crushed our daughter to death with her car, as easily as someone might stamp on a spider. Before driving off without so much as a backwards glance.'

Every time I close my eyes, I still hear the screech of those tyres, the sickening thud as two tons of unforgiving metal collided with two stones of innocent flesh and blood. My daughter's flesh and blood.

'I think it might be too traumatic. What's happened has made you poorly enough. It'll almost be like reliving that day.'

'I relive it all the time. No, I've got to be there. Nothing and no one is going to stop me. Hang on.' I swipe at my phone as it starts ringing from my bedside table beside the photo of my daughter. I really can't come to terms that in her photo is the only time I'll see her smile until the end of time. 'Hello.'

'This is DI Moor of West Yorkshire Police,' the authoritative voice announces. 'We've just had word from Leeds Crown Court about today's hearing.'

'Oh?' I really hope it hasn't been adjourned. Or that she's managed to negotiate a plea bargain. As it stands, she's been charged with causing 'death by dangerous driving,' and 'leaving the scene of an accident.' In my mind, at the very least, she should be standing trial for manslaughter. And the words, 'leaving the scene of an accident,' barely contain the enormity of the barbaric way in which she abandoned what she'd caused.

'I'm afraid an extensive psychiatric evaluation has been carried out and the defendant has been declared as unfit to stand trial,' the DI says.

'What does that mean?' I clutch my throat. They should put me in a room with the woman. I'd deliver my own kind of justice.

'It means that a trial of facts will be held in her absence.'

'A what?'

'It's likely she'll still be found guilty, but rather than a criminal trial, the proceedings will switch to be dealt with under the Mental Health Act.'

'You're joking. So she doesn't even have to face up to what she's done?'

'I've been told that she's quite ill. She's already hospitalised, but as a result of these proceedings, she's likely to be detained for some time longer under section 37 of the Mental Health Act.'

'She should be rotting in a prison cell after what she's done, not in some cushy hospital. I just can't, I just can't...' I'm gasping, my anxiety at its highest since it all happened.

I relax my grip as the phone is lifted gently from my hand and my husband takes over the call.

41

'This is safe to eat, isn't it?' One of the hen sisters gives the porridge a suspicious look as I place it on the table. 'I haven't done anything to upset you, have I?' She laughs, but her laughter rattles with nerves. Great, everyone, even them, seems to have turned on me now that the truth's out about my connection with Katina.

'Enjoy your breakfast.' I say through gritted teeth as I move to the next table with a plate of croissants.

'Is Tracy's body really in the utility room?' Brittany looks at me with widened eyes. There's no sign of her phone to suggest she's recording again, but it could be on her lap beneath the table.

'It's being stored behind a locked door until help can reach us.'

'You couldn't make it up.' Olive shakes her head as she spreads blood-red jam onto her croissant. 'Come on a relaxing wellness retreat.' Her voice is shrill as she spreads her hands out in mock invitation. 'But be warned, you might be spending more time than you bargained for in corpse pose.'

'That's enough.' Sienna's standing by the door, her hand on one hip. 'We're doing everything we can to take care of things. This is quite simply a stomach virus.'

'Well, I don't want her,' – Madison jabs an accusing finger in my direction, – 'anywhere near my food for the rest of this retreat. If it wasn't for the snow, I wouldn't even be staying until the end.'

'Us neither,' one of the hen sisters pipes up from the next table.

'You know she's going to sue you, don't you?' Madison looks almost gleeful as she watches Sienna's face fall.

'Who?'

'Katina. When I poked my head in there earlier, she said she's had the worst day of her life since she started with this, and that someone's going to pay. Namely you. I assume you've got adequate insurance?'

Sienna turns her back, pretending to be busying herself pouring a coffee at the sideboard. But from this angle, I can see her face. She's going to either erupt with rage or burst into tears.

'I bet Alexander would be suing too if he wasn't already married to the facilitator.' One of the hen sisters laughs.

'I think you need to be doing something about the levels of trust you have in your staff.' It's Madison again.

'Right, this is how it's going to be.' Sienna swings around. I hold my breath, wondering what's coming. Whatever it is, it's bound to involve me. 'Your peace of mind is of paramount importance to me; therefore, Aneka will *not* be involved in any of the food or drinks preparation for the remainder of your stay.' She looks at me pointedly, and I open my mouth to ask what the hell else I'm supposed to do while we remain trapped in this lodge. 'It's not that *I'm* suspicious of her in any way, but if it sets everyone else's minds at rest, that's what matters.'

'So I do all the work myself?' Nova scowls. There is no winning with the woman. She moans when she's offered help, and she moans when it's taken away.

'I'll see if Vince is up to helping you when he's awake, Nova.'

Vince hasn't uttered a word to me since yesterday. Either he doesn't trust what he might say, or perhaps the extent of his grief means he doesn't want to talk to *anyone.*

'I can help in the kitchen,' Carley offers. I've only got a couple of treatments booked in.'

Carley, who's been so friendly towards me during the two days since we arrived, also hasn't said two words to me this morning. I need to take her to one side and find out what's going through her head.

Just because I didn't hit it off with Tracy and Alexander, and just because Katina and I have a negative association, shouldn't give everyone free license to automatically blame me for all that's gone wrong.

One thing's for certain. I can't remain in this room another moment with everyone looking at me as if I'm the angel of death. It feels like it used to when I was at school. Especially after I became pregnant. Ostracised by the others. Forced to eat and spend time alone. I've always been lonely. And I'm absolutely sick of it.

Blinded by tears, I race towards the kitchen, keen not to show them all how much they've upset me.

'OK, Aneka.' Sienna comes after me and leans against the fridge as I tear off a piece of kitchen roll. 'As I just said in there, I no longer want you having access to the kitchen.'

'But I haven't even had any breakfast.' I'm trying to ignore the fact that Nova's standing at the sink, hanging onto our every word. She has her back to us, but no doubt she'll be wearing a grin the size of Brazil.

'You can help yourself to breakfast in a moment from the dining room,' Sienna replies. 'But perhaps you should eat in the chapel or in the hallway so as not to upset the guests any further, then after that, I'm afraid I'll have to put you on some rather unpleasant cleaning duties.'

Oh God. I know exactly what's coming next.

42

'I'M REALLY SORRY, but *someone* has to do the cleaning.' To be fair, Sienna does look apologetic. 'I paid a huge deposit for this place,' she continues, 'and if I don't get rid of the mess from Tracy and Katina's room and the snug where Alexander has been ill, I'm going to lose every penny.'

'I can't.' All thoughts of breakfast fade. 'Please, I really can't face cleaning all that.'

'Like you keep saying, you've got two children.' She gives me an odd look. 'Surely you're no stranger to clearing up when *they've* been ill.'

'But they're my children. It's completely different.' I can hardly tell her that the prospect of cleaning anything that's been excreted from her husband's insides is the most abhorrent thing of all.

'I'm really sorry, Aneka,' she repeats. 'But Nova's work is in the kitchen, so I can't ask her. Carley's giving her a hand in there, and she still has her own appointments.'

I'm tempted to ask why *she* can't clean up all the mess. It's *her* retreat, *her* deposit and *her* bloody husband.

'I'm going to continue with a semblance of normality.' It's as if she's read my mind. 'And will continue to lead the activities for the guests in the chapel, which only leaves *you*. Like I said, I'm really sorry.'

I still don't know what to say, so I say nothing. Cleaning shit and sick is the very last thing I can face today. But she's leaving me with no choice. I should have just stayed inside my freezing sleeping bag when Nova woke us this morning.

'We just can't leave the mess that's been made for the cleaners.' Her voice takes on a more pleading edge. 'We need to get rid of it ourselves.'

It's the inclusive language she's using which gets me. *We* just can't leave the mess. *We* need to get rid of it.

'Besides, it's the deposit that I'll be paying you with – you need it before Christmas, don't you? Plus, there'll be a couple of hundred extra for you, since it's such an unpleasant job I'm saddling you with.'

She's using money as her carrot to dangle. But I can't deny that a couple of hundred extra pounds wouldn't be a Godsend. Perhaps I can do this. I'll cover my clothes with an apron, I'll wear gloves, and I'll make some sort of face covering so I can't smell anything. I will try to pretend I'm clearing up after my children. Mind over matter.

'What about the sheets and towels?' I think of the washing machine and tumble dryer in the utility room. I can't go in there.

'You'll have to just step over Tracy.' Sienna's voice relaxes, probably in the knowledge that I'm going to comply with her request. 'I don't really want anyone in the utility room, but obviously, we'll have to make an exception. You can clean her up a bit as well if you don't mind.'

I search Sienna's face. This must be a warped joke. *Clean up a dead person*? However, she looks completely serious. 'Just wipe her over to get the worst of it off. And those clothes she was wearing. They should be easy enough to get off and throw into the washer with the sheets.'

'But why?' Has this woman taken leave of her senses? I've gathered that she's eccentric, but this is a whole new level of crazy.

'We could still be waiting several days for help.' Sienna pulls a face. 'Can you imagine the smell in there if we don't manage to clean her up beforehand?'

'But she's behind a locked door.'

'Honestly, it won't be long until the smell starts to seep along the hallway. And it will only take you a few minutes.'

'It's not the time that's bothering me. It's just, well, I'm not an undertaker, am I?' Talk about stating the obvious. 'Wiping down and undressing a corpse isn't exactly in my job description.'

'It's just as well you don't have a job description then.' Her dimples deepen as she smiles. 'Remember when Vince spoke on the phone? He relayed back to me that you'd be willing to do anything I asked. I know this was the last thing either of us would have ever expected, but here we are.'

'I know I said that, but—'

'I hate having to give you this job, really I do, and if it wasn't for the deposit and your money riding on it, and—'

'OK. It's OK. I'll do it.'

What choice do I have? Like she's said, there isn't anyone else to do it.

And I desperately need my money.

I brace myself at the door of the room from which we dragged Tracy's body out yesterday. Followed by Katina when we helped her down to the sofa. I know exactly what's behind it. One, two, three, go.

Even with the face covering I've fashioned from a thick

pillowcase covering my mouth and nose and tied around my head, I gag at the stench. Lurching across the room, I throw the windows open, noticing with a shred of hope that the sun has come out, making the woods beyond our lodge look even more Christmas card perfect.

And at last, it's stopped snowing. Perhaps within the next few hours, we'll be able to move our cars. I can understand Sienna continuing to run the retreat as if we haven't got a dead body lying only metres away in the utility room while we're snowed in, but surely, as soon as an escape is possible, we'll all be out of here.

But being out of here is what's beginning to scare me. What happens when the police arrive? They won't just let us walk away, not with three people violently ill and one of them already dead. And once they learn one of the sick women is my ex-husband's new girlfriend, their attention will turn to me.

Madison will be first in line to point the finger when she gives her statement. She'll relish the chance to spin her theory that I've been poisoning people simply because I served most of the meals.

And it won't stop there, they'll all be only too happy to reveal every run-in I've had with Alexander, Tracy and Katina since the start of the retreat. One by one, they'll hand the police as many so-called motives as they can cobble together.

But I can't worry about this yet – I just need to take everything as it comes. I turn back to the task at hand, retching the whole time. I can't believe I've been given this job.

I strip both beds, most grateful for my rubber gloves as I stuff the sheets and the pillowcases inside a bin bag, ready for laundering. The buckets by each bed will be easy enough to wash out in the ensuite, it's the congealed splatters on the carpets which will be nastiest to clean.

I carry the buckets across to the room, one in each hand,

gagging with every step. Then, as bile bubbles into my throat, I dump them on the floor.

I need to get out of this room. I need to breathe. Grabbing the bag filled with sheets, I hurtle to the door. I'll get these into the laundry, then I'll come back. I just need a break from this stench for a few minutes.

I lean into the landing wall, breathing deeply in an attempt to compose myself. Oh God. There's also the 'task' Sienna's given me to carry out when I get to the utility room. How the hell am I supposed to remove a dead person's clothing?

I'm not sure how long I stand, here on this landing, trying to regulate my breath. Nova's disco beats echo from the kitchen, and the rise and fall of a film can be heard from the sun room. Carley must be doing her massages in one of the bedrooms.

It's no good. I've got to do what I've got to do. I'll get Tracy's clothing off her for the wash as instructed, get out of the room for a breather, and then go back in again to clean her down. These tasks have to be broken into chunks. It's the only way I'll be able to complete them.

I edge along the corridor that runs behind the kitchen as though I'm heading towards my doom. This has got to be the worst job I've *ever* been given. But I've no choice. Sienna all but said that I wouldn't be paid before Christmas without the return of her rental deposit.

As I get closer to the utility room, a shadow skims the wall in front of me, stopping me in my tracks.

'Who's there?'

Carley emerges from behind a cupboard door.

'What are you doing?'

'Getting fresh towels from the cupboard,' she replies. 'What about you?'

'I've got to put these sheets in the wash.' I tug the key to the dreaded utility room from my pocket. I badly want to voice my woes at my current job at hand. Perhaps she'll offer to help, or at the very least, she'll sympathise. After all, Carley's my friend.

But I'd better establish something else with her first, since she barely uttered a word to me in the breakfast room earlier. 'I'm glad you're still talking to me, Carley. I was starting to wonder. You've gone a bit quiet.'

It's more of a question than an observation. Hopefully, she'll pick up on the inflexion in my voice.

Carley takes a deep breath.

'What's the matter?'

'It's just that.' She hesitates. 'It's just that I'm going to have to tell the police what I know – as soon as we can get through to them.'

'What do you mean, *what you know*?'

In the dim light of the passageway, I can see how uncomfortable she is.

'I saw you, Aneka.'

43

'You saw me, *what*?' I look at Carley in horror.

She hesitates.

'Tell me.'

'Look, I know first-hand what a lech Alexander can be, and I know Katina and Tracy were being absolute bitches. But—'

'It's some kind of virus that's got them. It's got nothing to do with anything *I've* done.'

'Sienna's only been saying that for the benefit of the guests.' Carley folds her arms as if trying to create a barrier of protection for herself. 'She's said it purely to keep them calm. I mean, if they seriously get it into their heads that someone on our staff is capable of poisoning them, all hell will break loose.'

'It already has broken loose, don't you think?' My voice rises. 'We've got a dead body in that room.' I point at the door.

'I hardly need reminding.' Her eyes are steely as she continues to fix me in her stare.

'Look, all I want to do is to get out of here and to get home to my children.' I no longer care about Sienna giving me more work. I just need the money for *this* work. Then I need to leave.

'What's going on?' Sienna appears at the end of the corridor.

'Carley says she saw me do something.' My voice is a squeak. 'And she really can't have done, Sienna, because I promise I haven't done anything wrong.'

'Listen to me.' Sienna takes hold of my arm, probably to pause my gabbling. 'Carley, I'll speak with you in a moment. Just let me have a quick word with Aneka.'

Carley looks hesitant, but after a beat of silence, she walks away, her plait swinging out behind her.

'What is it?' I turn to Sienna.

'You and Nova will inevitably be questioned by the police.' Sienna thrusts her hands into the pocket of her hoodie. 'After all, it's the two of *you* who've prepared and served most of the food.'

'But I haven't done *anything* I shouldn't have.' My voice rises. 'Just because there have been people I don't particularly get on with on this retreat, doesn't mean I'm going to start poisoning their food.'

Sienna pauses. 'But it's more than just *not getting along with someone*, isn't it?'

'What do you mean? You do believe me, don't you, Sienna?' Nobody else seems to, so I'm desperate to keep my boss on side.

She looks uncomfortable. 'We need to park this for now and leave the questions to the police.' She pushes her fringe from her eyes. 'How are you getting on with the cleaning?'

I asked her whether she believed me. But she never answered.

'I'm about halfway through,' I reply. 'But—'

'Sienna, come quickly.' Vince's voice echoes along the corridor. 'Something's wrong.'

Sienna sets off at full pelt, and I hurry after her. Vince is waiting outside the lounge.

'It's Alexander.' Vince is breathless. 'We need to get him to a hospital, sharpish. I'm no expert, but there's something up with his liver. He seems alright in himself, but he clearly hasn't looked in a mirror.'

I hover near the door as Sienna strides across the room. 'How are you feeling, love?' She takes her husband's hand.

'Better than I was, just a bit woozy. You know, like I'm not really here. But at least I've stopped feeling sick.'

Against the dark fabric of the sofa, I can see from here why Vince called her in. Alexander's skin has turned the colour of a banana. As he stares back at Sienna, and as I edge closer, it's apparent that the whites of his eyes are the same shade of yellow. He's jaundiced, severely so.

Katina is fast asleep on her side, facing the other way. It's probably just as well. She'd only panic if she were to turn over and see the colour of her fellow patient.

'I'll be back in a moment.' Sienna isn't showing her reaction, evidently not wanting to cause Alexander any alarm. She frowns at me as she crosses the room. 'You shouldn't be in here, Aneka.'

I follow her back out into the hallway.

'What's going on?' Nova emerges from the kitchen.

'It's Alexander.' Sienna pulls the door behind her. 'There could be something wrong with his liver.'

If it were my husband, I'd be panicking like hell, but she's as cool as a cucumber.

'Doesn't anyone have a four wheel drive that might stand a chance through this snow?' Nova looks close to tears.

'As I've said before.' Sienna gestures towards the drifts through the window. 'It's too dangerous to even attempt to get a vehicle along that track.'

'That's your husband lying on that sofa,' she hisses. 'You can't just leave him to die. You've got to do *something*.'

Sienna looks as if she's been slapped. It's probably Nova's use of the word *die*.

'Plus, as we now know.' Carley's avoiding looking at me. 'Katina's pregnant. It's not just her life that needs saving.'

'I don't mind trying to find the nearest house or road on foot,' I offer, before remembering that the only footwear I have with me is the trainers I'm wearing, and my only coat is my thin mac. But anything beats the job I've currently got in progress. I know it's risky to go out there, but I'm at the point where I'm desperate to get away from these people who are hell-bent on using me as a scapegoat.

'I can't allow *any* of you to put yourselves at risk. It's my retreat, so *I'll* try.' She looks sideways at Vince as if she's trying to gauge his reaction. Perhaps she's secretly hoping he'll attempt to stop her. 'I've led retreats at this lodge before, so I've a far better chance of finding my way out. Plus I've got boots and a decent coat in the car.'

'You shouldn't go on your own either,' I say. 'Can't Vince go with you? It isn't like he's doing much else.'

'I've been keeping an eye on those two,' he snaps. 'Plus, do I need to remind you that my girlfriend has just died?'

Sienna's expression becomes even more grave. 'If it doesn't look like I can get onto the main road or anywhere near a house, I'll come straight back. I won't be taking any risks.'

'If you really think you *can* get to a phone, you should probably try.' Nova's face is serious.

'Alexander has no idea how ill he is.' Sienna looks back at the lounge door. 'I can safely say, just between us, that this is way more than a stomach virus.'

'As everybody already knows.' Carley narrows her eyes in my direction.

'We've no idea *what* it is,' I fire back. 'But I do know that *none* of it is my fault.'

The way they're all looking at me makes me want to bang my head against a wall in frustration.

Within ten minutes, Sienna's dressed for the outdoors and is ready to brave the snow. I'm lurking at the back of the small group that's gathered in the hallway. No one wants to involve me in any conversation, and everyone seems to have me hung, drawn and quartered.

'I'll be heading in *that* direction, just so you know.' She opens the door, and even from where I'm standing, the furthest away along the hallway, there's an icy blast. 'There are a couple of turns to navigate before reaching the road, and then I'll try and flag someone down.'

'There isn't going to be anyone driving today.' Vince sounds incredulous.

'Just let her try.' Nova turns to her son.

'But come back if you don't feel safe, Sienna.' Carley wrings her hands.

Sienna turns to look back at us, and I'm certain I can see tears glistening in her eyes. Perhaps she wasn't expecting to be permitted to go alone. Or maybe she's just worried that Alexander won't be alive by the time she returns.

Carley glances to where I'm standing. 'You really do need to keep away from everyone, Aneka.' Her voice is as frosty as her expression. 'And I understand Sienna's given you a job?'

I shrink back. Really, I don't see what difference it makes whether or not I clean up the mess. It's a matter of time before a thorough investigation of this place will be underway, especially if Sienna manages to find the road and get the attention of a passing motorist.

And really, I'll welcome this investigation. However much the others try to blame me, I'm certain that no amount of their so-called 'evidence' will be enough for the police to bring charges.

They'll need proof, not hearsay. Forensics, not hunches. I'll be absolutely fine.

Won't I?

44

THE LOUNGE IS in darkened silence, and I'm still hanging around in the hallway, not really sure what to do with myself. It's freezing in the chapel, I have no room of my own to go to, and I've been banished from the kitchen, which is where Nova is. Carley's in the dining room, killing time playing some board game or other with Olive and Brittany. The hen sisters are in the games room, and Madison has skulked off to her room. Vince has gone back to playing Florence Nightingale.

And Sienna still hasn't come back.

Tracy, as we all very well know, has now been dead behind the door in the utility room for nearly twenty-four hours. I haven't followed Sienna's instructions to clean her up. I can't do it. If it's her dignity she's trying to preserve, the undertakers can take care of that.

Vince emerges from the lounge, his eyes hollow and his shoulders hunched. 'I'm no doctor, but I'm not happy with how Alexander's doing. Even in the faint light, he looks even yellower, and he's really floppy.' He rakes his hand through his fringe.

Vince is talking to me, which might mean he's not

completely on the same page as the others. I hope so, as I've never needed a friend more than I do at this moment.

'You do believe I'm not responsible for any of this, don't you?'

'I think I believe you.' He raises his eyes to meet mine. 'You don't strike me as the type to go around poisoning people. Especially pregnant women.'

'I've only just found out that she's pregnant.'

He gives me a strange look. That sounded wrong. It's true, I *have* only just found out, but I shouldn't be saying things like this in the context of her being poisoned.

'Is Alexander talking?' I stare at Vince's bare feet, noticing how long and bony they are.

'He's sleeping. He doesn't seem to have any idea of how ill he is. Mum's sitting with him.'

'What about Katina?'

'She's barely woken all afternoon.' Vince pulls a face. 'Mum flicked the light on for a moment to check her. She's also starting to look jaundiced.'

'I wonder where Sienna's got to. She's been nearly two hours.'

'If she doesn't come back soon, I don't know what we're going to do about her. It's pitch black outside.'

'There's not a lot we can do, is there?'

'I'll have to go looking. I probably shouldn't have let her go, but I thought she'd find her way.' He rubs at his gingery chin. He doesn't look to have shaved since he arrived here two days ago.

'Not in the dark. It makes no sense if you end up lost out there. She'll be fine.' I glance at the fireplace. In light of what's been happening, nobody's bothered to keep the fire burning. I shiver. It seems to be getting colder and colder in this place.

'Everyone's desperate to leave.' Olive steps from the dining room into the hallway. 'We can't carry on like this for much longer.'

'It's *them* that can't carry on like this for much longer.' Vince gestures towards the open door. 'Oh my God.' We exchange glances as another ear-splitting scream emerges from the lounge.

'Quick, someone, help.' It's Nova.

Something's happened.

I pursue Olive and Vince into the room, and everyone else pours in after me.

'I can't wake him.' Nova looks panic-stricken. 'I can't find a pulse. I don't know what to do. Alexander,' she bellows. 'Come on, wake up. Help's coming.'

'Just look what you've done.' Madison elbows me as she passes. 'You shouldn't even be in here, looking at the results of your actions. I hope when Sienna arrives back with the police that they throw away the key.'

Vince crouches beside his mother and probes around on Alexander's wrist. He looks up at us all. 'I think he's gone.' His voice is hoarse.

'What do we do?' Nova staggers to her feet, tears running down her face. I didn't think she was capable of so much emotion, but then she's hardly made a secret about her soft spot towards Alexander.

'Only staff should be in this room.' Carley seems to be taking charge of the situation. 'Come on, everyone out – please wait in the dining room.'

'This is the stuff of nightmares,' Madison moans as Carley ushers her towards the door. 'And I've been feeling sick all day. If I find out she's poisoned me...' I turn to see her pointing straight in my direction.

For a few moments, none of us speaks.

'Get her out of here as well.' It's Carley's turn to point at me.

'I don't believe it was *her* fault, Carley.' Nova raises her face from where she's silently sobbing beside Alexander and looks from him to Carley. 'If anything, it could have been mine.'

'How on earth do you work that out?' Vince is standing behind his mother, his hands on her shoulders. 'You shouldn't say things like that.'

'She's being ridiculous,' Carley says. 'Look, I'll see to the guests – I'll take them into the chapel.'

'To do what?' Nova asks.

'I'll lead a breathing exercise with them or something. 'We have to keep going until Sienna gets back or until the police arrive and tell us otherwise.'

I rush to the door after Carley. 'It really wasn't my fault,' I shout after her, my broken voice echoing along the hallway.

'Stay away from me.'

'Do we cover him over and leave him where he is?' Nova says as I return to the room. 'Or should we lay him beside Tracy, where no one has to keep looking at his body?'

'There's enough room for them to lie side by side,' I reply.

Vince doesn't look at me. I might as well have not spoken. He turns back to his mother. 'When Katina wakes and sees Alexander has died, imagine how that will affect her. We *do* need to move him.'

'*If* Katina wakes.' Nova glances at him and then returns to holding Alexander's hand. It should be Sienna at his side. Not Nova. Where the hell has she gone? And who's going to break the news that her husband has died?

'It's not just Katina who'll be freaked out if we leave him on the sofa,' I say. 'We've got the guests to consider.' I don't add, *and me. I don't want to look at a dead body either. Especially his.*

'We'll carry him into the utility room.' Nova wipes her face with the back of her hand. 'I think that's what Sienna would decide.'

'Let me help.' I step towards them.

45

THEN

'COME ON, *love, you really need to eat something.'*

The sound of my husband's voice at the bedroom door invites fresh tears to my eyes.

'Why don't you get a quick shower while I fix you some soup?'

I turn away from him to face the wall. I don't want a shower. Or any soup. I just want to be left alone.

'Lying here won't bring her back. And she wouldn't want you to be this destroyed by what's happened.' I sense his weight beside me at the edge of the mattress.

'It's alright for you.' I twist around to look at him. 'You've no idea what I'm going through.'

'Of course I have.' His voice cracks. 'She was my daughter just as much as she was yours.'

'You didn't carry her inside you for nine months. You weren't the one in charge when that nutter mounted the pavement.'

'But you're being punished just as much as that woman.'

'That's just it.' I sit up in bed. 'She hasn't been punished. She killed our baby, and she's getting off scot-free.'

'She isn't.' He sits on the edge of the bed and takes my hands in his. 'She's been forcibly parted from her own child, hasn't she?'

'But eventually, she'll go back to her.'

'Plus,' he continues. 'She's got to live with the guilt of what she's done for the rest of her life.'

'Look, I know you mean well, but I really just want to be left on my own.'

'We'll have other babies, love. It won't be this hard forever.'

I kick my legs out straight. 'How can you even say that?' I shout. 'How dare you? I don't want other babies. I only want her.'

'You've got to let this go. You're making yourself ill.'

'Just leave me alone,' I shout. 'I can't take it anymore. Just leave me the hell alone.'

46

Nova weeps during every step of the transfer from the lounge to the utility room, with Vince carrying Alexander under the shoulders, and I have him by the feet. As men go, Alexander was a small version of a man. Weasel-like, I thought, but in death, he certainly takes some shifting across the hallway.

'What an utter waste of life.' Nova unlocks the door to the utility room. 'I can't believe he's dead.'

'Careful,' Vince yells as one of us bashes something with the door upon entry to the room. 'Lay him down for a moment.'

It's Tracy's head.

Her eyes are glassy and staring. Yet I'm certain they were closed when I was in here putting her soiled sheets in the washing machine. Judging by the expression on his face, Vince can hardly bear to look at his so-called girlfriend. I don't know how long they've been together, but he seems to be functioning fairly well.

I tuck my nose inside my jumper. I've done so much cleaning today, I should be immune to the stench. I'll probably smell disinfectant, mixed with diarrhoea, vomit and death inside my nostrils for the rest of my life.

Vince goes in backwards, once again, taking hold of Alexander beneath his shoulders, and I pick up his feet to assist. This is where the term *dead weight* must come from.

Finally, we lay him next to Tracy.

'Why hasn't Sienna come back?' Nova gestures towards the front of the building as Vince drops into a crouch outside the utility room door. 'Where the hell is she?'

'I'm going to have to look for her.' Vince raises his eyes to his mother.

'Over my dead body,' Nova replies, then catching my eye, she says, 'on second thoughts, perhaps not. That was a stupid thing to say.'

My mother would no doubt be amused to learn that I'm currently in the frame as a double murderess, having poisoned three of the least-liked people at this retreat. She always said I was capable of anything. If I were to be charged and found guilty, she'd be able to say she was right after all, there was always something nasty inside me. She'd probably arrange to be paid by one of the tabloid presses, telling them she could sense my psychopathic tendencies from a young age. *She was always falling out with her friends*, she'd tell them. *She was a loner*, she might add. *Not to mention a thief and an attention-seeker. She even drove her own father away.*

I need air. It's freezing out there, but I'm climbing the walls inside this lodge.

Out here, all feels perfectly normal. Steam curls around the lid of the hot tub. The fairy lights between the sauna and steam room twinkle invitingly, and the snow glistens in the faint light of the moon.

Through the window into the chapel, I can see the guests,

all laid out on their mats in the candlelight, no doubt being supported to 'breathe their way through their anxiety' by Carley.

It feels like a lifetime since I was being asked to administer oils and head massages. No one wants me anywhere near them. Which is why I'm surprised it wasn't *me* who was sent out into the wilderness instead of Sienna. Nobody, other than my kids, would have cared if I'd gone off track and frozen to death in the surrounding woodland or if I'd slipped into an icy lake.

The door to the lodge is open as I reach the porch. Vince is standing in the doorway, probably hoping that Sienna is suddenly going to materialise out of the darkness.

'Someone needs to look at this.' Nova's voice echoes from the lounge as I step onto the doormat.

'Oh God, it must be Katina,' Vince slams the door.

As I hurtle across the hallway, following Vince towards the lounge, all I can hear is the anguished voice of my boy, *No Mum, you can't go. Something bad will happen. We're never going to see you again.*

'Some wires have been cut behind the curtain.' Nova points at the coloured wires held with cable ties beneath the window. 'I drew the curtain right back so I could look out for Sienna. That's when I saw them.'

'What are they?' Vince crouches in front of the wall. 'What's been cut?'

'They lead to the wifi box by the looks of it.' We follow her gesture to the right of the wall, along the skirting board. 'It's no wonder we haven't been able to get online or make any calls.'

Vince looks at me as if I might have the answers.

'It was working when we first arrived.' I don't even know why I'm bothering. It's not as if anything I say can form the basis of an argument. Certainly not as far as the others are concerned. 'My daughter phoned me about an hour after I arrived.' The pool of sadness inside me opens up some more at the memory of us speaking.

'She's right.' Nova frowns. 'Sue from next door also called to make sure I'd arrived safely with the weather being so horrendous.'

Vince is frowning as if he's trying to make sense of the wires.

'Can you fix it?' Nova looks at him with the hope of a young girl presenting her punctured bike to her father.

'I haven't got any tools,' he replies. 'Plus, look at all those wires. It's like spaghetti junction. I wouldn't know where to start. You know I'm no good with this kind of thing.'

As Carley enters the room and heads over to our point of interest, Vince checks his watch and glances at the window.

'It might be too late to save Tracy and Alexander,' Nova whispers. 'But surely we can give Katina and her baby a fighting chance?'

'Those wires have been deliberately cut.' Carley crouches beside Vince. 'And clearly, it was done well after we all arrived.'

Vince and Nova exchange glances.

'I hope you don't think it was me who cut them.' I rock onto my knees. 'Cutting the wifi off is the last thing I'd have done.'

'Sienna could be lying face down in the snow,' Carley says. 'If she was heading in the right direction towards the road, she would have made it there ages ago. Whoever's done this has also put *her* life at risk.'

'She'd have surely come across a house or a motorist in all this time,' Nova glances out at the black sky. 'We really need to have a look at these wires before we do anything else.' She bends towards them.

'No, leave things alone,' Vince rises to his feet. 'There's been enough disaster during this retreat. You electrocuting yourself won't be a good idea.'

'You can't electrocute yourself on internet wiring,' I reply.

'You'd know, wouldn't you?' Carley sniffs.

The rest of the group has gone through for dinner, which Nova is serving while we try to sort this. I say 'we.' I'm just loitering while Carley and Vince continue to pace between the cut wires and the router. I'm not sure how the guests can muster an appetite now that there are two bodies piled up in the utility room, but who am I to judge?

Carley checked on Katina a few moments ago. She's lying in the recovery position and seems to be doing OK. For now, she's sleeping.

'Why don't you just leave me to figure this out?' Vince continues to stare at the cut wires. 'Go and get some food. I honestly don't need any help.'

'Two heads are better than one.' Carley turns the box off at the mains. Her reference to *two heads* evidently means she doesn't want me to be involved.

'If we can't get electrocuted, why's the router plugged into a socket?' Vince asks.

'Because it's powered by electricity,' I tell him. 'But it's a really low voltage that passes through the cables.'

'She could be telling us anything.' Carley doesn't look at me as she speaks. 'I don't trust her anymore.'

'I haven't done what you think I have,' I reply. 'Why would I put getting home to my kids in jeopardy?'

'You can say what you want, but you had every reason to slip something into the food of all three people who've been so ill, especially Katina.' Carley spins around on the floor so we're face-to-face.

'If I were that way inclined, Madison would have been first in the firing line.' I force a laugh. 'As would Nova.'

'Let's just focus on getting this up and running, shall we?'

Carley's face darkens. 'Though like Vince said, we haven't even got any tools.'

'Have we got some scissors?' All the times I've fixed plugs over the years, having to do everything myself because George was never around, should now give me a fighting chance of being able to sort this. 'I promise, if you let me at it, I'll have the wifi back up and running within ten minutes.'

47

'THE TWO OF *you* will be next,' the man who's introduced himself as DCI Kirk, the Senior Investigating Officer, announces as he points from me to Madison.

I'm surprised how quickly the police arrived after I managed to rejoin the wires in the router, and we were able to call 999. Clearly, the report of two dead bodies took priority over any other reports they may have had.

I answered the door, and the first two officers were nice to me, almost sympathetic when they first arrived, but that was before word went around of me being the prime suspect. After that, although it was subtle, attitudes towards me seemed to change like the wind.

'Are we under arrest?' Madison looks to be almost enjoying the situation. 'Because I shouldn't be.' She points at herself. 'As everyone's told you, there's only one person you should be arresting.'

'We'll be the judge of who to arrest,' the officer replies in a gruff voice. 'Just have a seat.' He points to the window seat in the hallway. 'Until your car arrives.' He makes it sound like we're waiting for a taxi to take us to the pub. If only. However, I wouldn't choose Madison as my companion if she were the last person on earth.

A man, suited and booted from top to toe in white, nods at DCI Kirk as he passes him at the door, seemingly poised to take a look at what lies behind the perfectly painted matt white door along the hallway. I hope he has a strong stomach.

From all the crime dramas I've ever watched, I imagine that the analysis of the affected stomach contents would form the biggest part of any prosecution. But will there be anything left to test?

The ghostly faces of Tracy and Alexander will haunt me forever, but I'm grateful that I won't be forced to spend another night in the creepy chapel while their corpses lie just feet away.

However, I'm now worried that I'll be spending the entire night in a police cell instead.

The police have separated us, which they didn't do when they first took charge. It was as if they wanted to watch our interactions for a few moments before they waded in. Olive and Brittanny left in the first police car due to the meltdown Brittany was having. 'I just need to leave. I can't stay here a minute longer,' she was gasping.

'Breathe, for goodness sake.' Olive looked panic-stricken as she swerved her focus from her daughter to one of the officers. 'She suffers from anxiety. If you're shipping us out of here, she needs to be first. And she also needs to stay with me.'

Two of the three sisters will travel to the station together, and the third will travel with Nova. Vince and Carley will be last. It's become obvious why I'm next. I'm the person here of the most significant interest.

'Do you think you'll find Sienna?' Madison's voice is faint as she stares from the window.

'As you can see, we're doing everything we can. You really shouldn't have let her go out there in this weather.'

'It had nothing to do with me,' Madison replies.

The first thing Carley did after the wifi was fixed was to try calling Sienna. But it went straight to voicemail. Vince then went looking around the periphery of the lodge. After ten minutes, he was back, stamping the snow from his boots on the doormat.

'There's absolutely no sign of her,' he said. 'And I'm risking it continuing to search. We'll have to hand it over to the police.'

That's what the roar out there is now. The police helicopter is circling the grounds of the lodge and the woodland, using its thermal imaging capability to seek her out. The officer was right, we shouldn't have let her go, but that was before the problem with the wiring was discovered. Things until that point were feeling pretty desperate.

As yet, Sienna doesn't even know that her husband's dead. I only hope that Nova, Carley or Vince gets to her before the police to break the news. It will come better from someone she knows.

I wonder who will break the news about Katina to George.

She should have reached the hospital by now. I watched as she was stretchered out, not looking as jaundiced as Alexander did, but well on her way. The paramedics were grim-faced, which possibly reflects her chances of coming through this alive. As for Katina, she looked terrified. It was agreed not to tell her of the search that's underway for Sienna in the snow, nor has anyone confirmed the news about Tracy's or Alexander's death to her. She has enough of a fight on her hands.

Several less senior officers have been hanging around each of the pairings of staff and guests since we were all separated. I'd hazard a guess that they've been tasked with listening out for nuggets of conversation that might slip between us.

While we've been out here in the hallway, Madison's made several snide comments about what I'm supposed to have done, but I've stayed quiet. I'll have the chance to defend myself in my interview. The last thing I'm going to expose myself to is a catfight with the likes of her.

'It looks like your car's here.'

There's a rumble of an engine and a crunching over stone as a large police vehicle threads its way from the end of the track to the centre of the car park. I turn away from the window as the headlights momentarily blind me.

Then I reach for the one and only bag I brought to the retreat, which I managed to grab from the chapel minutes before the police arrived. I'm dreading this interview, yet welcoming the chance to get away from this lodge more than I've ever welcomed anything.

'Leave your belongings behind. Coats, shoes, mobiles, wallets and keys only. You'll hand those in at the station.'

'Why can't we take the rest of our things? What if—'

'In case you haven't noticed, this house is now a potential crime scene,' the officer snaps. 'Nobody's moving anything other than their essentials.'

'Someone should tell him it's a bit late for that,' Madison mutters. 'Enough has been moved as it is.'

As I shrug my coat onto my shoulders, I look over to where the Scene of Crime Officer has entered the room of death through what looks like a sheet. It's shrouding all vision of what's going on in there. I've not heard anyone gagging, but these people will have seen all sorts and will be hardened to death's smell even when it's as bad as it is in there.

'Will I be allowed to go home after my interview?' Madison asks as we follow DCI Kirk from the building. I just wish I were climbing into my own car and heading home. I've been in these four walls for forty-eight hours, and it feels like a lifetime.

'That depends on what the pathologist reveals,' he replies. 'As well as what you divulge in your interview.'

'What if there's nothing to 'divulge'?' I sketch quotes in the air. 'What if—'

'Again, we'll be the judges of that.' He cuts me off as he opens the rear door. He's a rude man, this DCI Kirk. 'On the journey, also consider whether you'll require a solicitor present at your interview. This can then be organised when you arrive.'

'I definitely want one,' I say quickly.

'You'll definitely need one,' Madison mutters.

48

I'M surprised I haven't worn the floor of this cell down with all my pacing. It turns out that duty solicitors don't rush on a Saturday night to offer their services to someone who's the prime suspect in a double murder investigation.

But they're here now, and he or she is being briefed by DCI Kirk before they take me into the interview room.

At least the kids won't notice my absence until tomorrow, by which time, I'm praying I'll be back at home. I have no idea how I'll get from where I am at Skipton Police Station, and it's really looking like I'll have no means of buying Christmas presents. But somehow, I'll make it up to the kids. That's if I ever *do* get home.

I have to find out what the police have on me first.

After what feels like forever, keys rattle, and the door is opened by the desk sergeant who read me my rights when I was first brought to the station. I've been swabbed, photographed and fingerprinted like a common criminal and keep thinking I'm going to suddenly wake up and find all this is a bad dream.

I asked whether the others were being dealt with in the same way, and was told to focus on myself.

'I'm Janet Downing.' A tired-looking woman in her early forties rises from her chair behind the interview table and stretches her hand out in a greeting. 'They've given us twenty minutes to complete my paperwork with you and discuss what's been happening on your retreat. So we'd better be quick.'

She goes through my income, my right to Legal Aid, since this is a criminal matter, and gets me to sign some forms so she can represent me, all at breakneck speed. I had to beg, borrow and steal money for the legal process concerning my divorce, but now I'm presenting myself as a 'criminal', it looks like the money's laid on to cover my necessary expenses.

'Now for the case against you, Aneka. It looks like most of the others have already been questioned and released. They're just speaking to one last guest from your retreat as far as I know. And obviously, you.'

'I didn't do anything.' I'm sick of saying this. I'm beginning to sound like a stuck record.

'If that's the case, stick to your story and you'll be OK.' Her voice is breezy, and I want to tell her that this is easy for her to say. 'There's no better defence than the truth.'

'Will they let me go after my interview?'

'Most probably,' she replies. 'The two deceased people still need to undergo a post-mortem and the toxicology examinations, so it's unlikely they'll bring charges against *anyone* before those results have been received. Plus, the search is still ongoing for Sienna Milner.'

'Oh God, haven't they found her yet? It was late afternoon when she set off to find help.' I glance up at the clock, which is ticking around to 11 pm. If Vince's fears were correct and she's fallen, by now she'll have died from hypothermia. Even as I walked from the lodge to the police car and the car to the station, the cold felt like a million knives stabbing into every pore in my body. No one could survive for very long in this snow. Especially as the temperature dips even more overnight.

'It's not looking too promising. Were you close?' I don't like the solicitor's use of the past tense. It's like Sienna's already been written off.

'They *are* still looking, aren't they?'

Janet nods. 'As far as I know, but the detective will be better placed to answer that question.'

49

THIS IS the first time I've ever been in a police interview room, and my heart is pounding so violently it feels like it might rattle the table as I lean over it.

DCI Kirk enters with a stern-faced woman who introduces herself as Sergeant Claire Maynard. As they sit, the air in the room seems to tighten around me.

My rights are read out again, for the third time today, each word a reminder that I'm not a witness. I'm under arrest. I'm a suspect.

After initially spending an hour in the cell, I nearly changed my mind and refused a solicitor, thinking it would speed things up. Thank God I didn't. Janet may only be the duty solicitor, but she has a quiet ferocity about her, a woman who looks ready to fight on my behalf. And right now, that's more than I can do for myself.

The DCI fires questions at me like bullets from a gun. Thick and fast, one after the other.

'How did you come to be working for Sienna Milner?'

'What was your role on the retreat?'

'To what extent were you involved in the food preparation?'

'What were your relations like with the other staff?'

'What was your connection with Katina Hendersen?

'Why didn't you divulge this information to your peers?

'How often were you left alone in the kitchen?

'Who's looking after your children?

'What were the circumstances behind your marital split?'

'What was your relationship like with Tracy Naylor?

And lastly, the big one.

'What were you placing on the top shelf of the freezer when you first arrived at Whispering Pines?'

'Erm, nothing.' I stare back at the officer.

'You were seen entering the kitchen and placing an item on the top shelf. You were also described as checking around yourself as you went in. Perhaps making sure the coast was clear?'

'Oh, that will have been my migraine hat.' My shoulders sag in relief as I realise what he's on about. This must be what Carley was referring to when she claimed to have 'seen me.'

'Your *what?*'

'I suffer from migraines, particularly when I'm out of my comfort zone.'

Like now. I rub my head. I'd probably feel better if I'd eaten and drunk something, but so far I've refused all offerings since I was brought in, other than water. The limp sandwich and watery tea were more than I could stomach. They went dry and cold and were taken away again.

'You put a *hat* in the freezer?'

'It's an ice hat, it does something to reduce my blood vessels. Why, what's the freezer got to do with anything?'

'We're still working to establish this,' he replies. 'But in the meantime, most of the guests and staff seem to have corroborated each other's stories, saying that you're the most likely culprit for contaminating people's food.'

'They're using me as the scapegoat.' Tears well up in my eyes. It's the story of my life.

'But there *are* some discrepancies in what's being reported, which we need to examine.'

'Such as?' Janet picks up her pen.

'The interview with a guest is still underway with my colleagues, but I'll be able to let you know more shortly.'

'There's a mobile phone allegedly containing evidence,' Sergeant Maynard adds, 'so you'll need to bear with us while we extract that evidence.'

'But there wasn't any phone or wifi connection at the lodge.'

'Like I said, bear with us. We'll be able to let you know more by the morning.'

'What does that mean?' I sit up straighter in my chair. 'Can I go home?'

'I'm afraid not,' she replies. 'We're authorised to hold you for twenty-four hours. By then, we should have enough information to know whether we'll be charging or bailing you.'

Tears erupt from my eyes. 'You're holding me overnight for putting a migraine hat in the freezer?'

'No, I'm afraid things are way more serious than that.' DCI Kirk packs papers into his file and clicks his pen. 'So for now, we'll return you to your cell, and we'll be back in due course with a few more questions. Interview suspended at 11:25 pm. I'll give you a moment with your solicitor.'

'Isn't there anything you can do?' I turn to Janet. 'Please, you said you'd be able to get me out.'

'Because you've actually been arrested,' she replies. 'The sergeant's right. They're able to hold you for up to twenty-four hours, and can even apply to the court for an extra twelve hours.'

'I can't stay here for all that time – I'll go mad.'

Sympathy is written across her face. 'I'm on call in the

morning as well, so as soon as they're ready to ask more questions, I'll be right back.'

'But can't I go home to my kids? Can't I just come back in the morning?'

I don't know why I'm even asking this question. I have no money to get home and return in the morning. My car is still at the lodge with its empty tank, and there's no one I can ask for help. My friend, Ruby, made her feelings clear on Thursday when I spoke to her, and as for George, well, by now, he'll have heard about Katina's predicament and no doubt he'll be aware that I'm being held at the station in connection with it.

I dread to think what's going through his mind.

50

THEN

I can't do this anymore. I need to be with my little girl. Every second of every minute, I'm filled with shame that it was her that car hit and not me. I should have protected her.

I can't live with myself, and I certainly can't live without her. Perhaps it wouldn't have been quite so impossible if the woman who did it had held her hands up to what she'd caused.

But she's never even said sorry.

Nor has she been punished.

The police let me know that she's coming up for discharge next month. How can I stick around, knowing I could bump into her and her daughter at any moment? I don't know what I might do to either of them if I passed them in the street.

I'm so depressed. I guess since the day it all happened, I always knew this day would come. The day I end my own life.

I hope you can forgive me. I hope you can go on and be happy again. But I hope more than anything that you'll find that bitch and make her pay.

51

THE SO-CALLED bed in this police cell is no better than the airbed in the chapel back at the lodge. I've spent the night staring into the darkness, every clang of a door ricocheting through my body.

Each drunken shout echoing down the corridor has been a stark reminder that this is where people end up when their lives go off the rails.

It's three days until Christmas. Those locked up alongside me were probably out celebrating, caught up in the pre-holiday madness, never imagining their night would end in a cell.

Just like I never imagined mine would.

Two people are dead. By now, Katina could also be dead. Sienna too, for all I know. And they think I'm the common denominator.

I thought I'd hit rock bottom when my bank card was declined in the supermarket. But this is way beyond that. This is the bottom of the bottom. And the only way further down is if they charge me. Then convict me and chuck me into a prison.

I force myself upright, the thin mattress crackling beneath

me. I could lose my children. And the darkest thought slips in before I can stop it – maybe they'd be better off without me.

'We have more information,' Sergeant Maynard stands in the doorway of my cell. 'DCI Kirk and I can either speak to you now before we go off duty, or you can wait for the officers who are taking over our shift to ask you a few more questions with your solicitor present.'

'I'll wait for the solicitor.' There is no way I'm going into a police interview without a solicitor at my side when I'm being questioned over a double murder. I'm surprised they're even giving me the choice. I bet they've been hoping that being here overnight will have ground me down to the point where I'm willing to allow them to wipe the floor with me.

I accept the lukewarm tea and cold toast that's set before me in the cell. If I don't get something into my belly, I'm going to keel over. And I have no idea how long it will take for Janet Downing to return as she promised.

DCI Kirk and Sergeant Milner have been replaced by two even stonier-faced officers who introduce themselves as DC Robyn Grant and Sergeant Alan Wallace. I listen as I'm reminded that I'm under arrest and am yet again read my rights.

'Have you found Sienna?' I should probably be more concerned with saving my own skin, but I can't seem to stop worrying about her. It's definitely fed into my insomnia.

'I'm afraid not,' the DC replies. 'I'm sorry to say that unless, by some miracle, she got to warmth and safety, in which case, I'm sure she'd have made contact, the outlook isn't looking very promising.'

A vision of Sienna's dimpled smile emerges in my head. So

filled with vitality and a yearning to improve the lives of others, I can hardly believe she could be lying somewhere in that vast woodland surrounding the lodge, having frozen to death. She went out there trying to get us some help, and look what's happened.

'And Katina?'

'She's gravely ill,' DI Grant replies. 'It's looking like a liver transplant could be her only chance of survival.'

If I were truly under suspicion, maybe the officers wouldn't be divulging all this information. They'd be way more cagey. Janet, my solicitor, hasn't spoken yet, so perhaps she's thinking the same. I'd like to ask the officers about Katina's baby, but it's probably better if I don't.

'The toxicology results are back,' DI Grant begins, 'and alongside discussing those, we'd also like to ask you about this.' She nods at Sergeant Wallace, who slides something from a folder.

'For the benefit of the recording,' he says. 'We are showing exhibit A, which was recovered from the belongings of Aneka Martin when the premises were searched.'

I frown as a bag is slid across the table. 'Oh my God.'

52

'Exhibit A contains a toxin, deadly when consumed by humans, known as Death Cap Mushrooms. Have you seen this bag before, Aneka?'

I sit up straighter in my seat. 'No.'

They look like ordinary mushrooms. I'd have never known the difference.

'The two victims at the retreat died from amatoxin poisoning as a result of consuming a quantity of these mushrooms. A third victim, Katina,' he glances down at his notes, 'is also at a high risk of losing her life.'

He's now referring to them as *victims*.

The sergeant peers over the top of his glasses. 'Have you ever heard of death cap mushrooms?'

I stare back at him. 'No.'

'Can you explain how the polythene bag containing four of these mushrooms came to be among your belongings?'

'I have no idea. Someone must have put it there.'

'We understand from the other guests that several of them ate an omelette during their first breakfast at the retreat.' DC Grant taps her pen against her chin. 'Who ate the mushrooms?'

'Tracy and Alexander,' I reply. 'But *death cap mushrooms*. Where have they come from?'

'That's what we're hoping you'll tell us.'

They're trying to trip me up. 'Like I said, I've never even heard of them.'

The officers glance at each other.

'OK, so you've found 'evidence' in my client's belongings,' Janet says. 'But it isn't forensic evidence. There's nothing to suggest the bag wasn't planted there.' She drives her pen into her notepad as she speaks. 'Good luck with convincing the CPS to bring charges on that basis.' Her voice is filled with sarcasm.

I'm so relieved I waited for my solicitor before being interviewed again.

'They grow natively in woodland through the autumn,' DC Grant ignores Janet's comments. 'And as with all mushrooms, they freeze well.'

'So,' – Janet looks thoughtful, – 'you're suggesting that my client picked some death cap mushrooms in the Autumn and froze them, all ready to poison her ex-husband's new girlfriend on a retreat she didn't even know she'd be working on until she was offered the job just the day before.' Janet points her pen at DC Grant. 'You're also suggesting that Aneka was planning to poison two people she never even knew existed.'

'She's had run-ins with all three of them since she arrived at Whispering Pines,' she says. 'It's common knowledge.' DC Grant shifts her attention from Janet to me, clearly waiting for my explanation.

'It was nothing serious.'

'Am I correct in believing Alexander locked you out in the cold on the first night? And Tracy, I understand she accused you of stealing?'

'I can't deny that I didn't like either of them,' I reply. 'But I would never have poisoned *anyone*.'

'We've been speaking to George, your ex-husband,'

Sergeant Wallace takes over. 'Understandably, he's devastated at how ill his girlfriend is, and even more so when he learned that you were there, serving her food.'

'So he also believes I've poisoned her?'

'He was shocked you were even at the retreat and said it couldn't possibly be a coincidence.'

'But that's exactly what it was. Like I mentioned in last night's interview, my friend Ruby put me forward, as I was desperate for Christmas money. Vince telephoned me the day before and offered me the job.'

'Well, this is the thing. We've checked with your friend, Ruby, and she knows nothing about putting you forward for *any* work.' DI Grant lifts her eyebrows as she waits for my reply.

'Of course she does.' My heart is thumping. 'There must be some misunderstanding.'

'George told us about the run-in the two of you had with Katina present outside your house, only the day before the retreat. He described you as being extremely jealous and bitter over his new relationship.'

'I just wanted my maintenance money for the kids.' I slump down in my chair. This is going from bad to worse.

'Whatever you know about the harvesting and serving of these mushrooms, Aneka, it would be far better for you to be honest while you have the chance.'

'It's always better to confess than to be found guilty.' The DI adds.

'You will not browbeat a false confession from my client.' Janet's voice is as hard as nails. 'She's just told you she had nothing to do with these mushrooms. So unless you can prove otherwise, move on.'

'Like your client just told us,' Sergeant Wallace's voice becomes softer. 'Her ex owed her a ton of money, which he was no doubt spending on Katina.' He turns back to me, with false sympathy etched across his face. 'Then, on the retreat itself, she was extremely unpleasant. Tracy accused her of stealing. And Alexander locked her outside in the cold in the dead of night. She could have easily frozen to death.'

'I didn't take those mushrooms to the retreat.' My voice rises. 'It could have been Nova. She clearly had a thing about Alexander. She might have got angry at him for stringing her along. Plus, she didn't much care for Tracy. She makes little secret that nobody could ever be good enough for her precious son.'

'But there'd be no reason for Nova to poison Katina, would there?'

I haven't got an answer.

'Nova's been released as it happens, pending further questions,' DI Grant says. 'In fact, *you're* the only person we've kept overnight.' She nods towards me.

'Who cooked the garlic mushrooms which Katina ate?'

'I did.' I hang my head. 'Nova told me to. She said she'd spotted them in the freezer left over from the omelettes at breakfast. What would I have gained from doing something this awful?'

'What would *anyone* have to gain from killing another person? Revenge, satisfaction, control...'

'We're not disputing that you placed your migraine hat in the freezer,' Sergeant Wallace goes on. 'What we believe, however, is that it was a smokescreen for placing the bag of mushrooms beside it when you first arrived at the retreat.'

'It wasn't. I didn't.' I drop my head into my hands.

'So how did that bag end up at the bottom of an Aldi bag containing your belongings?'

'Someone must have planted it.'

'We're going to have to see what the Crown Prosecution Service comes back with.' DI Grant rises to her feet just as there's a knock at the door. 'Yes, what is it?' She strides across the room.

After several agonising moments, she returns. 'We may have further evidence,' she explains. 'But for now, we're going to return you to your cell.'

'No, please, I can't go back in there.'

'It should only be for a short time,' she replies. 'Depending on how long it takes the CPS to reach a decision.'

53

THE TWO OFFICERS who've been interviewing me must have either gone off shift or gone onto something else, for a completely different officer appears in the doorway of my cell. She looks almost disappointed as she rattles the keys in the lock.

'You're being bailed, pending further enquiries,' she announces.

'Why? What's going on?'

'We've received information which implicates someone else in our investigation,' the officer says. 'And that's all I've been authorised to say.'

'Does this mean I'm no longer a suspect?'

'Not exactly, but just now, we're unable to bring any charges against you, nor can we give you any further information, therefore, we're releasing you on police bail.'

'Really?' Oh my God, I'm getting out, I can go home. And here was me panicking that they might be about to extend my stay to thirty-six hours.

'So if you can't tell me now who else is implicated and how, then when *can* you tell me?'

'Your solicitor will be in touch as soon as we're able to discuss this.'

'But I need to know now. I can't live with all this hanging over me. Especially over Christmas.'

'Our investigations will be concluded as soon as possible.'

I've never been so relieved to step back into the real world. I might be practically penniless, my phone might be dead, and I might be standing outside a snowy Skipton police station with no way to contact my children, but I'm free. All around me, Christmas lights glitter through the morning gloom, and shoppers hurry past with bags full of gifts, their laughter and chatter a world away from where I've just been.

I can't call the kids, but I can get in a taxi and head home. The paths and buildings are laden with snow, but roads look reasonably clear around here. Perhaps Hallie hasn't spent the full thirty pounds I left. Maybe the neighbour, whose dog I've walked more times than I can count, will lend me the taxi fare. And if not, I'll swallow my pride and beg the driver to let me pay later.

Whatever it takes, because getting home is the only thing that matters.

'Are you all ready for Christmas?' The driver glances at me via his rear-view mirror. Yes, I look dishevelled after practically a full night and day at the police station, but he has no reason to suspect that I can't afford to pay him when we reach Otley.

I don't know whether to laugh or cry at his question. 'Pretty much,' I reply. What else can I say? 'You?'

'I've just got to buy something for the wife.' He laughs. 'I'll be joining the desperate men brigade on Christmas Eve. We're easily spotted, wandering around shopping centres full of wide-eyed fear.'

I force a laugh back, remembering how George was once the same. George. I still have him to face. Who knows what my phone will yield once I get it plugged in?

'Have you enjoyed your weekend?' Trust me to get a driver who wants to engage in conversation. When at the moment, I just want to sink into myself and chew over everything that's going on. Just because I've been bailed doesn't mean I'm off the hook. The desk sergeant even told me not to go far when I signed for the return of the belongings they'd confiscated.

'It's not been too bad,' I reply. *What a question.* I could tell him the truth, but he'd never believe me. That I'm under suspicion for the murder of two people by toxic poisoning.

And that a third person is clinging to life while a fourth person is missing, and the way things are looking, she's presumed dead.

'What time are you working until?' It's the question we always ask taxi drivers when we're avoiding an uncomfortable silence. Either that, or *have you been busy?*

'Oh, I'm on until eight,' he replies. 'Which is good. There'll be lots of Christmas shoppers wanting rides home in this freezing weather. It just takes a bit longer to get around on the icy roads.'

'Just here thanks.'

Miraculously, my debit card works on the first attempt of offering it to the driver. Perhaps my luck is beginning to change.

'Mum, Mum.' Barnaby hurtles from the lounge and launches himself at me as I step into the hallway. 'Where have you been? Why wouldn't you answer your phone? I thought you'd left us forever?' He might be eight years old, but he's still quite capable of clinging to me like a limpet. I wrap my arms around him. I've never needed a hug more than I do this morning.

'I told him you'd be alright over and over again.' Hallie appears at the top of the stairs, her hair wrapped in a towel turban. 'We've been worried, though, Mum. We've tried ringing and ringing. Ruby said she didn't have a clue where you'd gone, and asked me to ring her the moment I got hold of you. She's been on the phone several times since.'

This is the second time Ruby's been mentioned. The police even said they'd spoken to her and she had no knowledge of me doing any job other than my cleaning and shop work. They said she's never heard of anyone called Sienna.

'Hang on – it was Ruby who recommended me for the job. She should have known exactly where I was. I don't understand this.'

Hallie shakes her head. 'She's been as worried as we have. We were going to give it until tomorrow for you to come home, and then we were going to go to the police when we could say you were a day late.'

'Why are you wearing those clothes, Mum?' Barnaby lets go of me and stands back. It's a fair question. If I'd had some money, I could have bought something, instead of heading home in the police station jogging bottoms and jumper they rustled up. But it's better than a paper suit, I've heard they make some people wear.

'You look like something out of 24 Hours in Police Custody,' Hallie laughs.

'I erm, I spilt something and didn't have anything clean.' I can hardly tell them that everything I was wearing has been bagged up as evidence in the case of their dad's girlfriend's attempted murder. I'm not going to tell them anything until forced.

'Dad's been ringing today,' Hallie goes on. 'He sounded really strange. He worried me.'

'Why, what was he saying?' I might have known he'd get onto Hallie, looking for me.

'Nothing much, but he sounded angry. And like he might be crying. He just wanted to talk to you.'

'I'll call him shortly, but first,' I open my arms out. Barnaby shoots back towards me, and Hallie, not as receptive to my hugs as she used to be, descends the stairs, less reluctantly than usual.

'When are you going shopping, Mum?' Barnaby steps back. 'We're sick of toast and jacket potatoes.'

'Tomorrow,' I reply.

I'll get some cash from somewhere, even if I have to sell a kidney to do so. But given the organ failure Katina's in, maybe this thought is in poor taste.

'I just want to have a bath and spend some time with you guys today.'

54

THE CHILDREN HAVE GROWN accustomed to me being back at home and have slipped effortlessly into their usual routines. Hallie has presents to wrap, bought with her babysitting money, she was quick to point out. Meanwhile, Barnaby is glued to YouTube as if nothing in the world has shifted.

But everything has in mine. The house hasn't changed, yet everything feels different. What I once saw as shabby and worn now feels like a sanctuary. These familiar four walls have never looked so precious. Especially now I'm facing the possibility of a prison sentence.

My phone lights up, finally charged enough to drag me back into reality. Twenty-six messages flash on the screen. A surge of guilt rises instantly, as no surprise, most of them are from Hallie.

> Hi Mum, what time are you ringing us?

> Why's your phone off, Mum?

> Mum, Barnaby's really upset. Can you call soon?

> Muuuuum!!!

The next day, there's one from Ruby.

> Why are your kids worried about where you are? Is it something to do with this job I'm supposed to have recommended you for? The one I know nothing about?

There's more from Hallie and another from Ruby, and then George.

> What the hell have you done?

> How are you going to live with yourself?

> I hope they throw away the key.

I need to speak to him. Against my better judgment, I hit the button next to his name. He answers after the first ring.

'You.' I've never heard his voice sound so strangled.

'I can't imagine how I could have been married and had children with such an evil bitch. How come they've let you ring me? Is this the one phone call you're allowed?'

'I've been released on bail.' In contrast to his, my voice is low. I don't want the kids to hear me arguing with their father. Not again. Besides, they know nothing of my predicament, and I'd prefer to keep it that way until such a time as I'm forced to tell them.

'You've what?' He bellows. 'You've killed two people and you've been bailed?'

'I haven't killed *anyone*.'

'Why are you whispering? Don't you want the kids to hear

what you've done? Well, let me tell you, as soon as I leave this hospital, I'll be coming round to enlighten them.'

'It wasn't me,' I reiterate. 'You've got to believe me.'

'You turn up at some event where my girlfriend's going to be,' I didn't think it was possible, but his voice is even louder than a moment ago. 'And you expect me to believe a word that comes out of your mouth. She's barely holding on, Aneka.'

'You know me, George, you know—'

'She's carrying my baby. Did you know that? Is this why—'

'You've got me wrong. I swear you have.'

'If the police aren't doing what they're supposed to be doing with you, then I will.'

'But, George, listen—'

The line falls silent. I can hardly believe the magnitude of our conversation. We're not just discussing a missing payment or his access to our kids. I'm being accused of attempting to murder his girlfriend and unborn baby.

The Christmas tree looks almost magical in the dark. With only the fairy lights glowing, you can't see how sparse the branches are or how the decorations are fraying with age. Hallie rarely watches TV with Barnaby and me, but tonight she's here, pressed in close on one side, Barnaby on the other, as we watch a Christmas film together. And in this small, imperfect moment, I feel it with absolute clarity – none of the things I was worrying about before all this really matter. I don't need money to be rich.

'I'm glad you're home, Mum.' Barnaby hasn't even complained about only having beans on toast for dinner this evening. But our days of living in poverty are numbered. If I've taken one lesson from this awful weekend, it's that it's up to me to make my life better.

I can blame my mother's rejection, my dad walking out when I was a toddler, my grandfather's death, or George's absence to my heart's content, but the only person who can improve my life is me. There's nothing like lying on a concrete slab overnight to improve one's clarity.

Not for the first time in the last few minutes, a movement catches my attention outside. There's a gap in the curtain, too small to make out who could be out there, but large enough to be sure that it's not just someone walking past the house.

The kids don't notice the way my breath catches in my throat as the shadow becomes visible again.

Someone is watching us. Hanging around outside wouldn't normally be George's style, and yet, I can't imagine who else it could be.

I've felt his presence out there for the last ten minutes, that prickling awareness all the way up my spine.

The moment I glance up, the shadow whips out of view.

'I'm just popping to the loo,' I say, forcing my voice to stay light as I rise from the sofa.

'Shall we pause it?' Hallie asks.

'No, I've seen this film loads of times.' The last thing I want is silence in the house. If George is out there, I don't want the children to hear what might be said.

At the front door, I twist the latch and open it just enough to peer outside. A blast of icy air bites into my skin. The street's empty, save for a solitary car inching through the slush that's collected in the ruts between the tyre tracks. It turns the corner, and the street is still again.

Too still.

A metallic clink echoes from the back of the house. It's the unmistakable scrape of metal against brick. A ladder, maybe? My stomach drops. George wouldn't enter our home by ladder.

Shit.

Did I close the window after my bath? If someone's going to try and get in through an upstairs window, I need to stop them.

I dart outside and pull the front door closed behind me. The alleyway between my house and next door is narrow and pitch-dark. I creep along it, my heart hammering.

At the high wooden gate to my backyard, I reach over and slide the bolt across, looking up at the house as I go. There's no sign of any ladder.

I hesitate. I shouldn't take this on myself. I should call the police. But after everything that's happened this weekend, would they even rush to help me, or would they push me to the bottom of the pile?

I've barely stepped into the yard when a shadow hurtles out of the darkness. Somebody slams into me, driving me back into the cold concrete wall, exploding the breath from my lungs.

55

THEN

'She's being discharged from the psychiatric hospital, but she's moving to another part of the country,' the officer tells me, his tone letting me know there'll be no disclosure as to the whereabouts. 'The powers that be have clearly deemed her fit enough to live a normal life.'

'What about my normal life?' The words leave me through gritted teeth. 'Why should she get to go home and play mummy? Because of her, I've got nothing. I've got no one.'

'As far as I know, her four-year-old lives with her grandfather,' the officer replies. 'She'll be having some weekend access, but that's it for the foreseeable future.'

'At least she still gets to see her daughter.' I'm shaking with anger. I always knew she'd be discharged eventually, but now that the time's come, I want to destroy her as much as she's destroyed me. 'If it wasn't for that woman, my daughter would have just celebrated her seventh birthday. And my wife...' My voice fades.

I can't find forgiveness. I'm unsure if it's forgiveness towards my wife for ending her life and leaving me completely alone, or forgiveness towards myself for not realising how close she was to the edge.

We were still in our twenties, so I thought we'd eventually have another child. We had plenty of time. We'd always mourn the child we lost so tragically, but that, in time, the grief might fade.

However, with the lack of punishment that was meted out to our daughter's killer, the grief only intensified for my wife.

Therefore, it's up to me to dish out my own punishment. I'll ruin her life. I'll ruin her daughter's life. One way or another, I'm going to get justice.

'How much counselling have you had, Vince?' The officer's voice is gentle.

'I don't want counselling. I just want to meet her. What's it called, you know, the process where a killer has to face the people they've hurt?

'You mean restorative justice? I'm afraid that won't be possible, Vince. Things are extremely fragile for the family right now. She needs a period of adjustment to continue to recover. Postnatal depression, to the extent she had it, can be a challenge to come back from.'

'What about what I've had to come back from?'

'Listen – Vince—'

But I end the call. I don't want to hear any more of his platitudes.

It might take months, it might take years. But sooner or later, I'll find her daughter.

And I'll use her to make as much misery as that woman has for my family.

56

IT TAKES a moment for the world to stop spinning after being slammed so hard against the wall. I blink hard, trying to focus on the hooded figure towering in front of me. It's not George, this man is taller.

Then the shadows shift, and I see his face.

Vince.

'What are *you* doing here?' I gasp, relief flickering for a second before it snuffs itself out just as quickly. Vince is far from pleased to see me, judging from his expression. 'How did you find my house?'

'I know more about you than you think, Aneka.'

Something in his voice is wrong, like all the warmth I saw in him at the retreat has been stripped away.

'What's going on? Is everything OK?'

'Everything has *never* been OK.' He steps closer, his foot crunching into the snow as his breath forms clouds in the freezing air. There's a calculated stillness to him. 'Not since I lost the only two people I've ever loved.'

Two people? 'If this is about Tracy—'

'It's nothing to do with her,' he cuts in, his voice chillingly calm. 'And I already know the mushrooms had nothing to do with you.'

My breath catches. 'Then what is this? Why are you looking at me like you want to kill me?'

'*I* picked the mushrooms,' he says simply, pointing at himself. 'Back in October. Death caps, as they're called. I harvested them, dehydrated what I couldn't freeze, then I brought them to the retreat.'

'What?' For a moment, my brain refuses to compute. 'You knew what they were?'

Surely there has to be some mistake here.

'I've been watching you for months,' he continues, as if I haven't spoken. 'Tracking you. Waiting for my chance.'

'Tracking me? But why? We only met on Friday.' I wrap my arms around myself, the thin fabric of my jumper no match for the plummeting temperature out here.

'We met *properly* on Thursday,' he interrupts, 'after I'd been able to confirm it was *you*. I've been searching for years.'

'But why?'

'You went and changed your name. You moved away. But you changed your name back. Good move.'

'I don't understand.'

'Did you really think our meeting was just a coincidence?'

My mouth feels as dry as bone. I lick my lips. 'I got divorced. That's why I went back to my maiden name. But why is that even relevant?'

His expression twists, not with rage, but with what looks like pain. 'Your mother,' he spits the word out, as if it poisons his mouth, 'she killed my daughter.'

'I...what are you talking about?'

'Thirty years ago,' he continues. 'The bitch left my four-year-old girl dying in the road. She just drove off like she was nothing. Vermin in the gutter.'

A chill seeps into my bones. The story. The accident my mother would never speak of. Grandad occasionally hinted at something but wouldn't be drawn out. It was always taboo, and whatever had happened, she always blamed me. She said I made her ill.

'That accident— I was only a baby. She was ill—'

'She wasn't ill. She was drunk and drugged and selfish. And your family made sure she never faced justice.' His voice cracks, then hardens again. 'My daughter died. My wife killed herself six months later. Your mother took everything I had. And then she got to carry on. She got to raise you and to pretend she was the victim.'

'But I hardly ever saw her. My father left when my mum went into hospital. My grandfather brought me up. And she blamed me for everything.'

'You got to grow up and have children of your own. My daughter never even made it to Christmas morning.'

'Vince... I'm sorry. I truly am. But you coming after me isn't justice for what you've lost.'

'But it's balance,' he replies. 'I want your mother to feel what I felt. To watch her daughter die. Slowly. The toxins from death caps can take hours, even days, while the liver fails. She should have been at your side, watching you die like I had to watch my little girl die.'

Ice threads through my veins.

'But you wouldn't eat what I put in front of you,' he continues quietly. 'You refused the quiche. You refused to let me cook you an omelette. So others died instead. Tracy. Alexander. Perhaps Katina.

'But *Tracy*? I thought—'

'I hated Tracy. She was a leech – sticking to me, refusing to let go. As for Alexander – well, he was always in the way of me and Sienna being properly together. She just wouldn't leave him.'

My heart lurches. I remember Vince's disappointment when I refused his food offering that first evening at the lodge – the quiche, which I think had mushrooms in it. His insistence that I should sit down and have something proper to eat.

'I had no idea you were involved,' I whisper. 'I thought Nova or Madison were framing me. Never *you*. I thought you were decent.'

'They *were* framing you,' he says. 'Because I led them to that belief. If I couldn't get you to eat the mushrooms, I'd get you to take the blame for the others getting sick.'

'You're deluded. It won't stick, you know. They've no *forensic* evidence on me.'

'If your mother could feel a fraction of the pain she inflicted on—'

'I haven't spoken to the woman in years,' I plead. 'She wouldn't even care—'

'She'd have heard about it on the news,' he says softly. 'And I'd have made sure she'd have known it was because of what she did to me.'

He's talking in the past tense. Like he suspects already that his plan has failed.

'Vince, come on. We can talk about this. You can't punish *me* for something my mother did.'

'I've got nothing left to lose,' he snarls.

'What are you talking about?'

'Someone filmed me planting the bag on you. So I'm done for.'

They've got him. Thank God for Brittany. There were times when her constant filming irritated me. But without her footage, the police could have been throwing away the key.

'The police will have me either way,' Vince steps forward and a glint of metal appears in his hand. 'I've lost my wife and daughter. My life has been worthless ever since. Even Sienna doesn't want me.'

'Vince, please.' I step back, slipping in the snow, but I'm out of space. 'My children are inside. They need me. They haven't got anyone else.'

His face is unreadable. 'Neither have I.'

He lifts the blade. I'm done for.

57

THE BACK DOOR RATTLES. Then the key turns in the lock from the inside. No. No, no, no.

'Stay inside!' I shout, my voice cracking.

But the door swings open. Barnaby steps out, framed by the glow of the kitchen light spilling across the yard. 'Mum? Why are you—'

He flicks on the outside light, and the full horror of the scene is exposed. A hooded Vince, looking from me to my son with hollow eyes, still clutching his knife.

'Oh my God.' Hallie appears beside Barnaby and promptly freezes.

'He's been outside my school,' Barnaby gasps.

'What? Just both of you please, get inside and lock the door.'

'You should listen to your mother.' Vince's gaze locks onto my children with a calmness that's as terrifying as his weapon.

'Hallie – lock yourselves in. Now!'

But Vince is already moving towards them in a swift, almost predatory lunge – shoving my children backwards. I rush after him, jumping onto his back, and in that single motion, we're all propelled into the kitchen in a blur of scrabbling limbs and breathless panic.

Barnaby hits the floor with a cry. Vince steadies himself against the kitchen counter before coming back at me. His arm hooks around my shoulder, the knife glinting inches from my face.

'Mum!' Hallie's scream pierces the air.

'Stay back!' I shout, but she's already inching towards us. 'Please, Hallie. Keep away from him.'

'Your grandmother doesn't deserve such lovely grandchildren,' Vince hisses, his spittle spraying through the air and landing on my cheek.

'They don't even know the woman. You're wrong about it all.'

'Balance, remember,' he snarls.

Then everything happens in an instant. Vince suddenly lets go of me and lunges at Barnaby. My maternal instinct kicks in, and I grab at Vince's arm with both hands, twisting his wrist with a strength I wasn't aware I had. He jerks back, trying to wrench free.

The knife's wobbling in his grip as he tries with all his might to drive it into me. But I'm pressing his arm back with every ounce of strength I can muster.

He freezes. For a second, I don't understand what's going on or why his arm's gone limp. It takes a moment to believe what I'm seeing, as blood blooms across his side, the grey of his joggers turning crimson.

In his battle to swerve the knife into me, he's driven his own blade into the flesh just above his hip.

He gasps, his eyes widening in disbelief. The knife drops from his hand, clattering onto the tiles. For a fraction of a second, there's shock in his eyes. Followed by pain and the realisation of what he's done. Coupled with fury, as though even this is also my fault.

Hallie darts forward, pulling Barnaby away as I grab Vince's arm to stop him from collapsing to the ground. 'Don't move,' I tell him, my voice shaking. 'You've cut yourself deep.'

He tries to push me away, leaving a red smear across the cupboard door as he lets go of his side. 'Don't touch me.'

I catch him as his legs buckle - still straining against his weight.

'The police are coming,' Hallie shouts. 'I hit the SOS button on my watch when I realised something bad was happening.'

I'm so proud of my girl. I should have known.

Vince's breathing is ragged as he continues to lose blood, but he's very much conscious. However, he's in no state to try again. To have another go with the knife. 'This isn't over. This won't be over until you and your mother pay for what she robbed from me.'

'It's very much over,' I reply. 'And thankfully, that injury's not going to kill you, Vince. You'll soon be able to answer for *everything*.'

I glance towards the hallway where emergency lights are flickering the wall with blue. They're here.

Barnaby clings to Hallie, and Hallie clings to the doorframe as I dart to the door to let help in.

Officers flood our tiny kitchen. Paramedics drop to their knees beside Vince. An officer pins Vince's arms to the floor as at first, he struggles. But he's too weak to struggle for long as handcuffs are locked half onto one of his wrists, and the other half snapped onto the wrist of another officer. Bandages are pressed hard against his wound. He cries out in pain, low and guttural. I hope it hurts like hell.

'You're going to be alright,' the paramedic tells him. 'We'll get this looked at.'

DI Grant's voice is calm and deliberate as she leans in. "Vincent Ward, you are being placed under arrest for two counts of murder, one count of attempted murder and conspiracy to administer a noxious substance. You do not have to say anything—'

And this is before they lay any charges against him for what he's done here, tonight.

Vince turns his head toward me, rolling his head against the fridge, his eyes clouded and his face grey. For just a moment, something like grief passes through them, and I almost feel sorry for him. Almost.

With one hand cuffed to the officer, he's helped onto a stretcher. Thank God he's still alive to face up to what he's done to the people from the retreat. And what he was intending to do to me.

As the stretcher is carried into the street, Hallie slips her hand into mine and Barnaby presses himself into my side. And with the slam of the front door, it hits me – how narrowly we escaped becoming Vince's idea of justice.

His atonement and his revenge.

EPILOGUE

'HOW ARE THEY BOTH DOING?' Sienna cradles the mug I hand her and sinks into the armchair, her movements slow, as if every breath still has to fight its way through her shock.

'Hallie's coping,' I say. 'She'd already pressed SOS on her watch, the second she realised Vince had a knife. She keeps saying she's fine, but I'm watching her closely.'

Above us, my daughter's music thuds through the ceiling, loud, defiant, and alive.

'And your son?' Sienna asks softly.

Barnaby's in his room, glued to his game. Normality has inched its way back into our home over the last forty-eight hours since Vince's appearance.

'He'll need counselling,' I admit. 'He's been anxious for months. It turns out that Vince has been hanging around the house and his school, watching him. But he didn't want to tell me as he thought I was already worried enough about other things.'

'I'll pay for whatever he needs,' she says immediately. 'I've realised how much you struggle, and I want to help.'

'You've got enough to deal with.' I reach forward and touch her hand. 'So enough about me – how are *you*?'

'I don't think it's all hit me yet.' She's staring into the fire. 'It was far from perfect between me and Alexander, but the reality that he's gone, permanently gone...' Her voice cracks. 'I keep expecting him to walk in with one of his smug little remarks.'

'I'm here for you,' I tell her. 'If there's anything I can do.' I know this is what so many people say as a platitude when someone's bereaved. But I really mean it.

Sienna nods, blinking rapidly as though keeping her grief in check. 'When I fall apart, and I will at some point, at least I know there are people who'll catch me.'

'Can I ask you something?'

'Of course.' Sienna's voice rises with what sounds like interest.

'Why did you want me to clean Tracy up? You know, along with the rest of the mess?'

'I guess I panicked,' she replies. 'I wasn't really thinking straight. It was my way of keeping hold of some semblance of control. I'm sorry. I was out of order.'

The clock on the mantelpiece ticks loudly in the silence. My gaze drifts over to the fire, and my mind drifts to Katina. I can't pretend to like the woman carrying my children's half-sibling, but I'm silently praying she makes it through her transplant.

'She's been in theatre for nearly four hours,' Sienna says, noticing where I'm looking. 'Her family says she's got a good chance of the operation being a success.'

Her family. I wonder if she means George.

'I still can't believe what Vince did,' I whisper as tears sting my eyes. 'But at least George has stopped blaming me. He told me that Katina being pregnant has made him determined to be a better father. And he's promised to get the money he owes me before the new year.'

'I always knew there was something dark about Vince,'

Sienna says. 'I only slept with him once, but he wouldn't let it go.'

'I gathered something must have happened between you.'

'What did he say?'

'I just got the impression that he wanted you more than you wanted him.'

'It was a huge mistake.' She seems to be studying the pattern on the carpet.

'Did you know about his past? Before you, you know.'

'I knew about his wife and daughter. But I didn't know he'd been searching for you.' There's an apologetic edge to her voice. 'You, *or* your mother.'

'The mushrooms were picked for me,' I say quietly. 'I wasn't meant to be coming home from that retreat.'

'I know,' she replies. 'Nova's found evidence of his research on his computer. It seems that when Vince's initial plans didn't work, framing you would still be revenge in his eyes.'

'It nearly worked,' I admit. 'Even you doubted me.'

'I'm ashamed to say, I did.' Sienna winces. 'Just for a moment. Do you know,' – she sits up straighter in her chair. – 'I should really check on Nancy. I still don't know how Vince got rid of her – creating the vacancy for you in the first place. I thought it was odd that she'd let me down at the last minute. And then by some miracle, Vince has discovered you.'

'He told me my friend, Ruby, had put me forward for the job.' I reach for my tea.

'He could have just plucked her name from your Facebook page.'

'I know. Anyway,' I slap my palms against my jeans. 'What happened to you that night? We thought you'd fallen into the river or frozen to death.'

'I got lost.' She pulls a face. 'Everything, as far as the eye could see, was white and disorientating.'

'But where were you?'

'I found a boarded-up farmhouse and managed to get inside and to set a fire going.' She sighs. 'Thank God for that lighter I kept in my pocket for the meditation candles, and for being able to melt snow to drink.' Sienna has a faraway look in her eyes as though she's bringing to mind a different lifetime. One in which she was unaware that Alexander was dead. 'The next morning, I walked and walked until I eventually found a road.' She presses her hands flat to her knees. 'And all the while, my husband was lying dead in the utility room.'

Silence falls between us, only broken by the hum of the boiler and Hallie's music continuing to echo through the floor.

'Did you really think I could have poisoned them?' I ask eventually.

'I honestly thought you had a motive,' she says. 'Alexander and Tracy were cruel to you. Then, with Katina, you kept your history a secret from me. So when I heard that bag of mushrooms had been found in your things...' It's her turn to reach across and squeeze my hand. 'But all that matters now is we know the truth.'

'What's happening with Vince?'

'He's had stitches in his hip and he's going to be alright. He'll be discharged tomorrow, but it's Christmas Day, so his first court date won't be until after Boxing Day. They'll definitely remand him, so I've been told. There's no scenario where he'll walk free.'

A wave of relief passes through me so powerful that I have to close my eyes. He can never threaten us again. Or my mother.

Sienna reaches into her bag and takes out an envelope. 'I also came to pay you.'

I hesitate, embarrassed. 'You don't have to—'

'Of course I do,' she interrupts, pressing it into my hand. 'There's a thousand pounds in cash. I'll transfer another thousand when you send your bank details. Just take it.'

Emotion rises like a living creature in my throat. It's not just about the *money*. 'Thank you.'

She nods toward the corner where the tree sits, lopsided and threadbare. 'There's still time to save Christmas for them.'

I smile. The tree doesn't matter. What matters is filling the cupboards. Putting presents under the tree and giving my children a safe home to wake up on Christmas morning in.

'I never knew the full truth about my mother.' I shift my gaze back to Sienna. 'How she drove off that day, leaving a child in the road like she was nothing. But my grandfather always said she was sick, and that the postnatal depression had stolen her mind. Which is why she's always rejected me since.'

Sienna nods. 'It sounds like your mother was punishing herself. Not only for what she'd done, but for the life she couldn't face. You were a reminder of everything she didn't deserve in her mind.'

My attention rests on the photo above the fireplace, Hallie at ten with Barnaby at two. They're so gorgeous and innocent. They're everything I fight for. But now I know the truth about my mother, maybe there's even more fight to find within myself.

'I might try again to contact her,' I say. 'Now that I know the truth, perhaps I'm ready to forgive her. Maybe I can help her to forgive herself.'

Sienna studies me. 'Whether she does or not, it sounds like you've already broken the cycle.'

After Sienna's gone, I stand in the hallway for a moment with the envelope of money in my hand, feeling calmer than I have for months.

My mother's rock bottom lasted decades. Mine ends here, in our little house, with my children happy and safe and the vision of our battered Christmas tree in the corner.

And I know one thing with absolute certainty. Rock bottom is a place I refuse to revisit.

Before You Go

If you enjoyed *The Winter Retreat*, I would be so grateful if you could take a moment to leave a review on Amazon. Reviews are the lifeblood of authors like me, and help other readers discover my books.

This was my 26th psychological thriller, and there are many more dark and twisty stories on the way, including my first release of 2026, which will be announced shortly.

Visit my website to explore my other thrillers and be first to hear about what's coming next...

BOOK CLUB DISCUSSION QUESTIONS

1. Did knowing the prologue outcome at the start add to the tension, or would you have preferred going in unawares?

2. Do you think Aneka's decision to hide her history with Katina made her more or less sympathetic as a character?

3. How did the isolated winter retreat setting contribute to the suspense? Could this story have worked in any other environment?

4. Aneka struggles financially, emotionally, and psychologically while trying to be a good mother. What does the book suggest about the lengths a mother will go to protect her children?

5. How did your perception of Vince shift throughout the story? Was there ever a moment you felt sympathy for him, despite his actions?

6. Sienna presents as calm and spiritual, yet she contributes to

tension at the retreat. How trustworthy did you find her, and did your opinion of her change?

7. Several scenes play out in near-darkness, snow, or silence. Which setting detail stuck with you the most and why?

8. How did the mushroom poisoning element affect your trust in the characters? Who did you suspect first, and when did your suspicions change?

9. Do you feel Vince is a villain, a victim of his own grief, or something in between? How does the novel challenge your concept of justice?

10. The ending leaves Aneka contemplating forgiveness for her mother. Do you think she should reach out or walk away for good?

11. Snow is often associated with purity, yet here it traps, isolates, and conceals. What do you think the snow symbolised in the story?

12. The retreat is marketed as a place of healing, but instead becomes a place of reckoning. What does the novel suggest about the facades people maintain?

13. Which twist shocked you the most? Looking back, were there clues you missed?

14. If this book were to continue in a sequel, what unresolved element would you most want to explore?

ACKNOWLEDGMENTS

Thank you, as always, to my amazing husband, Michael. He's my first reader, and is vital with my editing process for each of my novels. His continued support means more than I can say.

A special acknowledgement goes to my wonderful advance reader team, who took the time and trouble to read an advance copy of The Winter Retreat and offer feedback. They are a vital part of my author business, and I don't know what I would do without them. The Winter Retreat is my twenty-sixth full-length novel and it becomes harder and harder to think of first names for my characters. Therefore, I'm really grateful to members of the group who offered their own names up for me to use! They are:

Aneka (Aneka Lewis)
    Hallie (Put forward by Karen Kilburn)
    Barnaby (Put forward by Sally Cave)
    Ruby (Put forward by Clare Farthing)
    Sienna (Put forward by Julie Walker Dombrowski)
    Alexander (Put forward by Juanita Ramirez)
    George (Put forward by Liz Hodges)
    Vince (Put forward by Elizabeth Sanguedolce)
    Nova (Nova Read)
    Carley (Put forward by Maggie May)
    Katina (Put forward by Michelle Jane)
    Tracy (The Killer Thriller Book Blogging Mama)

I will always be grateful to Leeds Trinity University and my MA in Creative Writing Tutors there, Martyn, Amina and Oz. My Masters degree in 2015 was the springboard into being able to write as a profession.

And thanks especially, to you, the reader. Thank you for taking the time to read this story. I really hope you enjoyed it.

ABOUT THE AUTHOR

Q: Where do your ideas come from?

A: I'm no stranger to turbulent times, and these provide lots of raw material. People, places, situations, experiences – they're all great novel fodder!

Q: Why do you write psychological thrillers?

A: I'm intrigued why people can be most at risk from someone who should love them. Novels are a safe place to explore the worst of toxic relationships.

Q: Does that mean you're a dark person?

A: We thriller writers pour our darkness into stories, so we're the nicest people you could meet – it's those romance writers you should watch...

Q: What do readers say?

A: That I write gripping stories with unexpected twists, about people you could know and situations that could happen to anyone. So beware...

Q: What's the best thing about being a writer?

A: You lovely readers. I read all my reviews, and answer all emails and social media comments. Hearing from readers absolutely makes my day, whether it's via email or through social media.

Q: Who are you and where are you from?

A: A born 'n' bred Yorkshire lass, now officially in my early fifties. I have two grown up sons and a Sproodle called Molly. (Springer/Poodle!) The last decade has been the best: I've done an MA in Creative Writing, made writing my full time job, and found the happy-ever-after that doesn't exist in my writing - after marrying for the second time just before the pandemic.

Q: Do you have a newsletter I could join?

A: I certainly do. Go to www.mariafrankland.co.uk or click here through your eBook to join my awesome community of readers. When you do, I'll send you a free novella – 'The Brother in Law.'

Printed in Dunstable, United Kingdom

74185547R00156